SUNDOG

The story of an American foreman,
Robert Corvus Strang, as told to

JIM HARRISON

D0061616

BANTAM BOOKS
TORONTO • NEW YORK • LONDON • SYDNEY • AUCKLAND

SUNDOG

A Bantam Book / published by arrangement with
E. P. Dutton, Inc.

PRINTING HISTORY

E. P. Dutton edition published May 1984
Bantam Windstone Trade edition / July 1985

Windstone and accompanying logo of a stylized W
are trademarks of Bantam Books, Inc.

All rights reserved.
Copyright © 1984 by Jim Harrison.
Cover artwork copyright © 1985 by Skip Liepke.
This book may not be reproduced in whole or in part, by
mimeograph or any other means, without permission.
For information address: E. P. Dutton, Inc.,
2 Park Avenue, New York, N.Y. 10016.

ISBN 0-553-34188-X

Published simultaneously in the United States and Canada

Bantam Books are published by Bantam Books, Inc. Its trademark, consisting of the words "Bantam Books" and the por-
trayal of a rooster, is Registered in U.S. Patent and Trademark
Office and in other countries. Marca Registrada. Bantam
Books, Inc., 666 Fifth Avenue, New York, New York 10103.

PRINTED IN THE UNITED STATES OF AMERICA

O   0 9 8 7 6 5 4 3 2 1

to Russell Chatham

"Eternity is in love with
the productions of time."

WILLIAM BLAKE,
*The Marriage of Heaven
and Hell*

SUNDOG
JIM HARRISON

"A swift but deep read, ultimately inspiring in a way all too rare in contemporary fiction."
—*Detroit News*

"His stories move with random power and reach, in the manner of Melville and Faulkner."
—*Boston Globe*

"A feisty, passionate novel . . . A kind of intellectual detective story." —*Newsday*

"A writer with immortality in him."
Bernard Levin,—*The London Sunday Times*

"A contemporary writer who can mix the narrative-descriptive style of an early Hemingway with the interlocutory style of a mature Faulkner . . . *Sundog* provides the reader an opportunity to see a landscape that has not been as fully described since Hemingway's 'Nick Adams' stories."
—*New Haven Register*

"With a style at once gritty and elegant, Harrison ironically achieves a harsh yet lovely evocation of the spirit of a person who made a difference."
—*Booklist*

"Among the very best fiction writers in America."
—*Playboy*

Bantam Windstone Books
Ask your bookseller for the books you have missed

AUTHOR'S NOTE

For three years this project has offered the gravest doubts, not the least of which is whether or not the subject of this book is still alive. But that is only the most recent consideration in a long list of questions, none of which will ever be adequately resolved. Frankly, I have nowhere to stand, but then I have come to realize through the unwitting efforts of my subject that I shouldn't have been caught standing in the first place. It is an unnatural act. Fluidity and grace are all. The contemporary mage James Hillman has told us that the notion that there is a light at the end of the tunnel has mostly been a boon to pharmaceutical companies.

Of course, all disclaimers bear a strong odor. Why should I care if I was duped? Novelists are renowned fools in this respect—they listen to what a person is saying with little or no attention given to why he or she is saying it; thus my effort to write a book that is "true" might be the falsest of my inventions. Perhaps the true story of Robert Corvus Strang is not to be found in the thousand or so pages of transcribed tape I have winnowed down into a book. I decided only recently to alternate his story with my own observations of what went on during our five months of taping—purportedly the last five months of his life.

I felt compelled for reasons of readability to edit out information of a highly technical nature on the building of hydroelectric dams and large Third World irrigation projects. I have also banished certain speech idiosyncrasies Strang got from talking over the radio in all the godforsaken parts of our world, which is not shrinking as fast as I previously had thought. "That's a negative," or if I asked how to spell *Azula*, I would receive "Alfred Zebra Ursula Lock Alfred," or something daffy like that.

It all started in a locker room at a club in Palm Beach, both locales being highly unlikely. I was in Florida for the winter trying to get over the effects of a divorce and declining health, and working on a book about game cookery with a friend who lives there. I suffered deeply from gout at age forty-five. A rather fancy clinic would feed me fruit juices, elixirs of herbs and animal glands, then sink me in a whirlpool tub for the incautious sum of a thousand dollars a day, plus extras. After several hours of this, I would toddle off to plan the next test recipe for our book, say a slab of foie gras, or oysters Bienville, some grilled doves and roasted pintail ducks, assorted fruits and cheeses to add a health note. In Palm Beach you notice that wealth, like poverty, seems to blur the peripheries, and the spectrum is delimited to the torpor of the middle range. Even imaginary ailments demand unique treatments. Only later, when I neared bankruptcy due to this project, did I regain my health.

On to the locker room, the sort of locker room that would pass for a parlor in Grosse Pointe. A half-dozen men between forty and sixty were drinking after tennis games truncated by rain. I watched the quarrel develop as a polite, observant outsider. A young scion announced that he was bored with life, to which a wise old tycoon responded, "That's because you retired before you did anything. When's the last time you got out of town?" The younger man said that in the past year he had been in Beverly Hills, Palm Springs, Aspen, Deauville, plus a month at the Carlyle in New York City. "Those are all the same places," quipped the older man. "Maybe so, but then the television doesn't present the outside world as an attractive place." The old man stood up and nodded his assent, and everyone seemed relieved. Anger, after all, represents bad manners. Then he said, "Television never gets off the Interstate unless there's an explosion. The world wasn't designed to be an attractive place. You should meet the man that used to be my son-in-law. Compared to him you're all asshole fops. That includes you." He was pointing his finger at me, and my temples ached with panic. I'm so weak-stomached about criticism that I only read reviews after someone has assured me that they're laudatory. "I read your books. They're nice enough, but you might try writing about someone who actually does something." Then he left, whistling a show tune, and somebody asked me what the word *fop* meant. Naturally, an hour didn't pass before I began checking up on this ex-son-in-law to whom I compared so unfavorably.

There was a casual stupidity to this little argument, especially in that the reading public likes to feel superior to rich people and their ostensibly artificial problems. That doesn't concern me here. That afternoon was the rather nagging and painful beginning for me of a long voyage back toward Earth, however simpleminded might be my arrival. Rather than jump at the challenge immediately, I wrote a few letters to this son-in-law, Robert Strang, none of which brought a response. I checked the map and discovered the nearest airport to his place in the upper peninsula of Michigan was some hundred miles away in Sault Ste. Marie.

I put the idea on hold and went off to Key West for my annual tarpon fishing trip, which was severely marred by gluttony, alcohol, painkillers for the gout, and other such things that keep me awake for long, sleepless, tropical nights and have done so for over a decade. Only it didn't work anymore, and I sat in a dark room for three days with palm fronds rattling against the eaves. Then a postcard of a snowbank from Strang was forwarded from Palm Beach. In response to my rambling notes he only said, "I don't get what you're talking about. Robert C. Strang." I was so desperate at the moment that his terse sentence was all I needed to get started.

In bringing to a close this small introduction, I should thank numerous doctors, civil engineers, and certain companies involved in international construction projects, but they weren't, finally, germane in understanding our man. I am, however, thankful to Doctor Bryce Douglas for pointing me to a Harvard University Botanical Museum leaflet by Richard Evans Schultes with the imposing title "De Plantis Toxicarüs E Mundo Novo Tropicale Commentationes I." This leaflet identifies the plant *Aristolochia medicinalis*, which is a native Venezuelan remedy for epilepsy and other seizures, and which helped give me insight into the core of Strang's unique personality. Whether he is still alive or not is obviously beyond our control, but not beyond our interest. I must somehow content myself with having known a man totally free of the bondage of the appropriate.

CHAPTER I

So I moved slowly north, passing through dozens of springs, virtually traveling north with greening spring herself overhead and below, pausing here and there to wait for her and for my own courage to gather. You see, I was on the verge of doing something truly different in my life, something totally unexampled. Usually I drove north along the Eastern Seaboard to New York City and, later in June, to our cottage near Sag Harbor. My wife would fly ahead, lacking my affection for long drives. But now I had lost both the modest New York co-op and the Sag Harbor property to her in the divorce—not so much lost, but gave them up in an attack of kindness, much to the disgust of my lawyers and accountant. She was shocked but happy, what with a boy and a girl in their early teens from a previous marriage. My motive, oddly, was the memory of an unhappy move from Marquette to East Lansing, Michigan, at age twelve. The experience marked me deeply, and since I loved these children and had recently reread the great Dostoevsky, I had become at the same time serene and captious. But then this is not my story, and I will keep my intrusions to a minimum.

On impulse I had bought one of those large, involved, four-wheel-drive sporting vehicles and felt a little silly on the seven-hour drive from Key West to Palm Beach. Later, I decided, I might add some sensible plaid shirts to my wardrobe, a pair of boots, perhaps a hat with a feather in it. The vehicle had delayed me three extra days in Key West while I waited for the addition of cruise control; my gout-ridden right toes could barely handle a gas pedal.

I had been corresponding a bit with the older tycoon mentioned previously—I have promised not to mention his name because of his prominent political and financial affiliations. This seemed unnecessarily cautionary at the time, but later, when the situation became explosive, even grotesque, the stipulation appeared sensible. In any event, our tycoon had invited me to stop by for dinner, an event I had anticipated because of the reputation of his cook. The real reason for the invitation was that his daughter, the ex-wife of our unmet hero, was home for a week and he thought I might speak to her. I was ill-disposed to her because she hadn't answered a letter, but also curious when I heard she was a doctor specializing in tropical medicine for the World Health Organization.

"The deepest feeling of all is that there should be more," he said, from behind a small but billowing cloud of Havana smoke.

"There *is* a lot more. You just can't see it from anywhere you bother looking," she said. She was a mean woman, though she clearly loved her father. She had managed to ignore me in a way that couldn't be ignored. I was flushed, almost uncomfortably past enjoying my food and wine. There was an urge to present some fresh, invented credentials to supplant the ones she had apparently dismissed. I kept trying.

"But isn't it inherent in the idea of personality to wear blinders of some sort? You maintain that your father and myself are ignorant of a world that is the target of your intensest curiosity. Perhaps we are. Unfortunately, in the gunnysack holding all the possible attitudes on earth, the most offensive one that can be drawn out is that of moral superiority."

"Right!" she laughed. "I hate it. This town forces me into it."

"That's why it puzzles me that you won't talk about your former husband. I told your father that when I've been fishing or hunting in Costa Rica, Ecuador, Africa, wherever, I've met such people and their energy fascinates me. It rarely occurs to people like myself just who actually goes into a jungle and builds an immense dam or who engineers the irrigation of thousands of acres of desert. All I simply proposed is that I write about this man, say for *Vanity Fair* or *The New Yorker* or *Atlantic*, because it would be good for us to see this aspect. . . ."

"Maybe you could bring some Giorgio Armani models along, and they could sweep across the top of a dam and Scavullo could shoot them with a leg up against a turbine, or with a group of dark, smoky Brazilian workers."

"You're not being fair." Now I was more than reasonably pissed off.

"I'm being quite fair. It's such silly, scheming bullshit. We've become like the French. Everything must be *incroyable* or *bizarre*. If the information is sufficiently novel, it's a twenty-minute buzz while the bath is being drawn, sort of a three-dollar round-trip ticket before bedtime. Your type is drunk on novelty, not reality."

"You're the most unbelievable bitch I've ever met." I gulped my Calvados and choked. The father roared with laughter and pounded the table, then I somehow began to strangle and hyperventilate at the same time. The room began to dim as if by a rheostat, and I was facedown in my pear sorbet and chèvre cheese. I barely felt their hands on my shoulders as they helped me, with the aid of a black butler, to a sofa. As my vision cleared, I became drenched with cold sweat. She ran out of the room with a certain alarm in her eyes.

"I'm very sorry," I said, trying to get up, but my arms felt numb like rubber ganglia.

"Don't say a thing. Evelyn is hard on people, to put it mildly."

"I'm so sorry." She had returned with a medical bag and the trace of a smile. I was too frightened to be angry, and she had softened to the point of becoming attractive. She intently checked my heart rate and blood pressure, during which I could see most of her breasts. Somehow they looked like serious breasts, the sort that an effete writer would never get to tinker with.

"Not to panic you, but you're in terrible shape. Very high pulse rate, blood pressure 165 over 112, at least thirty pounds overweight." She slapped my tummy. "You could support an African village on what you spend on your gut." Then she gave me a sedative and denied me a nightcap. I was sent up to bed with two kindly handshakes.

In the morning I was alone in the house, except for the servants. To my delight, the butler delivered an ample breakfast along with *The New York Times*, *Wall Street Journal*,

Washington Post, and the *Miami Herald* for spice. There was also an envelope from Evelyn which I opened immediately.

Father chided me for bitchiness which was the reason, he reminded me, that mother was exiled to Rancho Mirage for a death tan. Not quite sure what to say about dear Strang. I had met him several times, then got to know him when I treated him for schistosomiasis. Haven't seen him since the accident, but reading the company's report the prognosis isn't good. Also the herbal remedy he tried for his petit mal epilepsy, otherwise totally controlled, has further cast him askew. He's had a dozen or so tropical diseases in the past twenty-five years and is pretty much physically burned out.

This isn't very helpful. You might key on what he calls the theory and practice of rivers. If you want to get into gossip, Strang understands women better than any man I have ever met.

Meanwhile, I looked in on you early this morning and you were grasping your penis like a seven-year-old waif. Follow the enclosed diet or you'll never see fifty.

Con amore,
Evelyn

The diet turned out to be suitable for someone with the disposition of a Gandhi, a Sister Theresa, a Gautama Buddha —some tiny, brown, selfless person. I, however, resolved to follow it and skipped lunch, supplanting the meal with a hundred-mile-long sexual fantasy about the good doctor Evelyn. If I weren't a gentleman, I might let you in on the details. I was heated up to the point that I reached for a bottle of La Begorce in my snack container. The wine broke down my food resolve, and consequently I swerved off the Interstate south of Macon and followed the red dirt road to Home Folks Barbeque, indisputably the best barbeque shack in the United States. Of course, I had been planning this move subconsciously for an entire day. Despite our well-advertised standard of living, a certain heartiness was gone out of American life. I've always insisted that *cuisine minceur* was the moral equivalent of the foxtrot. On my way south in January, I had stopped at Home Folks for an enormous take-out order. Some of the sauce had spilled indelibly on the marble tile floor of my Palm Beach rental, costing me several thousand of my damage deposit. A pungent sauce, to say the least, slathered over racks of pork and beef ribs. A sauce not to be confused with those hokum béchamels served over gaily decorated baby hamsters in New York City, home of the most otiose food faddism. Strangely, Doctor Evelyn seemed to peer up from the glistening pool of sauce, and I called for a doggy bag.

Crossing the Ohio-Michigan border, I again lost the sense of my quarry and the good sense behind the pursuit. The otherwise fair May afternoon turned dark and blustery with the arrival of a northern front, well advertised on the radio but somehow unexpected. I imagined Michigan as some huge, bruised mitten, floating in the hostile frigid waters of the Great Lakes. Above the Straits of Mackinac, the Upper Peninsula sat alone, perhaps the least-known land mass in the United States. In this age where every niche on earth has been discovered and rediscovered countless times, there is an open secret why the upper Midwest is generally ignored: it is relatively charmless, and it competes with Siberia for the least hospitable climate on earth. Perhaps I'd stop and see my mother, then head for Montana. Or Paris.

My spirits seemed to drag under the car when I noted an Irish setter, a big male, trotting up the median strip with a jaunty gait, as if Route 75 had been created for him. As I passed, he darted toward the southern-bound lanes, where an immense semi struck him square and he was hurled brutally upward and out of view.

It was a mile before I exhaled. My life narrowed to the gray, windswept highway, and my remaining support systems diminished into the ugliness of the blurred scenery. It was what a friend of mine, a former infantry lieutenant in Viet Nam, called the "old organ slide," where all sense of a personal destiny is lost. For a moment the dog had become the Irish setter of my youth, but then he had died at the end of my bed one winter night. And what had become of that shy, red-haired girl I had loved as a young man in New York? It was Merlin who invented the yo-yo which mirrored so perfectly those mood shifts, before he sank wisely back into the ooze of history. Otherwise we would have had an Eichmann trial for Merlin, and the world would have been attentive for a change.

I spent a disarming three days with my mother, mostly reading about the Upper Peninsula and studying maps, a wonderfully senseless vice. When a housecat can't figure out what to do, it merely sits down. We made an obligatory trip to the cemetery, since I wasn't going to be there for Memorial Day. (I had never been there for Memorial Day.) But first, at dawn, we went bird-watching, certainly her ruling passion. I had been worried about the apparent rate of her aging, but I could barely keep up with her as we looked for the first of the migratory warblers. These tiny birds, barely noticed by the world, were her obsession. We reached the cemetery before the gates were open and sat in the car drinking coffee from a thermos, waiting for the attendant. The earth had become lovely and pale green again after the storm passed through. A loutish gardener with a namepatch stating "Bert" appeared with keys, announcing to us, "The early bird gets the worm," a statement Mother thought wonderful and I thought in bad taste. She saw a vireo near the ten-year-old grave which she had cultivated with flowering crab and a mountain orange. My father had been a botanist, and I came up short of knowing more than a few trees and plants. I was embarrassed to be hungry.

"Let's go have breakfast," she said. She was always on the money when it came to actualities: death, worms, food, Mozart, and birds owned their anointed places.

Mother awoke me before dawn, under her lifelong conviction that all journeys should start as early in the day as possible. We were always the first to arrive at picnics, planes, ball games. I was red-eyed and frayed from a late night of studying notes and drinking an emergency pint of whiskey. The whiskey performed the function it was designed for—several hours of grace in which the drinker becomes convinced again of his viability as a human being; his personal narrative resumes structure, and the grace of knowing what one is doing returns.

We crept out the back door after a bowl of oatmeal and fruit—I had stupidly shared with her Evelyn's diet. Our stealth was to be my brief good-bye shot at bird-watching. There was a myrtle warbler building a nest at the edge of the backyard. The bird was minuscule, somewhat like a smudgy mouse with wings. Then we made a skirmish in a clearing near a swamp to see a male woodcock in its mating flight. She told me that they perform the dance from evening until dawn for two months in the spring. I watched intently, mostly because I have eaten these birds in France, where they go under the name *bécasse*. I told her so.

"How shameful, son. Think how they dance all night for

love, month after month. You've certainly neglected God's plan for your life. You've been divorced twice, and your health is a mess. And you eat these unbearably lovely birds. I still love you, but it's not always easy."

She gave me a kiss on the cheek, then went back to the woodcock, who wheeled higher and higher in gyres, with odd little cries in the first light, then returned toward earth in an amazing, fluttering spiral. I wished him luck. I waved at Mother from my absurd vehicle, but she hadn't turned around. I wished myself luck.

CHAPTER II

The lump in my stomach and chest, a combination of oatmeal and nerves, lifted after I passed Grayling and the forty-fifth parallel, a casual description of north. It was cool and clear, and the vast, hilly landscape of forest was a mottled canvas of hundreds of shades of pastel green, with tips of the taller trees buffeted and racked by a strong wind out of the northwest. The wind pushed up the paler undersides of leaves and made my vehicle buck and shudder in open areas. I listened to the notes I had made on my Japanese portable dictaphone and added to them. Large portions had been made rather optimistic and goofy by the whiskey.

TAPE 1: She's gone to bed with the usual string of wise instructions. I'm in Dad's study, looking at the glass cases of botanical specimens and the two walls of books, none of which piques my interest. Imagine at my age feeling vaguely naughty being here with a large glass of whiskey on the gradually warming track of Robert C. Strang. I have been given his employment folder by Evelyn's father, though with his remuneration politely blacked out. This isn't the case in the book or movie business where figures, generally inaccurate on the high side, are bandied about readily. Born in Engadine, Michigan, in 1935. Education limited to kindergarten and first grade by seizures caused by accident. Petit mal epilepsy now totally controlled by Tagonet and other drugs. After a half hour's study I see there has been no time allowed for vacations between 1953 and 1983. Holy Jesus. Started working for his older brother, a subcontractor, on the Mackinac Bridge. By age twenty he is helping building schools and missions in Kenya for the United Nazarene Mission, whatever that is, then on to Sudan on an irrigation project off the White Nile. Then to Amritsar for another irrigation project for a Swiss company, down to Hyderabad for a flood control project. Hospitalized for amoebic dysentery, returned to Miami for treatment. Then on to Baja California for work on La Paz Reservoir, a dam in Costa Rica, more dams in Peru, Venezuela, Brazil, becoming in his thirties somewhat a trouble-shooter for——Corporation—it would identify our tycoon. Two years in Uganda working on a dam project for the French, left when Amin came in. Back in Venezuela with a year's stop in Holland on their immense storm surge barrier called the Delta Project. Back to Brazil on the Tucurui Dam on the Tocantius River. Last two years ending with disaster in Venezuelan highlands. Whew. Old Pasternak said it takes a lot of volume to fill a life. Another glass of whiskey and a peek in the refrigerator. Part of a ham with a Do Not Touch sign. Ripped at it shamelessly. Back at the desk, I incriminate myself with a smear of ham fat on the glass top. What can one make of these incredible spiderwebs on the world map? Not much yet. I think of my own rather tepid trips, other than stray fishing and bird hunting expeditions. Dove hunting from a villa in Colombia, fishing from posh hotels in Ecuador and Costa Rica are not quite the same thing. Neither is sand grouse hunting in Kenya when your clothes and boots are warmed by a native in early morning chill. On down the employment record I see checks are regularly sent from the Houston office to Emmeline Strang in Manistique, Michigan, and to Allegria Menquez Strang in Puntarenas, Costa Rica. Nothing sent to Evelyn for obvious reasons. Two children by Emmeline, one by Allegria. A sudden image sends me whirling, so I pour an ample nightcap. It was against this desk at seventeen that I almost made love to my first love, "almost" because she was Methodist, thus the undies stayed on. Mom and Dad were at a convention in Ann Arbor. Over twenty-five years ago, Sheila was grinding against me, and we toppled over the chair. She wondered if she could get pregnant through undies. I brought a washcloth, and she rinsed off, rather prettily, right before my eyes.

There was a short traffic jam at the Straits of Mackinac approaching the bridge, and I nearly hit a station wagon in my Sheila reverie, swerving off into an exit as if that was what I meant to do all the time. At a combination coffee shop–restaurant I was told that the bridge was temporarily closed because of the gale. Once the wind dropped below fifty knots, the bridge would reopen. I felt more than a touch of claustrophobia in the crowded place. It was unlikely that anyone among the burly truck drivers, construction workers, sportsmen read novels. Not that they made a point of it, but save for one pudgy, manic waitress there wasn't a friendly face. I left and pushed against the wind down to the shore looking out over the Straits. The waves were mountainous, and the center suspension section of the immense bridge swayed a little through the binoculars. The sand stung my face, and I felt an intolerable loneliness. I might have been born up here, but I didn't belong. I couldn't begin to imagine Strang working on this bridge any more than I could imagine writing anything about such a person. We seem to live in unapproachable little arenas, none of them touching upon one another beyond some fragile, nominal sense of a language that isn't in itself especially common.

Another violent mood swing, but this one surprisingly positive: I had got back in my machine and treated myself to a sporty Bordeaux and a long nap. When I awoke I noted that the bridge was still not open. There was a group of north-woods types looking at my vehicle with envy. They wanted to know if I had a one- or two-ton winch. I only added it for pulling the tarpon skiff out of the water in Key West. If you leave a winch attached to your boat trailer, someone will quickly steal it for dope in that island paradise. I went in the bar and had drinks with these friendly yokels, who turned out to be from Detroit and headed north for brook trout fishing. After a number of rounds they admitted that when they became exhausted in their cross-country treks looking for fresh brook trout creeks, they would stop for a coke break, that is, a big snort of cocaine. I was amused by this new twist in the sporting community.

The real thrill was crossing the bridge, where my dogged spirit felt true fear again. I could barely hold the lane and was whipped back and forth with my stomach and heart jumping and thumping and sweat itching around my ears. The tumultuous water below looked at least a mile away. I yelled at the toll attendant on the far side, then sped off. I somehow enjoyed being frightened in something other than a plane—an Aeroflot in a runway pirouette in Leningrad, an engine aflame over the Sahara. The only other true fear I could remember was when I had taken what turned out to be a rather nasty ballerina down to Dominica in the Windward Islands. She had one of those improbable Degas physiques, with dimples on each side of her spine above her buttocks. We had gone on a hike to look at the flora and fauna and had become lost until after dark, and she had prattled incessantly about the dread fer-de-lance, which I had thought was only a resident, among the islands, of Martinique. By nightfall she had me convinced. We finally stumbled onto a road where, according to this dancing herpetologist, these giant vipers traveled at night. At her insistence, I shipped the little tart home the next morning.

By twilight, almost nine in the evening in this latitude, I was within an hour of the village of Innisfree—a devised name to hide its identity. I stopped and peed by a giant river, then crossed it, tipping my hat to a sandhill crane down in the elders. On the other side of the river, the road entered an enormous swamp some thirty miles in width, with very few other cars on the road. For a while the lack of any traffic caused a vertigo as if I had been abandoned. Apparently on a Thursday night in May in the Upper Peninsula no one goes anywhere, but then where would they go? You could enter schizoid Michigan in the Detroit metropolitan area, where the old West replays itself with over six hundred murders a year, the new mythology, not the quick-draw face-off, but the squalor of anonymous slaughter; then out Michigan's nether end, the U.P., as it's called, you enter a timbered-over, rock-strewn waste, a land so dense and desolate it became obvious to me that the most redoubtable survivalist couldn't survive.

Now I was driving straight into half a red ball that was the sun; immense crows swooped back and forth across the road looking for carcasses to pick. I remembered in a confusing moment that Mother had told me to look for the ravens that favored northern climes: My confusion was over a feeling of déjà vu, of a twelve-year-old boy being driven east, then south in 1953 to a faraway home he neither desired nor would ever feel truly at home in; and the boy in a state of petulance and anger staring out of the back seat of the car at this self-same swamp, and how he may have blocked those memories of the first twelve years until he no longer understood their language, which still somehow emanated, however weakly, but was suffocated with irony and mock sophistication. Now the ravens, the puddle ducks in the swamp, the geese wheeling to land in the distance, the dead raccoon and the setting sun, the road itself, cut clumsily but forcibly through the thirty intervening years, leaving them as badly lit photos. There was then, and there was now.

Innisfree barely existed, defying the prominence of the name on the map. Ever faithful to appearances, I neglected to check the population figures. Under a single streetlight—one of the crossroads was gravel—there was a motel that wouldn't be open for the season for another week, a wooden frame hotel with a single yellow light in the back, a darkened combination gas station–general store, a well-lit bar with a pickup and logging truck in front. Radiating out from this "hub," there were a dozen or so visible, modest houses, interspersed with the ubiquitous house trailers with their various, junky additions. Beyond this there was nothing but a hard, driving rain and the roar of what I knew must be Lake Superior out there in the night. In the darkness it all had the aura of one of those cheapish, gothic novels. Perhaps a little girl, possessed by de-mons or whatever, would eat off my tires by morning. I began banging on the door of the Idylwild Hotel, my only port in this particular storm. A middle-aged lady of Scandinavian descent answered. She was so dour it would not have surprised me had she flipped a hatchet from beneath her robe and sunk it into my forehead. She literally ripped open the door.

"What do you want, hey?"

"A room for the night. Please."

"Do you have a reservation?"

"No, but I'll take the room for a week." I brandished a fifty.

"You should have called ahead. I'm closed for the night."

"But I didn't know your name." I still hadn't been al-lowed across the threshold.

"I don't know why I pay good money to the Yellow Pages." She looked down at my expensive luggage, which was getting wet. "Your luggage is getting wet. Next time come earlier or sleep in your car."

"Thank you." I pushed in with a glad heart. Nobody could get me out of there now. In a grandiose gesture, I bought a half-dozen skin magazines from a rack.

"Hunters and fishermen buy those. Nobody from here ever bought one of those."

I looked down with despair at fifteen bucks worth of porky rumps with splayed apertures. Maybe there would be some articles. "I need directions for the morning to the cabin of Robert Strang—"

"Absolutely not," she interrupted. "He won't see anyone but these specialist doctors his company sends. You're no doc-tor, that's for sure."

"How do you know?"

[16]

"I've never sold a filthy magazine to a doctor. They come up here for natural beauty."

I drew some folders from my brass-latched Buitoni briefcase. "It is of the utmost urgency that I see Mr. Strang in the morning. There is a considerable amount of money at stake." She peered at the papers doubtfully, but I could see that she needed glasses by the red mark on her nose bridge. She drew a precise map, showed me to my room, and said, "Good night, don't let the bedbugs bite," one of my mother's perpetually repeated witticisms.

It was a night I would remember poignantly but not wish to repeat. Insomnia opens the door to previously untraced memories, makes a mockery of the good sense that possesses us at high noon, and any effort we make to channel our thoughts twists the energy, rebukes us with half-finished faces, sexless bodies; we learn again that our minds are full of snares, knots, goblins, the backward march of the dead, the bridges that end halfway and still hang in the air, those who failed to love us, those who irreparably harmed us, intentionally or not, even those we hurt badly and live on incapsulated in our regret. The past thrives on a sleepless night, reduces it to the awesome, distorted essence of all we have met.

These thoughts left me staring at my travel clock and listening to the gale on Lake Superior, which owned all the harsh throatiness of Kenya's grandest male lion, one of which had roared at our Rover's headlights, his entire massive head and mane drenched with blood.

Then it was that I heard an honest-to-god scream that jellied my bowels. I leapt to the window, grabbing the sill to steady the dizziness caused by the sudden motion. The bar was closing, and you could see the moon above the streetlight, and the sheen of the moon off the whitecaps foaming over the breakwall in the harbor. At first I couldn't see anyone, but then there was another scream, and a woman followed a large man into the circle of light. I couldn't see their faces, but her voice was hard and clear. "I know you fucked my little sister, you sonofabitch—" She dashed in and slapped him hard. He continued walking up the centerline of the highway through town. "I've got proof. She told me herself. 'I fucked him, Charlene, what you going to do about it?'" Now Charlene kicked her husband in the ass and grabbed his hair. He somehow continued walking, now nearly at the edge of the dark. "You did it to my little sister, you cocksucker, and I'm going to fuck everyone in town. I might just cut off your dick when you're sleeping. You'll be sorry." He had disappeared into the dark up the road when I heard him bellow, and she streaked back through the circle of light as fast as a deer. What did this Charlene's sister look like that this lummox gambled on endless grief?

My adrenals were pumping out a hopeless amount of poison, so I studied my notes again. It had been over a decade since I had done anything vaguely journalistic, and this project was becoming more doubtful by the moment. Early in my career I had interviewed a number of famous sporting and political figures, and it was difficult to decide which produced the maximum emetic effect—the narcissistic athletes, one of whom frequently beat off in the showers after a successful contest until an injury turned him into the eight-year-old he always was, or those android parrots that pass muster as public servants. An important interview blew up when I finally said, "I'm going to make a preemptive strike and call you a lying crook and asshole, sir." That brief moment of victory, however, didn't make up for years of boozy pressrooms and sodden by-lines.

What I began to wonder in the middle of this sleepless night is if our man Strang ought not be allowed the grace of his private gestures. He had lived and worked in a world that no one but its inhabitants knew. Certainly the world itself must be more than the collection, the accretion, of all we read about it. It is, after all, *The New York Times,* the New York *Newsweek,* the New York *Time,* the New York–Washington NBC, CBS, ABC, PBS. Every summer there is a photo of a farmer in a drought-ruined cornfield in the Midwest. That's why I had lived on the East Coast for so many years—all of "us" were there. Movies and entertainment TV came from the other dream coast. Now there was the immediate question of going back where I belonged.

It was my almost naive curiosity that kept me in town that night and the following weeks and months. By 4 A.M., with the gale outside subsiding, I began trying to sort out the ostensibly banal mysteries of personality. One need only dabble in psychoanalytic literature to see how deeply idiosyncratic we are. Catholics and Tantric Buddhists have been wise enough to accommodate this lushness in human impulse; Protestants must subdue their heretical yearnings. They belong to the cult of self-improvement and hammer at their poor souls as if they were tract houses. The point is we are all quite different, and everyone tells us we're not. There is this inescapable, incredible variety of perception and sensation, the little parcels of experience that add up to a whole not necessarily typified by any sort of symmetric unity, but the urge of life herself.

I put a pillow over my eyes in a vain hope of sleep. It became the kind of intensely private movie that no one but a professional would want to see. Then I heard a rooster crow for the first time in memory and was brought close to tears. A door slammed, and a diesel truck started. I went to the window naked and watched a logging truck roll out of town. In the first light the world was becoming red above the fog that eased itself across the lake, which for all purposes could be regarded as a sea or an ocean. I dressed quickly to enter this strange world. I waved good-bye to a magazine rump that stared, fleering up from the floor. It looked curiously more attractive than the night before.

CHAPTER III

It was a dawn to remember with a smile on your deathbed. The sky was a vivid red as if the forest had caught fire. I drove through clumps of pink fog, recrossing the river of the day before which lividly reflected the sky. The roadside and small clearings in the forest were covered with white blooming dogwood, around which mist coiled and released like unraveling white satin. I stopped the car and shivered, imagining that I might have died and this was some sort of afterlife designed by H. Bosch and Magritte, much less vulgar than Dali; or it was life lived within a brilliantly colored seashell from which one might not emerge.

As per instructions, I drove off the gravel road onto a two-track at exactly 15.2 miles on the odometer. There was a friendly sign that read KEEP OUT—TRESPASSERS WILL BE SHOT ON SIGHT. The road was narrow and muddy, passing through a tamarack swale where the water from a small but overflowing creek crossed the road. I shifted into four-wheel-drive and roared through with a neck-snapping lurch, causing the accumulated fatigue of a sleepless night to descend with force. There was a small clearing covered with a pale, bluish moss that looked attractive for a nap. I hadn't been this sleepless since my student days, or on those rare times I experimented with pharmaceuticals. It was a distortion similar to the actual hunger I had experienced in my late teens in New York City where as a neophyte bohemian I had bruised myself with what Rimbaud demanded of the poet, the "derangement of all the senses."

The Strang cabin was somehow more elaborate than I expected: first there was an open wooden gate, a grove of firs, then a large clearing on the river. It was an ample, old-fashioned, log house with a screened porch surrounding two sides and an enormous stone fireplace chimney from which friendly smoke emerged in a plume. The air smelled of dew, flowers, smoke, bacon, and coffee. Outside the door there was a battered, mud-covered pickup.

The trouble was, no one was home. A peek in the dark cabin revealed only the glowing coals in the fireplace. I carried my briefcase down to the river, where on a small platform an easy chair sat rather absurdly facing the river. I made myself comfortable, stared at the river, and opened my briefcase. The river looked wonderful while the briefcase appeared silly and alien, so I closed it and fell asleep, thinking of George Sand's notion that the world is divided between those who want to live in palaces and those who would prefer cabins.

First there was sun warm on my face, the itch of mosquito bites, and the cries of ravens overhead, and a soft voice. Later on she told me that my snoring had irritated the ravens and alarmed both of them as they approached from downstream. At first they had suspected a bear with its head in the garbage can. When I opened my eyes, I saw a lovely girl, medium in height, rather slender, with dark hair and eyes and olive skin. Behind her was a fat yellow Labrador in the river, swimming upstream with effort and trying to bark but choking on the riffles of water. Just behind the dog was a man standing thigh-deep in the water in a three-sided aluminum walker, the kind very old people or the injured use to get around. He held a bamboo flyrod. The man's appearance alarmed me: His hair was medium length but seemed to bristle in every direction, and his eyes were hazel-colored but cold, though this proved to be a misapprehension. He managed to give the impression of someone who is at the same time enormously vital and gravely ill: His skin was a splotched and faded bronze from the tropics, and his convalescence had taken too much of his weight, which made his wiry, corded musculature more apparent. I knew he was a little older than me, but I have never seen a man who looked so totally "used" by life.

"May we help you, sir? You're the writer?" she asked.

"Who else could it be? We thought you were a god-damned bear. This is my daughter Eulia. She's from Costa Rica, and she's here to see that her old man doesn't die alone. I'll shake your hand in a minute." The punctuation is my own, as his voice tended to end a sentence on the upswing and rush onward. He literally dragged his legs out of the water and threw himself down on the bank. Eulia stooped and drew off the hipboots, revealing a maze of braces on both legs. Then the fat yellow dog shook the water off herself and lay down next to Strang, nuzzling and licking his neck. He didn't seem to mind.

"Eulia, love, I'd give one hundred dollars for a cup of

coffee with some rum in it and one for the writer if he hasn't taken the pledge."

"That would be fine. I was a little startled by your sign out on the road about trespassers."

"Not mine. This place is my oldest brother Ted's. He retired up to Alaska. He hates the world because his daughter got attacked in Detroit by this gang of young hoodlums. She wrote me down in Brazil that she got over it by spending a month in this big church in Detroit where she's the organist. She just sat there and played Bach for a whole month without hardly sleeping. I'll play you one of her tapes."

Eulia was partway out the porch door with the coffee. She heard Strang and turned around to put on the tape. I trembled involuntarily as the music boomed out into the glade, complementing the purling sound of the river.

"Made you shiver, didn't it? Of course, Bach didn't get Esther over getting raped, he only helped her accommodate it. Tell me one real bad thing you ever got over?"

"Give me a minute. . . ." I was startled by the question. I accepted the coffee from Eulia, whose brow was knotted with concern. "Well, yesterday I got pretty upset that my folks moved from Marquette to East Lansing when I was twelve. That's not in the league of your niece, but it was real enough to me."

He had pushed himself up on an elbow to drink his coffee, then he averted his eyes which were squeezed shut in evident pain.

"Of course, those situations are pretty dramatic. They can be figured out. The worst suffering I see back here in the States is another matter. People here suffer terribly without knowing why. They suffer because they live without energy. They can't get anything done. They lame around. It's the real and secret source of their anguish. If you think a factory smokestack is ugly, just look at one with no smoke coming out of it. These folks have trapped themselves with the help of the government and companies. We had some of those Polish boys from Detroit down in Brazil, welders and iron workers, and they'd put a harder day in than anyone I'd ever seen. They were scared of snakes, so I brought over a small anaconda to show them how sweet they could be, but one guy just plain shit his pants and fainted on the spot."

Now he laughed as I leaned over and flipped on my tape recorder.

"If you don't mind?"

"Not at all. I can't comprehend why you and your people might be interested in what I say. In the old days some companies would request that we allow the CIA to debrief us as if we'd been in some place they were interested in. I'd sit there with a guy in a hotel room and he'd crank up a recorder like that one. Maybe I'd have been on a dam in Costa Rica or up the Amazon basin or in Nicaragua. So the guy would ask me questions and I'd answer the best I could. But he would quite often disagree, even if he hadn't been there. And I would say, I really don't know politics, but I'm just giving you observations. Are your Costa Rican workers unhappy with their government? I would answer that they rarely spoke of their government because they pretty much have always had a good one. Now my dad was a goofy, old creature, but he was somewhat of a follower of Thomas Jefferson, who said the government was a mechanism to allow us to live our lives freely. . . . But you know all of this. I doubt I can tell you anything you don't already know."

"What did you do about the CIA people?"

"Oh, I pulled their legs a few times and they stopped

bothering me. I invented a guerilla nicknamed Geronimo. I've read a lot about Indians, so I gave this imagined revolutionary group all the characteristics of the Mescalero Apache. You better keep alert, I'm a bit of a fibber."

Now he alarmed me again. He began to scat, to sing nonsense syllables along with the Bach, rather well, I thought, but his eyes weren't right. Eulia quickly gathered his head to her lap and tried to soothe him. She held a finger to her lips to silence me. Strang's right arm twisted and bulged; he tore up a sizable chunk of sod by main strength as his voice grew louder. In some very poignant way he had become the music, a sensation we have all approached, but not this violently. Eulia leaned over and kissed his mouth passionately, suffocating his song. It was not a daughterly kiss, and sweat popped out of my forehead and around my neck. Mercifully, the Bach tape ended though the kiss continued. I got up and strolled around the cabin with the dog. There was a small, lovely garter snake sunning itself near the woodpile. I leaned over to peer at it more closely, but the old dog darted in and ate it. I began to wish I was elsewhere. I decided to go back to the riverbank and excuse myself for the day, or forever.

Strang, however, had become the soul of composure. Eulia was singing him a Spanish nursery rhyme when I approached to say good-bye.

"I'm sorry." He turned to me and raised on an elbow from her lap. "Evelyn probably told you that before I hurt myself I took this medicine. I ran out of my regular prescription, and I only had a week to go, so I took a local remedy. Sometimes I'm not too goddamn smart. They had this flume problem over in Venezuela on the Rio Kuduyari. It was only a month's job, but I ran out of my pills. Well, these Kubeo Indians have this astringent root that they pulverize that they call "dakootome" for people who have seizures like my epilepsy. Afterwards, the company got some doctors and botanists to figure out what this *Aristolochia medicinalis,* as they call it, does to a person in the wrong dosage. It can be both insanity and paralysis. It can let up or not. So they haven't figured out if my legs are just injured from the fall or the herb, though with my mind it is obviously the herbal remedy, but—"

"It must be terrible," I interrupted, trying to put him at rest.

"Of course it is. But I figure it's my brain or my heart and soul, whatever. It's a bit like having a monster in your head that takes you everywhere, whether you want to go or not." Now he was laughing again, and Eulia looked desperate. "What do you know about irrigation and dams? Probably nothing. I got some books for you if you still want to talk."

He grabbed the aluminum walker and was up in a single movement. We made our way to the cabin as he continued talking.

"We better do our business early in the morning as I tend to short-circuit around noon. Then I have to crawl. A few weeks ago this doctor was sent up from Ann Arbor, and he started me crawling, which is supposed to repattern my brain and body to walk, if you get what I mean."

I had heard of the treatment and muttered something reassuring. I was given a stack of books. The cabin was full of stuffed animals and birds, and the railing and chairs had different furs covering them. Only the well-equipped kitchen was comforting. It was as if some half-crazed taxidermist had been turned loose, a hunch that later proved true in the person of Strang's brother Karl.

"I like this crawling." Eulia took his hand with a sudden movement, as if anticipating something unpleasant. "Eulia drives me to someplace of interest every day. I've been working on this particular creek. Me and the dog are going to trace it back to its first trickle. I've always been a creek and river walker. All land is determined by which way the water goes. I like to look at moving water. It comforts me deeply. I used to be a night swimmer, too, but my legs have gone bad. Once when I was a little boy I was swimming at night. I was trying to swim up on a loon, which is my favorite bird. The loon kept laughing and moving. It was wonderful with these northern lights shimmering back and forth across the sky at the speed of light. It helped me see where the loon was going, though she told me by her laughter."

He abruptly stood still as if he had become stone. Eulia led me to the door. "Please don't come back," she said. "You'll make him sicker. He becomes too excited."

When I drove away, my breath returned to normal. I was wet with nervous sweat and badly needed a drink, something to eat, and a long nap.

CHAPTER IV

When I got back to the hotel I washed up for lunch—certainly an unnecessary gesture—and called our tycoon—henceforth to be called Marshall—in Palm Beach. He was in a jolly mood as if he had conned this not totally anonymous writer into a state of distress in the most remote part of the United States.

"But the whole point is that his daughter from Costa Rica told me not to come back."

"Strang doesn't have any daughter from Costa Rica. He has a daughter in the navy, but she's stationed with NATO in Italy. Pretty, plump like Emmeline, a first-rate kid named Aurora, an awful thing to call a girl."

"I take it he likes the northern lights." I was making time, trying to get over the confusion about daughters. "What's the prognosis on this drug thing?"

"We haven't heard. There's a drug firm in Switzerland I have an interest in that's trying to isolate the nature of its effect. My daughter's sending you a medical history. I don't want you to lose interest. Frankly, I've known him almost twenty years, however slightly at the beginning, and I'd like to see him figured out."

After I hung up the outdoor pay phone, I looked up into the sun and pondered the manipulative powers of the very rich. I had always been secure in my trade, and a man had averred that I was a fop and said my life's work had been "nice," certainly the feeblest of intensives; then casting about for something to do I thought of a series about real life, a series about people who do the actual work of the world but are never written about. Years ago, for a lavish sum, I wrote a screenplay for an ultramogul about thoroughbred horses. This mogul never said anything much to me before or after the project except "Make sure our horse wins." Maybe he just needed something to read. If you have hundreds of millions of dollars, the true price of a screenplay is like a trip to a bookstore. And Marshall would be getting his story for free.

Lunch at the bar offered a rise in spirit. It was all-you-can-eat of fresh-caught whitefish, and I polished off five delicious pieces with cold beer. The rather ample waitress told me the record was twenty-three pieces, eaten by a four-hundred-pound logger, while the women's record was seventeen. An actor once said to me that only in the Midwest is overeating still considered an act of heroism. In any event, my dad had always insisted that fish was brain food, and I felt properly stoked for an afternoon of study, reserving the evening for snooping.

TAPE 2: Strang's books are nearly a dead loss: Golze's *Handbook of Dam Engineering, Irrigation*

Principles and Practices by Hansen, Israelsen, and Stringham. The third book, D'Arcy Wentworth Thompson's *On Growth and Form* is the only one more than vaguely accessible to the layman. It is about why everything on Earth is shaped the way it is, an idea that naturally never occurred to me. But what a tremendous idea! My only viable scientific observation is that I dream more on the waxing than on the waning of the moon. But dreams are certainly a dreary mess compared to the reasons why all things, animate and inanimate, are shaped the way they are. Of course, twenty pages of the book gave me a headache—such abstruse reading isn't my habit. It is midafternoon, and I wonder if Strang is crawling through the brush in search of his legs. There is nothing pathetic in the thought because there is nothing pathetic in the man. I was struck by his essential kindness toward me, toward his daughter, toward the dog, and this after being intimidated by his appearance and his comments on energy. But then I am sensitive to implied criticism to such a degree that I might roll or wobble through life like a perpetually intact egg. When I came back to the hotel after lunch, I looked overlong at a group of young nymphets playing computer games, one of whom could be best described as a ball-buster. My hostess behind the counter frowned on this stare, but it doesn't matter. What would I say to these girls? "What's your favorite color?" I have the distinct feeling that I'm in a foreign country, the sensation that this place has blurred my peripheries. It is strange how the world we think we know, the world we perceived in school, no longer exists. We think colonially. Perhaps the northern Midwest is another country, as is the Northeast, the deep South, Florida by itself, the Southwest, California by itself, and the Northwest. Why do they bother reading the *Detroit Free Press* up here when Detroit is four hundred miles away? Most of them don't. I am beginning to feel this disassociation strongly. When I got back to

the room, my skin magazines had been stacked
neatly next to my pillow. There is a sense of humor
afoot. If I squint my eyes, crystalline Lake Superior could be the Caribbean. Only it isn't.
Since I brought along two cases of well-joggled
wine, my main problems will be food and sex. Not
oddly, they're the same problems a lot of people
have everywhere on Earth. This gives me a slight
sense of community, the march of the codeprived.
If I touched a nymphet downstairs, I'd get a bul-
let from a deer rifle from an enraged father. Does
Eulia ever crawl through the ferns and up the
creekbanks?

I was surprised by a long nap, waking to a beautiful late spring
evening. I walked along the harbor beach to give an edge to
my appetite. Someone's little mongrel followed me, and I was
kept busy throwing sticks for it. Frankly, I was touched on
some stupid level that this dog wanted to play. When it followed me to the steps of the bar, I bought a raw hamburger
patty and took it back out the door, but the dog was gone.
There was the question of what to do with the hamburger. I
put it in the pocket of my bush jacket.

Unfortunately, the evening special was the same as lunch
—a move to a cabin with a kitchen was definitely in the offing.
I had scarcely picked the batter off my first piece of fish when
Eulia fairly strode into the bar, stopping in front of my table
without a greeting. I stood up so precipitately that I spilled my
beer. Her face was dark, and her eyes glistened with tears of
anger.

"You're to disregard what I said to you. Come out at
daylight. Please don't upset him."

[3 2]

She rushed out before I could respond. I was so upset I only poked at the rest of my food. She had worn the same sort of fashionable, sporty clothes that my obnoxious ballerina had worn. I ordered the first of many double whiskies and spent the night chatting about the world at large with the bartender-owner, who had an insatiable curiosity which made me an insatiable talker. I got up to go at closing time, and he squinted at me in such a way that I knew either some advice or a pronunciamento was coming.

"You be careful of those Strangs. They can be a rough bunch. I don't know nothing about Robert because he was always overseas. Now Ted got pissed off and moved up to Alaska a hundred miles from anyone. And Karl is over at the maximum security prison in Marquette. I'd a lot rather have an NFL football team after me than Karl."

"What's he in prison for?" I was a bit groggy from booze and incipient violence.

"That's not for me to say." He turned away and began counting the till.

CHAPTER V

I arrived at Strang's at 6 A.M. sharp, with the buffered senses of the habitual tosspot. The pickup wasn't there, but I could see Strang sitting on the easy chair at the river's edge. I guessed Eulia had gone somewhere and suppressed a dangerous feeling of disappointment; few people other than true students of love, of which I number myself, can recognize the first discomfiting, almost hostile signs. Strang didn't turn at my approach, though the dog wiggled her fat butt frantically.

"You should have been here a few minutes ago. Three otters swam by, really hauling ass. You know, jumping and diving as if the world were a circus. I'd like to introduce an otter to a porpoise. They might get along well."

"Why's that?" I sat down next to the snake-eating dog and flipped on the tape recorder.

"I read that the less animals have to work for a living the

harder they play. Life is fairly easy for otters and porpoises, which is the exception."

"I see that you never took any vacations. Are you good at play?" I was trying to throw a curve.

"Oh, bullshit. People are quite different. You can only draw very simpleminded conclusions from animals. My work was my play in that it always gave tremendous pleasure."

"Marshall said you used to rappel down the faces of dams."

"I was looking for pressure cracks. Dams have cracks just like boats and ships, only you can't let it reach a bilge pump stage." He laughed deeply at the idea. "I didn't like waiting for a sequence of hanging scaffolds so I borrowed this mountaineering equipment from an engineer. It was wonderful. I could bound around like a goat or bird. I had seven-league boots!" Now he turned and smiled as if I were a long-lost friend. "Eulia drove over to Marquette to get me some kneepads. I been wearing out my knees and trousers with this crawling."

"Should I ask you if you had a good crawl yesterday?" The dog eased herself into the river for no apparent reason.

"You might say I had a fine crawl. I covered too much ground and then had to get back. I goddamn near croaked getting back, and Eulia was crying. She admitted she told you not to come back, and I said that was bad manners. Nothing upsets me besides my brain."

"Did you see anything extraordinary? How long did you crawl?"

"About five hours or so. I was the hungriest I've been in weeks. Eulia made me a version of paella, and I feel asleep on a cushion before the fire. I dreamed about the time our whole family, all seven of us, went on a picnic because Dad's old Plymouth was going to turn over—you know, break a hundred thousand miles. Eulia wants to get another dog because Miss here is afraid of everything but birds. I said no, so she got me a machete to wear on a sling on my back. Yes, I saw something extraordinary. I was eyeball to eyeball with a fawn not more than a day old. I saw some bear poop that was steaming, so I changed course. I saw two male bluejays fighting. You're so low to the ground you revert a bit and you get some strange memories that could frighten you. There was this girl when I was twelve, the loveliest girl I ever knew on earth. . . ."

Then he stopped and drew his breath in sharply.

"What is it?" I had warmed to the conversation and hoped not to lose him after a half hour. There was also the consideration that Eulia wasn't there, and I had no idea what to do if he were to have a seizure.

"I just saw a bad picture. I was back in the woods on a cold, windy day late in October. I was near her house, the shack she lived in with her parents and sister. I was watching them pack their belongings on this flatrack truck. When they were nearly done, she went in the house and out the back door. She came out in the woods and kissed me good-bye. She knew I was back there because we had this signal like a raven's voice. That's where I was just now. I hope I'm not driving you crazy along with myself."

"Not at all. I find it interesting." I was making a vain attempt not to sound like a psychiatrist. He read my thoughts and laughed.

"I had to talk to a lot of those boys when they were trying to find something to counteract my self-doctoring."

We took a break, went into the cabin and cooked some breakfast. He positioned himself before the stove and expertly cooked some brook trout and scrambled eggs, warming some tortillas that Eulia had made. He rambled on about specifications for company jets, Central American politics, the machinations of the biggest of all construction firms that had been much in the news. I was more than a little amazed by the breadth of his reading. He was, after all, self-educated, according to the vitae that Marshall had given me.

"The thing is you have to read books or you'll drive yourself up the wall. All the locations are remote and have the aura of a huge hunting, or oil, or army camps where there's not going to be a war. We have all the movies and videotapes of sports and that sort of thing, but that becomes tiresome. So there's always a bunch that reads a lot on the professional staff, which I'm on by default, because I don't have any engineering degrees. This friend of mine broke into tears one day when the chopper didn't bring in his package of books. He got drunk and drove a dozer into the river."

"Wasn't he fired?"

"Of course not. Everyone thought it was funny."

We had a long, bizarre conversation about Saul Bellow's *Humboldt's Gift.* Humboldt himself seemed to represent Strang's notion of a writer, along with Thomas Wolfe. Talking about books drew out of him an unnerving idea of the nature of personality: We achieve our dimensions for very specific reasons we ourselves ordain. In other words, we already are, at any given moment, what we, in totality, wish to be. There were addenda to this pessimistic core, such as: Scarcely anyone at any given time can locate himself in a meaningful sense. He thought this was wonderful, and I took the brunt of this Socratic mood.

"You don't seem to know what you're doing up here, do you?"

"Of course not. I thought I'd do some journalism. Write about a subject I've never written about before."

"Pretty good, but you need some nouns in there for fuel. I can tell you think you're in either over your head or under your head. I can tell by the way you ate that you're worried about what you're going to do about food in town, and by the way you look at my daughter I can see you're worried about getting laid. Right?"

"That's one of the limits of out-of-the-way journalism." My ears were tingling, and if I weren't of a dark complexion, I would have been blushing. "I'm being active so I don't catch myself sitting around regretting. If I'm active rather than self-absorbed, then my regrets can't catch up to me. How about your regrets?" I made a lame attempt to get him off my case.

"The usual ones, like standing there in the woods with that girl. I really think the self-destruct system is something we build in." He gestured to his broken body. "It was about 1942 when I got my brother Karl to find out what petit mal epilepsy was. Dad wouldn't let me go to school for his own reasons. Karl was about five years older than me and tried to be as worthless as possible, like many preacher's kids do, but I loved him and he was my hero. So in the school library he tore out a page, page 654, of the 1929 *Britannica*, which was medically way out of date, but I didn't know it. It said if you had my disease you lost the last twenty years of your life. Karl said that wasn't too bad if you thought it over and he'd teach me how to really step on the gas. And he did in his own way. You might say he met the problem of my longevity head-on. I was about seven and he was twelve at the time. Now Karl pretended to be a little slow-witted so that they'd leave him alone at school, which he hated, but in reality he was full of all sorts of theories. He might have inherited this propensity from Dad, who was once a guest preacher over in Negaunee to a church full of Finnish Lutheran miners. He harangued them for hours, convincing a lot of the audience that Finns were the long-sought, lost tribe of Israel. Karl's favorite books were by Richard Halliburton—you know, *The Royal Road to Romance, The Complete Book of Marvels.* We were always going on hikes in the furthest reaches of the forest, looking for the lost temples of ancient tribes of Indians. Anyway, Karl busied himself on what he called equations to make my life livable. Since I would surely die, according to the *Britannica,* by the time I was forty-five, I had to speed up all the processes; he seemed like a bully to others, but he was full of compassion, at least to me. I kept those rules, written in a code gotten out of a comic book, until my luggage was stolen in Hyderabad. I didn't begin to understand India until—"

"Would you mind telling me some of the rules?" I had to interrupt, in that I am a perpetual creator of rules, codes of honor, programs, dos and don'ts, Calvinist self-laceration routines (without any ostensible results).

"Of course. They were partly childish nonsense about thirty percent less sleep, thirty percent more exercise, more hunting, more fishing, more adventure and travel, more money, and more sex—because Karl was somewhat a sex maniac."

"So did you follow this program?" I had one of those free-floating hangovers that made these adolescent dicta attractive.

"Seems like I did. I'm pretty wore out, aren't I? I'm forty-six, and I'm told I'll be lucky to see forty-seven. That puts me right on schedule."

"Would you mind telling me how you handled the sexual problem if you were in the jungle or desert or whatever?" I was eager to follow this direction, remembering Evelyn's note.

"It's easy. You save it up and bury yourself in your work.

Then every month or so they let you out, and then if you like, you can cut loose. It's not like this country, where the truly ordinary problems of love and death get suffocated. You people are partly at fault. An article about what women are really all about is as likely to be as inaccurate as one on what men are all about. Women are quite a bit different in every country. In most places, they've consolidated their power. A smart woman, or a black, or an Indian, has the perfect duty to go into the Lincoln Monument late some night when no one's there and blow the fucker sky-high. You get what I mean?"

"I suppose so." I paused, trying to think of a maneuver to get him back to sex.

"You want me to talk about my sexual experiences because you're hung over and ideas bore you at the moment. Right?"

"Absolutely. Isn't it where we're all the most confused?" I could see he had begun to frazzle.

"Maybe so. First, you come out of the jungle. Say you're in Caracas or Baranquilla, or Panama City or up in San José in Costa Rica. You're a bit like a hunter looking over a new territory. You don't get drunk because alcohol is mostly a sedative and you lose all your elasticity and resilience. You probably know some people, and you meet a woman, preferably not in a bar or lounge, because that puts an uncomfortable onus on the whole thing. You remember again what your oldest sister Laurel told you one New Year's Eve when she was drunk on homemade choke-cherry wine. You were about thirteen, and you stood there on the back porch watching the snow fall, and she said Corvus, she called me by my middle name, don't be like Karl. If you are kind and good and honest with a woman, and if she's not too screwed up herself, you'll get all the loving you can handle. I said what if they're screwed up, not quite knowing what it meant. Then you'll have to get quite dramatic if you want to love them, but you're better off looking elsewhere. That's all Laurel said. Anyway, you take them to a movie, an opera, a folk ballet, an art museum. You buy them some flowers and go to dinner. Make sure it's the very best dinner available. By now you will know by a look or a gesture if she's going to make love to you. It isn't mechanistic, because you like to do all of these things anyway, especially after months of mud and jungle, cement, roaring machinery and exhaustion. In other words, you're full of delight or, as the Bible called it, jubilance. You go to her place or to your hotel, and you kiss her. You kiss the soles of her bare feet and her toes and her ears, her neck and under her chin, her knees and the backs of her knees, her belly and bottom and sex and breasts and armpits and thighs, and then you lick all these places with all your heart, over and over. When you rest, sometimes you brush her hair, because your sisters taught you how. You listen carefully to what she says, and she listens to you. You keep this up as long as you can, or time allows, as long as she wishes to, because you just entered her life, and she might not want you to know the rest of it."

There was nowhere to go after that, so we just sat there staring off into the greenery across the river. An alder branch partly submerged in the current bobbed in the surge, but not metronomically. My first feelings of nearly bitter envy subsided as I stared at the moving branch. A group of ravens flew from their rookery down toward the delta, exploding in mock ire at our presence. The dog was stalking a frog lunch in the reeds, her body all aquiver as if her life depended on it. Strang's eyes were closed, and I looked with no little pity at his legs in their braces, the way they were twisted limply askew, and the ragged hole in one of the knees. I could imagine him strolling down an avenue in Caracas in a tropical suit with a señorita on his arm, or perhaps a wayward señora. He would be all eagerness and curiosity, a half-starved vassal being led into the castle's kitchen before a Renaissance feast. I began to wonder about how many men like him there might be, building dams and suchlike, that the rest of the world was largely ignorant of, like some crazed draft horses of progress. The dog turned suddenly from her frog-stalking and ran barking out the drive.

"My mind was so full of passion I fell asleep. That must be Eulia. I bet you didn't read those books I gave you."

"I'm trying." We turned to watch Eulia swerve into the yard with Latin aplomb, barely missing the picnic table. She stooped, then went to her knees to pet the dog. The glimpse of thighs beneath her skirt brought back the conversation with uncomfortable force. She flashed us a smile and drew some packages from the truck.

"I know you gentlemen have been talking wisdom, and how Robert is making sure there are twelve light bulbs in every house in the world." She knelt by his chair and watched him unwrap a package of knee pads. His face glowed with pleasure: Like all members of big families of reduced circumstances, Strang took great pleasure in giving and receiving gifts, however small. She turned to me and shook her head. "I can tell by your eyes that you misbehaved. Your body is full of poison. . . ." She ran up to the cabin, returning with a rum bottle full of green liquid and leaves and a small glass. Strang, meanwhile, had tried on the sort of knee pads some basketball players wear and was circling the lawn at a swift crawl. "Drink immediately!" The greenish liquid in the glass she offered looked worse than Pernod. "Drink it now. My grandmother taught me how to make it."

"I'm not sure I can trust you, let alone your grandmother." Always the cad, there was an air of irrepressible flirtation in my voice.

"Trust is for the feebleminded. It belongs with envy, jealousy and laziness. I can see that you have no *cohones.*"

Naturally, I drank the brackish liquid in one prolonged gulp. Strang pulled himself onto his chair, patting his knee pads with satisfaction.

"These are wonderful pads, Eulia." He shook his head at me as I coughed. "Boy, are you going to be fucked up. You'll eventually be fine, and you won't have a hangover, but you need genes from south of the border to handle that stuff. It's one-fifty-one rum with various herbs, including lots of resinous cannabis buds."

"But I don't like dope," I said plaintively.

I sat there pleasantly enough for an hour or so until I could recapture my basic motor abilities; it is an error to fight against narcosis and offer up any evil energy that might be lurking in your brainpan. You go with it, as the young say, because that exhausts the alternatives. It was a honeyed somnolence, somewhere between De Quincey and Thoreau: The diminutive chickadee, the bravest of birds, landed on my shoe for a moment, and we exchanged glances not the less meaningful for being silly. You don't get to be both the dancer and the dance very often. If the potion had been one octave more potent, I'd have panicked. I was so busy tracking my thoughts—more accurately, images—that I didn't turn around when they left for Strang's therapeutic crawl. I felt warm to the point of tears toward Strang and Eulia, battling as they were against this seemingly inevitable disintegration. There is nothing quite like a summer skirt with thighs under it, is there? I offered this voiceless question up to the river, as the actual skirt raised on the usual wings of imagination and she waded in the river shallows, every bit as graceful and halting as a blue heron. I could feel the coldness of the water on her brown legs. Maybe I could save her from a rabid bear and she would be grateful.

It was a lust for food that brought me out of this uncanny, waking nap. It is, after all, the sublimated reason why many of us leave the Midwest in the first place. Even Boswell, with his bold knife and fork, would enjoy Zabar's, Manganaro's, the fey Dean & Deluca's. For a young poet from the Midwest, the discovery of garlic can be as poignant as the discovery of Rimbaud and Federico García Lorca. Art without sensuality dwindles into the Episcopalian. But food is still pretty much a novelty, unbusinesslike, a signal of decadence in America: Nader, Nixon, Reagan, throw in Congress, sup at the same dreary table. Finally ambulatory, I sped toward town and the inevitable whitefish special. I felt a strong enough commitment to Strang, not to speak of Eulia, to find a cabin with a kitchen.

TAPE 3: New quarters on a lagoon which was formed, so I'm told, when the mouth of the river changed courses in an enormous gale. According to a paperback book concerning itself with local history, I have noted that in a century and a half of successive Novembers hundreds have died at sea. The question naturally arises, Why didn't these folks stay ashore in November? It is probably similar to deer, who can't seem to remember the previous November when thousands were shot. Historians are twirps when they fail to remind us that memory herself is in short supply on Earth. A self-styled anarchist waiter in one of my favorite New York restaurants maintains that politicians have rarely seen anyone die, hence death is only temporary as in the movies, hence war remains a matter of rhetoric. I am resisting an impulse to call this restaurant and have them ship some raw materials by overnight express. Mother slipped in one of those Third World-type cookbooks that specializes in fiber, which summons up an image of counterculture people boiling or braising rugs. Strang, however, presents a mighty lesson in mortality, a lesson I have decided to take advantage of. Every one of us has seen the phenomenon where a grotesquely homely old sculptor, painter, writer, inventor, owns an entourage of lovely ladies. Is it a kind of ineffable vibrancy or what? It is extremely irritating to more orthodox men who want to be rewarded for their hard work, their commonplace drudgeries, however successful. And some like myself who are quite literally not totally committed to anything find the phenomenon intensely curious. The wives of these vital creatures are often secure but cynical, a queen bee syndrome. On the other side (I've always hated the word *distaff*), successful actresses enjoy the same kind of attention. Strang has a peculiar attentiveness to life, to be banal. He takes it seriously but somehow with a light touch. The light touch idea is what is keeping me far from the civilities I love, a good meal, and an embittered career woman with whom to exchange caresses. A little while ago I tried to study Strang's dam handbook, along with a glossy folder Marshall gave me extolling his firm's expertise in overseeing these giant projects. I read how a dam in Brazil has taken a decade and thirty thousand men to build. Marshall told me scornfully that most people have no idea where electricity comes from. It's almost equally true with food, I responded. But many educated people find it unpleasant that either comes from anyplace. It is a philosophical inconvenience that rivers be diverted and controlled or animals de-

stroyed. If your mind changes itself fast enough,
the result is vertigo. Certain words, such as
satori or *epiphany,* or that old saw *conversion,*
come to mind. The Danish malcontent and humpback
Kierkegaard insisted that ""purity of heart is to
will one thing.'' On that note, I'll get ready for
the dance at the bar, which has advertised a live
band as opposed to a dead one. I've eaten a fibrous
soup of lentils, cabbage, and garlic and am waiting for health to arrive despite some recent bel-
ches that would have inflated the Hindenburg. Who
knows if the night might hold romance? I'd wager
against it heavily, but my like has been full of
self-fulfilling prophecies. I doubt I'll ever
see a cow without building a sentence around the
poor animal.

   Tape 3 cont. 3:00 A.M.: A word to the wise. Went
to the bar and was forced to dance because everybody dances. Soaked with sweat. Wrestled with a
woman my own age in car. She took advantage of me.
Just threw soup into lagoon. The bar owner danced
on the bar with the waitresses, one of whom fell
off without injury. Am eating raw hamburger with
black pepper.

CHAPTER VI

Another dawn, another tack which caught us by surprise.
Much later I realized it was the wild thunderstorm, abetted by
Eulia's singing in the kitchen. She played a twelve-string guitar
so softly that, with our backs turned to her as we faced the fire,
one could have sworn the music came from back in the forest.
When I had arrived and found Strang staring at his barometer
with delight, I remembered thinking rather dully when I left
my cabin that there appeared to be immense black mountains
to the west out in Lake Superior. So before the fire, whose
banal attributes have evoked so many questionable tales, I
prodded Strang into beginning his own:

————————

Late in July of my seventh year, I became quite suddenly
old. A thunderstorm did the job, which I didn't see coming

because of the ridge of hills on the north side of the lake where I was fishing for perch and bluegills. At the same moment my dad called to me from shore, the wind began to howl and lightning strike around the lake. But before the lightning struck the boat there was a moment or two of silence, I think, when birds and fish became hyperactive before the storm—fish jumping and rolling, swallows performing maneuvers that would shame the most daring pilot. I heard a roaring from behind the ridge and then saw the black clouds and the yellowish pall beneath them, and then Dad called, his voice barely beating an enormous thunderclap to the boat. I was only seventy feet or so from shore, fishing between a reed bed and a patch of lily pads, with their small, yellow buds and an occasional large, white lily, which can be smelled a long ways away. Anyway, Dad shouted, and then there was this immense white light and the oarlocks, my fishing reel, and the screws that held the old wood boat together, all begin to glow. I was pitched backward out of the boat and only remember crouching on the bottom of the lake near the roots of lily pads, with my hands grasping at the roots and muck. I ran out of breath and pushed toward the surface, which was a sheet of white light from the storm. It was raining so hard that the rain almost drowned me. I swam toward Dad's voice in the driving rain, my ears sounding like trumpets and my vision smoky and diffused, and that's how I got my seizures.

That must have been in 1941 in the summer before Pearl Harbor. "Remember Pearl Harbor as we go to meet the foe," everyone used to sing. Thinking back on that unique event—I mean the accident, not the war; wars are about as unique as cowshit or marriage—I realize how lucky I was to be a swimmer, particularly a night swimmer, as I was more than half-blinded at the time. I think I mentioned this night swimming to you. Starting at about age four, when Karl taught me I would swim anywhere the water was warm enough to bear, anytime I could get away with it, day or night. At our camp, that's what they call a cabin up here in the Upper Peninsula, I would slip out of the loft past four sleeping sisters and two brothers, down the ladder past my snoring dad and mom, and swim around the lake in the pitch dark. Karl knew what I was doing and told me there were werewolves out on the lake at night with heads of a regular wolf but with bodies like a black alligator, but I kept it up. It was this stubbornness that saved me in my accident in Venezuela, though I now question whether my current life was worth the effort.

———————

I must interrupt Strang's tale. The most extraordinary thing just happened. Outside the rain was coming down in dense sheets. Eulia announced to us that it fascinated her and she was going out in the rain. She quickly removed her clothes except for her panties and bra, which quite literally shortened my breath. But then seeing her out through the window, hugging her chest with her face tilted upward, the vision became nonsexual, numinous, with the effect of a fine pre-Raphaelite painting. Strang stared out the window as if only Eulia still kept him anchored to the earth. The few minutes had achieved an almost embarrassing intensity when she rushed back into the cabin and wrapped herself in a blanket.

"When I was a child," she said, "we had this dog that would hang around our shack outside Puntarenas. We fed him scraps, but he would never let us touch him except during a thunderstorm. Then he would crawl under the porch and we'd go in after him, and we could pet him because he was so frightened of the thunder. The minute the storm stopped he'd run off, but as long as it thundered he would be all limp and friendly like a baby. I loved him so much I'd pray for rain." She laughed at this thought and abruptly went up to the loft to dress.

———————

Isn't it strange that the place it rains the most on earth is an area of the Atlantic far off Trinidad and Venezuela? Torrential rains falling on the ocean, day after day. I like the whole idea for some reason. I've always been a student of water, especially rivers.

Dad, being a preacher of sorts, made hay out of my accident. He was really a crackerjack carpenter, profoundly religious, a layman preacher full of elaborate notions, often changing denominations with the shifts of his mind. He was a footloose man and didn't dwell on ancestors and relatives. I was the only one of the kids born up in Michigan; all the others were born in Chicago. I was what they supposedly call a love child, born when my mother was forty-seven, though that issue is somewhat confused now. Perhaps anyone's true biography is where they have arrived. Theodore was the oldest—named after one of Dad's countless heroes, Theodore Roosevelt. Then the girls: Laurel, Ivy, Lily and Violet—my mother was taken by flowers and plants. Next was Karl, and five years later me. I heard we were vaguely related to King Strang, the Mormon apostate scoundrel who, back in the nineteenth century, took over Beaver Island as a new country for his followers.

The petit mal epilepsy was caused, of course, by the trauma of the accident. It is an easily controlled infirmity now, but then during the war it was another matter, especially here in the outback. Dad didn't give credence to any doctor but the healing power of Jesus. Mother snuck me off to some drunken osteopath in the county seat who pronounced me hopeless. He shined lights in my eyes, which set off a seizure. "Three bucks, and get this kid out of here." This osteopath was later run out of town for killing a child with nosedrops, of all things. He killed the wrong child, the child of the school principal. Who can count the damage this fool did before then? When this sort of injustice ceases to make the heart ache and no action is taken, we become the country we are becoming.

So Dad kept me in his power until he died when I was fourteen. I don't want to make this a pilgrimage backwards, because that's what humans do, they make pilgrimages back to a way they never were. Karl was always calling Dad "Dire Portents," or "D.P." because Dad drove us batty with that phrase. Hitler without doubt was the Antichrist, thus Jesus would be returning soon to preside over the only Apocalypse we'll ever have. My youth was in the arena between Dad and Karl. Karl was under no one's control by the time he hit thirteen in 1942. He was a big kid and awesomely strong for his age. He knocked out a teacher in the eighth grade and that was the end of his school days. The problem was, Karl had a trapline, and he'd get up at 4 A.M. and sometimes would fall asleep in school from fatigue. The teacher was one of those bully coaches, and he jerked Karl awake by his hair, which got him knocked cold. Dad would pray for Karl during grace at mealtimes because Karl refused to be baptized. Dad would keep repeating the story of the ninety and nine, how the shepherd would search all night in the storm for the single lost sheep, all of this with the potatoes cooling and the fat on the sidepork congealing.

"Number one, I'm not a sheep. And number two, I've never been lost. I'm about as good in the woods as anyone," Karl would say.

Now my father wasn't one of these Bible Belt maniacs who doubles as a child-beater. He never raised a hand against any of us. We were sort of a sloppy, good-humored bunch, in fact. Karl couldn't make him angry, and Ted, when he was home, kept Karl from ever being truly insulting to Dad. Ted had the practical authority of being the oldest son and was already building houses by the time he got out of high school. Ted would pay Karl a dollar a day in the summers to dig well pits and foundations.

The real hold my father kept on me, as unlike other fathers as he was, was that I desperately wanted to go back to school with the kids I knew in first grade, but my disease kept me from doing so. Dad said he had a dream that Jesus would heal me if I did His will. If I did His will, then I could go back to school. Dad's interpretation of the "will" was to travel around the Upper Peninsula in an old Plymouth, testifying at churches about my miraculous accident. I did so right up until his death when I was fourteen, though it slacked off a bit toward the end as we had overcovered the territory and the invitations decreased and I had become a preacher.

I sometimes wonder if there wasn't some hidden pragmatism in my father's religion. After all, he moved up into this desolate area with a carload of children in the Great Depression. Thinking of it now, the situation reminds me a little of what I saw when I was working in India. American

[52]

people support their holy men the same way they do in India. Brother Strang and his fine Christian family were always getting a donation of a quarter of beef, half a pig, a few crates of potatoes, even a deer.

I admit this religion thing was frightening at times to a boy, though I enjoyed the travel and socializing since I didn't get to go to school. What was scarey is how carried away Dad would become. In fact, it would scare anyone that came in contact with it, though under the guise of religious ecstasy it was acceptable behavior. It's acceptable now with blacks by our educated whites, but the fact that poor whites behave this way is found somewhat embarrassing. That's because these poor folk are misrepresented by the gouging, venal television preachers. So we might be driving from Moran way over to Iron Mountain or Laurium. We'd stop to eat a sandwich or take a pee, and he'd grab me and swirl around an arm in the sky as if he were orchestrating nature.

"Look, son! Precious Jesus, look around you. Solomon in all his glory was not arrayed the way God arrayed these natural wonders. Look at the forest and birds and this creek. Let's pray, son." We'd kneel then in the grass off the roadside and pray, oblivious to any passing traffic. "O God of heaven and earth and the whole wide universe, look on my little son and these fits he has with kindness. He lived through your great miracle and nearly saw Thy face but didn't quite, or else he'd be dead. Your power got into him, and he testifies to your grace and majesty. Heal him so he won't die in some woeful frenzy. Help also his brother Karl who has not taken Jesus as his own personal savior and mocks Thee, O Father. Spare Karl from harm and make him come to you. Amen."

Karl, frankly, was no help. By the time I was eleven and maturing rather early, Karl would try to get me to squeeze these church ladies in the ass when they would smother me with kisses. It was beginning to be quite a trial when I'd help baptize people in a lake and you could see right through the nightgown the girls wore. Karl had bought some dirty pictures up at the Soo, that's what we call Sault Ste. Marie, and he made sure I saw them. The one that struck me the hardest was a photo of Hedy Lamarr, where she was swimming in a pond in the jungle and her bare bottom was raised out of the water. Dad burned Karl's photos in the kitchen stove, and he never was able to find that good one with Hedy Lamarr again.

Here is a story that might show you what Karl was like and the effect it had on me. In summers I'd earn extra money picking berries: huckleberries or blueberries, as they're sometimes called, blackberries, raspberries, wild strawberries. Before I could pick any to sell, I had to get Mother what she needed for the family for jams and preserves. I tended to shun the side of the village where the school was located and where the kids played ball in the summer. There is a specific cruelty to children that is really a veiled curiosity, and I was the brunt of it, except at church where everyone is compelled to behave. Some older girls even cornered me outside the post office and asked me to have a fit for them.

"Go fuck yourselves, you shitheads!" I yelled, which is how Karl taught me to respond. The girls thought that was the funniest thing they had ever heard.

It was while I was picking berries that I met Edith, the girl I mentioned as my first love. I'd leave early in the morning with two three-gallon cans and a smaller container and a crossbar to help me carry the fruit home. I'd take the path down past the old dump which led into the forest where the picking was the best. Edith was often there with her dad and mom. Her dad, who was older like my own, acted strangely because he had been gassed over in France in World War I. He busied himself digging up scrap iron in this deserted dump, a valuable item for the current war effort. Once he dug up the boiler and wheels for an old logging machine and really made a payoff. Other people in town tried it, but the work was too hard. He had to tunnel down in frozen sawdust and winch out the boiler right on Christmas Day. Anyway, Edith's dad would see me coming home with all of these berries and ask me how much I made at my picking. I told him, and he asked if I'd mind putting his daughter to work so she could earn her keep.

The first few days we scarcely talked, out of shyness. We were only nine or ten and were both outcasts, I suppose. By about the third day she had a ribbon in her hair and her bare feet and legs were comparatively clean. The main reason we got more berries than anyone else is that Karl told me where to go. He was big on drawing very precise maps, and his knowledge of the woods, gained from hunting and trapping, was exhaustive. During bird and deer season, when well-heeled hunters came up from downstate, Karl would sell them game so they could spend their time drinking and playing cards and still show off when they got back home. Early one morning Karl picked us up in Ted's truck just beyond the dump. He announced he had found what he called a mother lode of blueberries. Edith and me were happy because I had an order for twenty quarts from a lawyer's wife who always paid more than we asked. This woman was known to be a bit of a drinker, but she once invited us into her house for a Coca-Cola and played the piano for us.

I remember being a little upset that Karl stopped that morning. I was having the first burning infatuation of my life, and I know Edith felt the same way. Sometimes we held hands, and I imagined us as living in the books I read at the time by Horatio Alger, *Jed the Bootblack Boy* or *Sink or Swim,* that kind of book. Edith said she was going to be a nurse when she grew up and help those wounded in war, no doubt thinking of her father. Myself, I was torn between becoming a preacher in an enormous, big city church who would be given a new car every year and an occupation Dad preached against. He railed against the gods of Mammon and Moloch who built the Hoover Dam where a boyfriend of his, and dozens of others, had died in its construction. I read about this dam in Richard Halliburton and, since I had always been so protected, I felt the appeal of doing some truly dangerous work. What boy hasn't felt the call to commit an act of daring that will lift him out of the commonplace in the eyes of others?

Well, we were way down a gravel road and, turning off on a two-track, Karl turned to us with an air of foreboding.

"I suppose you ninnies, you two lovebirds, think I'm taking a day off to help you out? Think again, suckers. You might say I'm an archaeologist and you're my workers. You two are so goddamn dumb and scared you don't even know how to kiss and screw. Now Corve (my nickname), if you don't give Edith a little loving, she'll start looking for a real man like me." Karl was a fourteen-year-old at his worst, all hormones and braggadocio.

"If you touch Edith, I'll get your gun at night and shoot you in the head!" I literally screamed this and grasped

Edith's hand. She had begun sniffling, and I put my arm around her.

"Calm down, you little chickenshits. We're doing archaeology today, not screwing. You're absolutely dead-on right, Corve, to shoot anyone who screws with your girl. I was testing you to see if you had the courage to face up to what I'm going to show you. Last winter when I was trapping way back here along the edge of the swamp and was led out of the blizzard by a giant, fire-eyed dog known as Wendigo to the Ojibways, I saw something that almost burst my heart with fright."

Now Karl stopped the truck as the two-track winnowed down into no more than a game trail. Edith and me got out with our scalps tingling from Karl's apparent caution. He led us down the trail carrying three shovels and berry pails as if we were stalking the most crazed Bengal tiger. We reached the edge of an immense marsh that was blue with acres of berries. Karl pointed to a hillock and rock outcropping on the far side of the marsh.

"Last December, when the snow was falling hard, I was on that island in the marsh. It was late in the afternoon, and I didn't want to spend a night under a pine tree with my hands buried in the warm guts of a beaver to prevent freezing." Karl was a fan of Jack London. "I stood there in the fading light trying to figure out what to do and then suddenly I heard a deep, hoarse breathing, as if it were wind from some hellish cave. I turned slowly and leveled my rifle at whatever it would be." He stopped and shook his head dramatically, while we clutched at each other. "I'll tell you what it was, and I swear this on Mother's head—it was an open-mouthed white skull bigger than a car!"

I fairly tripped over poor Edith trying to run for it, then

paused out of love and grabbed her arm, but Karl was too quick and held us back with his muscular arms.

"Nothing doing, cowards. It's too late to turn back, besides we've been spotted. I actually brought you along to protect me. You two little Bible-thumpers are safe from dark spirits while I'm a nonbeliever and they can get me. It's like Dracula can't suck blood from anyone who wears a cross. Please help me."

The Dracula comment made matters worse as we shuffled along behind Karl. The merchants in our town sponsored free shows in the summer, putting a sheet up against a building next to a vacant lot. Our church was dead set against both movies and dancing, so Karl was the only one who got to go. Dad somehow didn't mind Karl reenacting the movies for us, and Dracula was his most powerful performance. The whole family was frightened by this blood-sucking menace from Europe. Dad offered a usual theory.

"This is surely dire portents of the Last Days. The Lord will not bear his children sucking blood out of each other's necks. Jesus said no man knows the hour of his return, but I'd say it was right around the corner."

"It's just a movie, Dad. It didn't really happen," Theodore said.

"If it's in a movie, it had to happen to get on a screen. I saw movies in Chicago before I was saved. I can tell you, Al Jolson never bit anyone in the neck."

Well, we reached the island after stumbling in the spongy sphagnum of the marsh. I had a lump in my throat, and Edith's cheeks were streaked with drying tears. Karl held up his hand as we stared into dense viburnum and tamarack to a small knoll with a clearing. Without question there are places in nature that own a certain unique spirit, that are so peculiar and individual that they draw us to them, not that they care, but that they stand out in the surrounding solitude and vastness of the forest and act as magnets to anyone who passes their way. This was such a place, and to this day, more than thirty-five years later, I remember it as well as any house I have ever lived in.

Now Karl began singing a no doubt phony Indian chant. I suspect he had managed to frighten himself a bit. Then he plunged boldly toward the clearing, and we hurried after him, not wanting to be left alone.

"Corve and Edith, this is where I saw the skull, big as life. It was about eighteen by ten feet, which would make the whole skeleton as tall as that fire tower over by Rexton. I would have to guess that the skull, for its own reasons, has sunk down into the ground." Karl scuffed at the dirt in the center of the clearing with his boot. "This might well be the tip of the nose. We better get digging right here."

So we dug our hearts out. By noon and lunchless, Karl excused Edith to go pick blueberries so we wouldn't get in trouble with her dad or the lawyer's wife. We continued probing for the nose tip and then the forehead, which would offer a larger target. Edith came back, announcing with delight that it was the best berry picking in the world; her feminine pragmatism had replaced fright with fulfilling an obligation. She watched us dig with condescension as if she had caught us whacking off. What saved the day was that under a damp bed of tamarack needles I found a large, yellowish-white bear skull. This was a rare find because up here porcupines clean the forest of all bones and antlers. If it weren't for porcupines, the forest would be a boneyard. Karl seized on the bear skull as a vindication of the day.

"I knew it, goddamit! This bear skull has the power to grow and shrink. I mistook it for a human in the blizzard. Corve, try to imagine a bear the size of the Mackinac Ferry. That's how big this sucker would be. It could eat the whole town and might very well do so." He looked around as if wondering what to do with it, then made us kiss it as he whispered more mumbo jumbo. Then he took his belt and hung it from a limb so the porcupines wouldn't get it. "This ought to scare the shit out of anyone who tries to trespass on my trapline."

I just remembered that someone said that the ultimate track that any creature leaves on earth is a skull. That's a wonderful statement, isn't it?

CHAPTER VII

The preceding was interrupted at midmorning of what turned out to be Memorial Day. Eulia was sunbathing on a cushion in one of those string bikinis favored in Central and South America: Suffice it to say that this suit would have fit, chipmunk-style, in one of my cheeks. Strang was bearing up well under the stress of telling his tale except for moments when he would lapse off into a reverie or the pain would overwhelm him. The pain, however, didn't stop him from his arduous afternoon crawls in the forest. The mosquitoes and blackflies endemic to this latitude had come to life, and his face and arms were covered with bites, despite the lotions used as a repellent.

"I don't see why you continue this therapy if it hurts that much?" I had asked.

"It's my only chance to see the world clearly, you know, to get better. If I just sat here and took all the drugs I've been prescribed, nothing would happen except narcosis. That's why

I get up at first light when the world begins again. I always have. Then you see everything before your mind is involved in the struggles of the day's work. Same thing happens if you work a night shift and sleep in the evening. You go to work after breakfast at midnight. The excavation might be three miles across and mostly lighted by spots, with the roar of hundreds of earth-moving machines, and the roar of the diverted river behind you. You jump into a pickup to relieve your man and see how the work is going. Maybe you are lowering a three-hundred-ton generator into the new shell of a powerhouse. You saw the old crane was breaking down and you located one in the Alps, which was out of the question, and another one in Terre Haute, Indiana. The crane in Indiana is shipped down the Mississippi, then out of New Orleans on a freighter, down to the coast here. If we're really in the boondocks, you have to cut the crane up and ship it in by Sikorsky freight helicopters. After a job is done, a lot of the big equipment is abandoned if you're back in the jungle. You might find natives living in the cab of a crane when you come back to check a breakdown. Or say you work all night getting an eighty-ton transformer down a hill with hawsers and an airbag. Suddenly it is dawn, and everybody is happier because the birds start up and there's less fear on the site. Once a group of us were up on the side of a hill moving loose boulders at night and one of my men was half crushed. I held his head and shoulders in my lap while waiting for the doctor. Then daylight came, and over our circle of Brazilians, with me in the center on the ground, a huge bird flew, circling for a moment. No one had ever seen it before except the half-dead man in my lap, who was smiling. I moved him a little for his comfort, but the back of his head felt like a cloth sack with gravel in it. Then his life gave way, and all those *católicos* knelt down and started praying. Later I found out the bird was an eagle that eats monkeys. Maybe the dying man, who was a smart fellow, smiled because he saw the irony there. So to answer you, I do the crawling because it's the only work at hand and I'm a worker and it's my only chance to get back to my real work. Maybe the treatment is a hoax, even a fatal hoax, but it's the only one I got to go on. Twice I've been on a project that never should have happened. There's no more pathetic thing than building a dam that shouldn't be there. It usually happens for political reasons. I always demand a transfer. I can't bear meaningless work. Now Eulia is a dancer, and she works out at least four hours a day, and it's hard to understand how she repeats this same routine every day. She says it's to be physically capable, when the occasion arises, to do what the choreographer asks, or to do the movements her heart or spirit might ask her to do. So that's meaningful work. What if you suddenly couldn't write after spending your whole life doing so? You're no spring chicken—what if you had a small stroke and everything else was fine, but you even spelled your goddamn name backwards, what would you do? That's what I mean."

"I understand," I answered, not without a tremor in my stomach. "Perhaps I'd hang in there a while and see if it was reversible. I'd be full of dread—"

"That's wrong," Strang interrupted. "You've got to beat the dread out of yourself, or you can't do anything for yourself properly. I've gathered together all the available information, and I'll give it a try until October. I've had other times in my life that seemed worse, but that was earlier. Now it's time for your sedative." Strang had become an accurate observer of my behavior and knew when I was desperate for a drink.

Back to midmorning on Memorial Day, with its sidelong glances at Eulia's bottom staring back at the sun in an equal trade of glory. My eyes were overdazzled, and my concentration inept. Strang took a break to fish in his aluminum walker contraption downstream near a log jam. His struggle against the current created a lump in my throat. Miss, the fat dog, watched him from the bank, then rushed barking along the bank and out the driveway. A big station wagon entered the yard with the dog behind it, as if it were only through her efforts that the car could move. A large woman in her early fifties got out, followed by a younger woman in a women's air force uniform and a sluggish-looking fellow, also big, in his late twenties, I would guess. They were all spiffy in their Sunday best: The man wore the sort of doubleknit suit and string tie preferred for formal occasions in the Great White North. He actually wore well-shined brown shoes and white socks. I felt snobbish and territorial at the same time, mistakenly, it turned out. Eulia got up from her brazen mat, all supple and greasy with lotion.

"May I help you?"

"I'm Emmeline. You know, Corve's first wife. And who are you, beautiful? You could start a public riot." She laughed the kind of deep belly laugh that makes everyone within earshot feel better.

"I'm Eulia." She offered a rare smile. I walked over, and we completed the introductions. They were openly pleased I had come that far to talk to their ex-husband and father. Robert Jr. strode down the bank and into the muck and reeds to help his father. Strang hugged them all, half pulling them over the walker, no mean feat as they were true heavyweights. They reminded me of people who had emerged whole from the time warp of the 1950s. Aurora cried after she kissed her father. Emmeline was distressed and beaming at the same time, while Robert Jr.'s face reddened as he glanced at Eulia, who was unnaturally pleased at the reunion.

"Bobby, you stupid shit, you're muddy to the knees," Emmeline said with another laugh.

"Guess I don't care one bit." He gave one the impression of a man who spent a lot of time alone. It turned out he was a logger.

"You sound like Uncle Karl. Emmeline, are you sure you weren't fooling with Karl when I was in Africa?" Strang's eyes sparkled with the question.

"Robert Corvus!" She covered her face and shrieked. "You know I was true to you for years. Who knows what you was doing with those jungle bunnies overseas? I'm taking my picnic and going home."

Strang reached over and tugged her by the arm. "You were the truest woman of my life. After you, it was pretty much downhill."

"Nobody said you had to spend all your time away," Aurora flared. I could see she held her own.

"I didn't drive a hundred miles to see you bitches try to tear Dad apart. Besides, I'm hungry. Aurie," he called her, "get the picnic basket."

"Get it yourself, you lamebrain bastard. You call me a bitch again, and I'll use judo." She advanced on him with a silly smile, chasing him to the car.

It was an oddly wonderful picnic. Eulia got dressed to Robert Jr.'s loudly spoken regrets.

"To be frank, Eulia"—he pronounced it Yew-lee—"I've never laid eyes on one like you in real life."

"Bobby here cuts down trees all day long. His wife ran off with a cosmetics salesman and left him with two kids. She was pretty awful."

"You should have brought your kids, Bobby. Jesus, am I too young to be a grandpa? Eulia, I'm a grandpa."

"What a wonderful thing to be!" I found out later that Eulia's happiness was due to the fact that she was from a big extended family and loved family confusion.

"I didn't want to tire you out with the kids. We know you're real sick, and we want to take you over to the hospital in Escanaba."

"Thank you. They're no doubt good at chain-saw wounds and sewing up drunks, but I got some special problems. It was a good thought, and I'll call if I need help."

Meanwhile, I was intent on the food before us. Emmeline had spread a fine Belgian tablecloth that I guessed Strang had sent years before. It was the kind of northern feast that accounts for the heaviest concentration of stomach cancer in the United States, a fact that deters no one. There were Cornish pasties wrapped in foil to keep them warm, smoked whitefish and lake trout, cold beef with a horseradish cream sauce, a container of home-pickled herring, and assorted pickles and relishes.

"You're too thin, Corve," Emmeline said somewhat defensively.

"I busted up my guts when I fell. They took out my spleen. I couldn't keep down food for quite a while."

"Our stepdad wanted to send over some flowers. He's a good guy, you know. He wanted to send over some flowers, but I said old Dad only likes wildflowers, so he picked these." Aurora reached into the cavernous picnic basket and brought out violets and buttercups surrounded by watercress strands.

"Please thank him for me." Strang buried his face in the flowers long enough to make us uncomfortable. "You didn't know my sister Violet who died. She didn't like violets, but she liked buttercups."

Strang and Emmeline went to the cemetery to visit the graves of father and mothers, sisters and brothers, a custom still followed religiously in rural areas of our country. I clearly saw that Strang didn't want to go, but it was a palliative offered after some odd unpleasantness over business accounts. Robert Jr. had gone off to the car after the meal and returned with a pile of ledgers. I had followed Aurora's signal and moved to the riverbank, where we sat with Eulia and the dog. Eulia spoke eloquently to the dog in Spanish, which made me curse my ignorance of that language. I began talking with Aurora who, as it turned out, was stationed in Naples, Italy, with NATO as an information officer. We spoke rather excitedly about the food available in all the different regions of Italy and about Waverly Root's masterpiece on the subject. Eulia asked how we could possibly talk about food after an enormous meal.

"Jesus, Eulia, give me a break. It's my favorite thing. Call me Miss Thunder Thighs. Luckily for me Italian men don't mind a little substance. One old goat calls me *piccola mamma*. Are you Dad's girlfriend?"

"Of course not. I suppose I am his stepdaughter. He is my favorite man in a world of worthless pigs."

"Thank you, darling." I suppressed an urge to oink, but was a little too hurt to respond comically. Aurora patted my arm, and Eulia kissed my ear, our first physical contact, and my ear burned with her breath. Meanwhile, I was practicing one of my minor, schizoid talents as a writer and listening to the conversation up at the picnic table with my cooler ear. Here is a somewhat garbled rendition.

"Dad, you could at least look at the books. We busted our balls to make a go of this."

"I've seen some of the figures. The accountant in Miami sends me figures every quarter." Strang was plainly keeping his low pitch while the other two voices were choked with emotion.

"I just always thought we were doing our best for you. I

mean, we always did real well because you put up the money—" Emmeline said.

"That had nothing to do with it," Strang interrupted. "Lots of money gets invested, and more than half of all enterprises go bankrupt. You both did well because you're smart and worked hard."

"I just thought you'd come back someday and be the head man or advise us, you know, when you retired. Now you're all busted up, and me and Bobby want to take care of you. We got plenty of money—"

"I don't need any money, Emmeline. The company takes care of you when you're injured. Ted gave me the cabin. And you already have a fine husband to help run things. . . ."

"He don't know anything. He's a good guy, but he's got no sense. Mom runs the whole show." Robert Jr. was red-faced and pacing.

"I just always thought you'd come back someday and live near us and we'd see you. I know we wouldn't be family, but I would see you. I loved you so much my heart just breaks." Her sobs were strong and full as her laughter had been.

Robert Jr. strode off toward the forest. "I can tell you one thing, goddammit. I'm not taking your goddamn money," he yelled.

Strang slid down the bench and put his arm around Emmeline. Aurora joined them and ran a hand through his hair. Eulia buried her face in her hands, and I gave her a frantic pat on the shoulder.

After Strang and Emmeline left for the cemetery, Robert Jr. walked out of the woods with an air between shame and embarrassment. Eulia had retrieved a bottle of whiskey and four glasses. We sat at the picnic table with all of them implicitly looking toward me and my seniority for wisdom. I passed.

"I guess I fucked up. I never thought I'd yell at my own father. He probably won't want to see me anymore."

"Oh, nonsense, Bobby. You're always like that. If you stepped on dogshit in the middle of the night you'd think it was your fault." Aurora had been out in the great world and was being sensible.

"We built up a logging business, and a motel and restaurant on his money. Now he doesn't want any part of us. Do you think my dad's got all his marbles?" The question was on the money, however inelegant.

"Not on the terms of nearly all of us," I hedged, then tried to confront the issue. "I imagine he liked being paid well all of these years, but he has no particular use for money. As far as I can see, he's never slowed down long enough to have time to spend money. I'm sure the only regret he's had is not spending much time with those he loved, so he wanted them to live well."

"I just don't know. Maybe I can at least get him down home to see my new skidder." Bobby talked as he fingered through his wallet and unfolded a clipping which he passed to me.

It was an Associated Press piece printed in the *Marquette Mining Journal* a half dozen years before: "Upper Peninsula Man Overseas Giant Brazilian Dam Project." It showed a photo of "head foreman" Robert C. Strang, rather shyly dwarfed by an immense dump-truck tire, and another of him pointing to a dam from the top of a powerhouse. I read it quickly and passed it back.

"I'd say that there's a man who knows what he was doing." Bobby drank down his whiskey with the air of a man who had made the winning point.

"Bobby, remember when he brought us down to Miami to this big deal hotel? We were about ten. We waited a couple days for him and went swimming all day in the hotel pool because you asked if we could. Then Dad came into town in old construction clothes, and he just called the clothing store in the hotel and they sent up new clothes for him. You wouldn't eat lobster because you said it looked like the hellgrammites you used for trout bait."

"I always thought Mom should have just waited for him like he was off to war or something like that."

"That's not fair," Eulia said. "My father went to Limón one day, and we never saw him again."

CHAPTER VIII

TAPE 4 : Back to my own cabin with an extraordinary
sense of relief. My god! Confrontations and anxiety are the given in the big city, but they seem
especially raw in a sylvan setting. Imagine a
prolonged and vicious argument between lovers in
a beautiful part of the forest. I will create one
because that's my business, as it were. Strang
caught me on the way out of the yard. He was plainly
exhausted.

"Beating a retreat, hey?"

"You don't look so hot yourself. A poet named
Lorca once said, 'I want to sleep the dream of ap-
ples, far from the tumult of cemeteries.'"

"That's a fine thing to say. Love and death
tire a man out. You just can't answer any of these
big questions, but you got to keep a weather eye
out for them."

"You want tomorrow off?"

"Oh, god, no. I thought we had some work to do."

There is a uniqueness to those who work very hard. Thoreau only pretended to loaf—every step of a walk was part of an idea. I remember reading about Rilke's pilgrimage to see Tolstoy. He told the great count that he wanted to be a writer. "Then write, for God's sake," replied Tolstoy. It is built into the arts that her participants, except for a few, are waffling neurotics. The distorted prism is the source of the energy. What did Shakespeare feel like after a good lunch and a stroll along the Avon? I doubt he regretted the extra chop or he wouldn't have eaten it. The other evening I bought a local Indian a few drinks to see if he would reveal any secret lore. Nothing doing. We can be reasonably sure that not all of these people are mysterious. He did give me three illegally small lake trout. As opposed to the lake trout of the warmer waters of Lake Michigan, the permanently cold waters of Lake Superior yield up a pink-fleshed, fatless fish. I poached the first, serving it to myself at room temperature with a fresh cucumber mayonnaise and a Sancerre. The second I broiled over wood and grapevine cuttings swiped from a grape arbor near the cabin. I basted it with lemon, butter and vermouth. By the dint of inordinate self-control I will save the third for tomorrow. Or not. Strang with his children: Real emotion can seize one with terror. As children we are guided around like little bears. We are taught essentials: not to piss our pants or bed, how to tie our shoes, to eat with our mouths closed, the reversal of which we practiced before the mirror to see what was so terrible about it. Mashed potatoes were interesting. But then many of us are released on the world as permanent orphans, or those who are only casually and insincerely, we feel, adopted. I have a few rich friends who were sent off to boarding school at age six. Mothers and fathers, lis-

ten! They never got over it, never. I was a hopeless bed wetter, then one morning I jumped out of
bed at dawn and ran downstairs in dry pajamas. Mom
and Dad, I shouted, I didn't pee the bed! They woke
slowly but treated this accomplishment as a tri-
umph. My life changed for the better that day. In
New York, it makes everyone glad to see those nursery school tykes marching down the street con-
nected by a long string. Some of them pause to
watch a bum gurgling down a bottle of Tokay, and
the string grows taut.

Last evening I drove around the countryside—
it doesn't get dark up here until after ten this
time of year—with a set of topographical maps
Strang loaned me. When we take breaks from his
story, he is trying to teach me about geology,
weather, natural history, physics and suchlike,
including the basic shapes used in structural engineering. He confesses kind amazement at what
little I know. We discuss humanism and my considerable knowledge of history, arts and letters,
music. He is no slouch in this area, either. The
textbook on dam engineering is the best tonic for
insomnia I've ever possessed. He is an unself-
conscious visionary of technology. He thinks the
"nuke" boys haven't perfected their lessons,
hence there will continue to be a need for the hydroelectric power. I was pleased when he said the
Glen Canyon shouldn't have been built any more
than we would allow NASA to dye half the moon pink
for research.

Stopped at the tavern for a nightcap. The bar
owner whipped out that morning's *Free Press* for
our discussion of current events over my bedtime
toddy. We never got past an account of government
research announcing that Michigan leads the
country in alcoholism, obesity and hyperten-
sion. It is second in smoking to North Carolina. I
light a cigarette and drop my lighter. My temples
pound when I bend over to pick it up. I take a gulp

[73]

of my drink and suppress a belch. Did I need that
platter of *roesti* potatoes with my fish? Did the
salad require two hard-boiled eggs, a tin of anchovies, and a half-cup of Parmesan? The bar
owner is a tad burly like myself. He drinks coffee
brandy with milk because of an ulcer. Oh, well. We
promise to discuss this further.

———————

A cold dawn with the wind shifting to the north in the night.
I tried to scrape frost from my windshield with my fingernails.
No wonder vegetable gardening isn't a big item up here, while
the making of gravy is a science. I began to mull over my sexual
deprivation when my eyes caught a movement ahead. It looked
like a beige, medium-sized dog, and I recognized it as a coyote.
I made a note to send my mother a postcard to announce my
nature sighting.

All was not well at the Strang cabin, and it took a while
to get started. He was in great pain and had allowed himself
a pill, which made him drowsy. Eulia was doing some stretch-
ing exercises in a flannel nightgown that revealed nothing. I
fetched some wood for the fire and filled the tank of the
ancient Kohler generator they used for power. The dog cornered a chipmunk but lay down as if puzzled by what to do
with the prize. Back in the cabin, Eulia was heating something
up at the stove that smelled delicious. One tends to approach
the cookstove of another with hands behind the back like a
tentative professor. It was a Spanish bean soup with sausage
and fat pork and redolent with garlic. Despite a diet I had
devised during a 3 A.M. spate of indigestion, I craved a bowl.

"We had a difficult time." Beneath her tan there were
shadows. "After they finally left—I don't blame them, really

—he was so exhausted he fell asleep on his river chair. I sat on the chair and brushed the mosquitoes away. Then I covered him with a mosquito net and came into the cabin and started this soup. Then later, out the screen door, I heard him crying, and I ran out there. Because of the net, he thought he was in Venezuela when his friend Jorge had his hand cut off. I heard the story. So when I made him realize he was at the cabin, he said we must send Jorge some money immediately. One day on a riverbank a peasant had come up behind Jorge and chopped off his hand because Jorge had made love to his daughter. It was almost dark, but there was a big moon and Robert wouldn't eat. He wants to get better because his company will start a dam in New Guinea this winter. So we drove up the road so he could crawl in the meadow in the dark and he becomes lost for several hours until midnight."

"I wasn't lost. I knew where the moon was and where it was going. I just forgot where I started out. I could always have followed the dog home." He pulled himself up into his walker and made his way to the kitchen table where Eulia was serving the soup. "I went too far down in the swamp and lost one of my knee pads. Then the dog ran off for a while when she heard coyotes. But here I am, all alive and sparkling. Right? And Eulia has made my favorite soup."

"Did you see anything extraordinary?" I couldn't begin to imagine crawling around in the forest and swamp at night.

"I just felt and heard things. I got my bearings when I found the river by the sound, and the spring a quarter a mile upstream. Then I was thrown off by the hairpin bend in the river where you hear it on both sides. This phenomenon can screw anyone up. Then there were northern lights, which by their intensity helped me determine the direction. When Dad got really crazy on his deathbed, we helped him out to the porch to see the northern lights. He said the northern lights were the blood of Jesus streaming in the firmament, which even scared the hell out of me. It went Karl's inventions one better. So I was down in the mire of the horseshoe bend, and the northern lights seemed to set off that bad herb I took. I sensed I was on a swampy island with a big river rushing all the way around it in a circle, which isn't possible. Finally I was able to listen to where the river sound was weakest and find the neck to higher ground. You flush a grouse before your nose, and it's thunderous."

This little rendition gave me vertigo. Eulia brewed some delicious but muddy Cuban coffee, and we made our way to the chairs before the fireplace. I could hear Eulia dressing in the loft but was too slow and preoccupied to invent a reason to glance around. Shakespeare himself would have twisted owl-like, knowing one had to seize the day, rather than creating reasons to seize the day. That came later. I began to feel a little dread at Strang's manic appearance.

———————

When that grouse flushed up in my face, I was reminded of a hunting story that got me some pills from a doctor to subdue my seizures. You see, because of my illness I wasn't allowed to have a shotgun. I was a fisherman, which was what helped draw me to the water. Dad swore we didn't have enough money to feed a bird dog. Karl said he would pay for the food, but Dad put his foot down, saying there were no bird dogs in the Bible.

This may sound a little bizarre, but I became Karl's bird dog, and it was the finest time of my life up to that point. I had a purpose to my life, other than my studies, for more than a month. I wanted to get Edith involved, but Karl said that one make-believe dog was enough. Dad was with Ted down in Manistique, building a school, or we might not have gotten away with it. Mom and the girls were all for it because they wanted me to get some pleasure from life. After my first few days running through the brush and getting my clothes all torn up, Mother fashioned me a canvas suit out of an army surplus puptent. Mind you, Karl wasn't taking advantage; we were partners in an operation that mixed the pleasure of hunting with profit. As with the berries, it was the lawyer's wife who bought most of our kill, and our family ate the rest. She gave the birds as presents to her husband's associates in the Soo and Marquette, earning him a reputation in the U.P. as a great hunter. She cooked us some woodcock one rainy afternoon in what she called a French sauce. It was fine, but we liked them best the way Karl called Indian-style: He built a spit over wood coals in the backyard and roasted the woodcock and grouse basted with butter and pepper. Ted had bought this book for us by Ernest Thomas Seton called *Two Little Savages*, and it was filled with information about such things. When Dad came home, he did some theological hairsplitting and decided that, since the birds came from God's bounty, the project was blessed.

Here was our routine: We'd find some good cover, usually strips of popple, which is what we call aspen, alder, dogwood, with lush groundcover of berries and wintergreen. Often this cover was around farms deserted during the Depression. We didn't waste our time if the area wasn't first-rate. We'd ride out in the morning on Karl's bike with me on the back and the shotgun and gunnysack strapped across his shoulders. I'd enter the thicket upwind of Karl so the birds would fly toward him. Game birds prefer not to fly into the wind. I'd give out a screech when a bird would flush and then hit the deck so I wouldn't get hit by the pellets. I would crisscross, casting back and forth across any patch of cover like a good English setter does. I carried a pair of gloves for when I'd have to crawl through a thorn-apple thicket, which grouse favor, because the thorns can go right through a hand. Once in a while I'd bark for the hell of it and to let Karl know where I was. I was thin and wiry but strong, and I can see and smell those thickets right now as surely as I can see you and Eulia.

And then there was a beautiful day that helped change my life. It was late in October, during a respite from the winter to come called Indian summer. It was a glorious day, around fifty degrees with a clear sky and a dull, soft light in the late afternoon. We were late in our best hunting ever— we had thirteen woodcock and nine grouse, and I had mentally picked out a pair of lace-up, high-top boots I was going to order from the Montgomery Ward catalog with my earnings. We were a good way from town, and I knew we would have to ride back on Karl's bike in the dark, but I didn't care. Then I heard bells and was a little frightened, because I knew Karl was a long ways off and I couldn't figure out why there were bells way out in the woods.

So I just sat there behind a downed tree looking up a culvert where the sound was coming from. The culvert was brilliant yellow from fallen maple leaves, and there was a large group of blackbirds, gathered to migrate south, feeding among the leaves. It was such a strange sight that I looked away, as I began to have that diffuse, dreamy feeling that often signaled a seizure. Then I would black out for a moment. I slouched down to further hide myself from the bells.

It turned out to be two English setters with bells around their necks. The female pointed me in my hiding place because I had handled so many dead birds that day I smelled like one. The male honored her point, that is, he pointed on trust in her rather than scent. I'd be goddamned if I knew what to do. Then two men entered the clearing and readied themselves to shoot.

"It's me," I croaked.

They both yelled in alarm, so I stood with my hands up like they did in pictures from the war. Then they laughed with surprise, only stopping when Karl swaggered into the clearing. Even at fourteen Karl was a showstopper. He had seen a movie about Jesse James with Tyrone Power and liked to affect the rakish manner of that outlaw.

"Hello, gents. Those are nice dogs. What do you think of mine?" Karl said, pointing at me. "If you're short on birds, we got some to sell. A quarter per grouse, ten cents a woodcock." Karl dumped our twenty-two birds out of the burlap sack for inspection.

"You must have shot those out of the trees or on the ground," one of the men said petulantly.

"Got a few of the grouse that way, but I've never seen a woodcock, not in the air, have you? How many you guys get?"

I picked that moment to have a fit, though not a bad one. I was petting the dogs, and one shook its head vigorously, and the flash of the shiny bell set me off. When I came to, moments later, the taller of the two men knelt over me. It turned out he was a doctor. The upshot was they gave us a ride home, and the doctor talked to Mother. Dad and Ted had returned to Manistique.

Early the next morning I was driven, along with Karl, by

a family friend who owned the hardware store, Brother Fred, over to the Soo to the doctor's office. Mother tried to pack us a lunch, but Karl insisted he wanted to spot me my first restaurant meal. In all my trips with Dad, testifying to the grace of God for not killing me with lightning, we had never eaten in a restaurant. As a youth in Chicago, he had suffered food poisoning, and God had not spared his life to repeat the mistake. Now Brother Fred was a sincere Christian but was a goofy sort, and he enjoyed the prospect of getting out of town. We weren't a tenth of the way down the road when Karl had him talked into going to a movie while I was at the doctor's for tests. We were sworn to secrecy, because Fred was an important force in our church, part of his power coming from his elaborate stories of his sinful past, including a trip to a burlesque show in Detroit, where shameless women "bared their parts for the world to see," the latter being a favorite of the male members of the church.

Sault Ste. Marie was a bit frightening to a boy during wartime. The Soo Locks handle more tonnage than Panama or the Suez Canal, and they were intensely guarded against sabotage by the Germans and Japs. This wasn't the usual paranoia, where even the smallest villages went through air-raid practice; a great percentage of the country's iron ore is from Michigan and the Mesabi Range in Minnesota, and it all went through the locks, and it was an armed camp.

We had reached the Soo in time for our lunch before the appointment. We sat in the Ojibway Hotel dining room, watching an ore freighter pass, with my stomach hollow and jumping with the thrill of this giant ship so near to us. I offered a silent prayer that I might be allowed on a ship one day. So then Karl knocks our hats off by ordering a beer for himself and Fred, who looked off weakly as an innocent victim, though he was fifty to Karl's fourteen.

"Sure you're old enough, cutie?" asked the waitress.

"Old enough to handle the likes of you any day of the week." Karl flashed a smile and patted her butt. Fred buried his face in his hands. I watched intently, not wanting to miss the ways of the world. We had big steaks, and they had several beers. Karl gave me a teaspoon of his, and it was made delicious by the fact that it was so evil. Then they dropped me off at the doctor's office with instructions to meet them at a neighboring park.

Well, I went through a number of simple tests. The doctor and his nurses were kind, and I was given an enormous canister of pills to take, one a day. The doctor said I'd eventually be able to function as well as anyone, but the cure would be gradual. Even now, he said, there was no reason I shouldn't be in school the same as anyone else, because I only had blackouts rather than true seizures. Then the doctor tried to throw a curve by hauling out a county map, and trying to get me to mark Karl's best bird-hunting areas. Now this is something one never gives away and shouldn't be asked, so I just marked places that were down the road from the good ones. Brook-trout spots are the same way: Breathe a word, and they'll be wiped out by those too lazy to hike for their own. I thanked the doctor, and he said he'd check me out next October when he was out our way.

Luckily, I was dressed warm, because I waited in the park until dinnertime for them to show up, and then it was only a weeping Brother Fred, who, so he told me, had fallen asleep only to find Karl gone. There was a note, however: "Dear loved ones. I have gone to serve my country whether at land or sea or air. Duty called me and my courage answers with a forthright yes. May the eagle ever fly above the flagpole. Your son and brother, Karl H. Strang." I was sent into a diner to get a sack of hamburgers for the beery, fat, tearful Fred. On our slow way home I had to reassure him a hundred times that it wasn't his fault. I had known, anyway, that something was afoot, because Karl had taken along his secret kit that held his hunting knife, arrowheads and dirty pictures.

It was probably good for me, because that winter I began reading and studying in earnest. Not that I didn't miss Karl terribly. In fact, I wrote him letters in wait for such a time that we'd hear from him. There is also the thought that occurred to me later in my life: Karl, as noble as he seemed to me as a boy, always ran so stridently counter to all authority, to the way we structure society, that he was doomed from the beginning. I don't just mean the cliché of the Midwest preacher's son sowing wild oats; I mean a hard-core, violent man, at odds with the world. I've wangled him out of prison twice, but I'm afraid this third time might be beyond anything I can do. Much has been made of Viet Nam returning us a lot of psychotics and uncontrollable young men. So did World War II, though not much was made of it because the currently popular cry from the heart was not in fashion then. Some of the crews I've worked on have their share of these men, now in their late fifties, and they're still a rough bunch, though most of these unregenerate types don't live all that long.

By this time, the middle of World War II, my sisters Laurel and Ivy were downstate with their husbands, working at the Chrysler Tank Arsenal. When the husbands were drafted, the girls kept on working in the factories. Laurel sent me a new book every week, a thrill not to be underrated during a U.P. winter. Ted was bitter about being rejected for the service, because his building abilities were such that he was put to work building primitive radar facilities all across the northern Midwest. Dad was with Ted most of the time, preaching wherever he could find a welcome and making more money than he had in a lifetime. If it weren't for Ted's efforts, Dad would have given it all away, a propensity I seem to have inherited.

That left Mother, Violet, Lily and me at home for the winter. Then Lily, who was only seventeen, ran off with a commercial fisherman from Naubinway. I was thankful that Violet stayed home, because she paid the most attention to me and was by far the best and most faithful teacher of the lot. Something just occurred to me: brushing hair. I always brushed the girls' hair for them in the evening from the time I was small. I remember a potbellied stove, a table with an oilcloth, and a radio which Dad wouldn't listen to except for, later, the war news as broadcast by Gabriel Heatter. I would brush all of their hair except Mother's They all had long hair, but Violet's was the longest. What wonderful sisters they were! I must be boring you. Just because we have invented clocks and calendars doesn't mean that's the way people keep track of their lives, do you think? One winter might be the winter you see through ice. You go out on a lake, and if it hasn't sleeted and blurred in freezing, you can wipe away the snow and look down through the ice as if it were a horizontal window. I saw muskrat and beaver swimming this way, also large pike, which was what we were looking for. It was Dad's favorite food, a mess of fried pike, and it was the single, truly pleasant thing Karl would do for Dad. Once I read a story about a farm kid whose pig broke through the ice of the farm pond and the kid could see the pig swimming under the ice, looking for a way to get out.

That winter damn near killed Mother, Violet and me and is the reason, I suppose, that I've spent my life working in the tropics. What happened is that we had a rare January thaw, then an ice storm that knocked out the power, not all that rare an occurrence. Violet had a bad case of the flu, and then Mother caught it. They could barely get around, so I took care of them as best I could, bringing them water and aspirin and emptying the chamber pots, because we had just got electricity out in the country and didn't yet have inside plumbing. I'd warm up chicken soup for them, but they couldn't hold food down. My main job was to feed the woodstove and keep a lantern lit. It was lonely with no radio and no one to talk to. Without thinking, I stupidly used all the dry wood from the woodshed. After the ice storm, the wind shifted north and we had the great blizzard of '44, which was a three-day blow with mountainous snows and subzero temperatures. I could barely see the drifts through the heavily frosted windows. Violet would stumble out, pat my head, and tell me to get at my lessons. I sat there with a world map and H. G. Wells' *Outline of History,* looking at a dead radio and listing to the wind howl, the house shudder.

Well, when I got around to replenishing the wood supply, I could barely get the door open, and the woodpile was under a big drift. I wasn't too concerned until I dug down and discovered the wood was all stuck hard together by the ice storm that came before the blizzard. I could barely knock off a single piece with continual swings of a sledgehammer. Now, to be frank, the shit was scared out of me. I had no one to turn to, what with two sick ladies on my hands, whom I loved and felt responsible for. I sat there in the pumpshed, looking at the three lonely pieces of maple I had left, crying and praying, neither of which did any good. It was midafternoon and early dark. It was obvious to me we would be frozen dead by morning even if I burned the furniture. The drafty old house required about a half-cord a day during a winter storm when you're talking fifty knots and up off Superior.

What saved us was the sudden memory of one of Karl's pranks. We loved to watch Ted blow stumps or dislodge boulders with dynamite—everyone in the construction business up here uses it because the U.P. is mostly rock. Karl wanted to blow up a beaver dam and lodge that was no longer in use; he had this elaborate notion, unless he was pulling my leg, that beavers lived in quarters that included a death room (where we would find bones and skulls), a kitchen for eating saplings, and a sleeping room. We stole a half a dozen sticks of Ted's dynamite and rigged it to a fuse, stuffing it a few feet into the dam. We used about four sticks too many—the whole setup became airborne, as it were, and a search of the area revealed no bones, or at least none that were intact.

I wiped away my tears and got the flashlight. I wallowed through the drifts out to a locked shed where Ted kept his gear, broke a window, and got two sticks of dynamite and a section of fuse. I dug well down beside the woodpile, chipped away the ice, stuffed the sticks into an opening, and rigged the fuse. I felt I should go in and warn the ladies. Mother was asleep, but dear Violet lay there bathed in sweat.

"There's going to be some noise, Violet."

"You go ahead and play. The noise won't bother me.

You get some venison from the crock, and maybe I'll have some, too." We kept venison buried in rendered beef fat to preserve it. I heard the French still do this with geese and duck.

Here goes, I thought, going back outside and lighting the fuse. I hoped the charge was deep enough not to break the windows, and I prayed not to have a fit and get my ass blown off. I scrambled for cover, and there was an immense, satisfying *WHUMP* as the woodpile rose up a few feet above the snow and settled, all broken apart. Then I spent an hour or so, until I couldn't move from cold and exhaustion, filling the pumpshed with wood. I couldn't have weighed more than eighty pounds at the time. Violet had a plate of venison and potatoes ready for me.

"I see you got us all the wood we need," she said. I never much liked winter after that nightmarish incident.

CHAPTER IX

I was disappointed when this winter incident ended. There was a wonderfully infantile pleasure in being told a story so directly from someone's life. The trouble with television, movies, most novels, with the rarest of exceptions, is that nothing is true to the life you have experienced, or true to a life you could conceivably comprehend: The pope conceals a bomb beneath his vestments that will blow up our president because the pope's hearing aid is controlled by the KGB, who also control the prez's harem of starlets with vaginas wired for sound; if the KGB pulls it off, the Arabs will give them fifty billion in free crude, plus this year's Canadian wheat harvest. That sort of thing.

Anyway, Eulia interrupted us, saying she wanted to cook and would I take Robert for his stroll? Of course. A little earlier, when she had returned from the post office, I had watched her out of the corner of my eye open a large package out of which emerged the vapor of dry ice. I sidled into the kitchen for a disinterested snoop.

"A little package from Marshall. Some boring food," she teased.

I spotted duck, veal chops, lump crabmeat, oysters, and stone-crab claws before I turned away with a yawn.

"You must crawl for your dinner." She slapped an extra set of knee pads into my hand with a trill of laughter.

"By all means." She had hit some seedy chord of masochism; my stomach quivered, and my ears reddened. Any literate man over forty-five is not a beat away from his own Blue Angel.

"These Latin girls know how to pique your interest, don't they? It took me years before I dared sit down and play a game of Chinese checkers with one of them. It either costs you a fortune, your heart, or you simply die when the game is over. A schoolteacher jumped off a cliff because of Eulia's older sister." Strang had noted my discomfort.

"He was a monster. He seduced a reasonably innocent student. Besides, the cliff was his idea, not hers. He had been warned against reading too much poetry." There was a mocking sadness in her voice.

I followed Strang toward the door, with an uncomfortable memory of my single year of teaching. "This is the race that gave us bullfights, the Inquisition, the gay colors of Goya and El Greco, the aural torture of flamenco, Franco, whatever." She gave me a harsh goose and pushed me out the door.

It was quite a trip, what with the dog wedged between our bucket seats like an overbearing tour guide. Strang made me a little uncomfortable by asking some highly technical questions about my vehicle, none of which I could answer. He studied the owner's manual, spieling off data on gear ratios and that sort of thing.

"Why did you buy it if you don't know anything about it?" He seemed genuinely puzzled rather than critical.

"I was in Key West. I was under stress from a northeast front that knocked out our tarpon fishing. It's the shore time that drives you crazy. I liked a woman who didn't like me. I saw a TV ad. The salesman bought me a drink. I had the money."

"Good answer. I was in Key West once to hire some divers for a project. There were an extraordinary number of homosexuals there in one place. It was like university people, or farmers, or rich people, you know? They all wanted to be in one place. I drove past the house of Tennessee Williams because a civil engineer friend of mine studies his plays. This engineer has been writing these plays on dam projects all over the world. His father wanted him to do something sensible. I like the one called *The Rose Tattoo*."

"How about the plays of the engineer?" The fact that Strang had read Tennessee Williams disturbed me.

"They are truly awful. Down in Brazil he had us all reading different parts out loud. It gave this welder, a top hand, the notion he could be an actor, and he disappeared. People can be truly amazing. For instance, you don't even understand the internal combustion engine that's been hauling you around all your life. I got this little theory, an utterly unimportant theory, that most people never know more than vaguely where they are, either in time or in the scheme of things. People can't read contracts or time schedules or identify countries on blank maps. Why should they? I don't know. There's a wonderful fraudulence to literacy. Yet these same people have emotional lives as intricate as that Bach piece my niece played."

Strang used the fact that my vehicle had four-wheel drive to get us into a nasty swamp he was curious about. Too wet for crawling in June. Then we went up a long grade through hardwoods and out into an immense barren area dotted with decayed white pine stumps, some over six feet in diameter. The amount of virgin timber left in Michigan wouldn't cover Central Park. It is a shameful heritage, as if someone in North Dakota might brag, "My ancestors killed all the buffalo to make Fargo and sheep possible."

Suddenly we were on a high bank above the river, and the two-track dead-ended. Strang strapped on his knee pads and literally bailed out, with the dog scrambling after him. What the fuck, I thought, and ran over to the bank, noting the river hundreds of feet below and the bushes waving on the way down to mark Strang's progress. I felt a bit lonely out there in the outback, naked is closer, so I opened a bottle of wine to drive away the road dust. Will the white Bordeaux change the wilderness like the jar in Tennessee? Hopefully. I looked wanly at the extra set of knee pads and knew that, in that I am an incompetent liar and Eulia would ask, I'd have to crawl a few feet. I had negligently taken all the snacks out of my cooler, so I would go lunchless. Abruptly I felt caught in the locus Strang had just described: I didn't know where I was, pure and simple. I restored the Bordeaux to my Igloo cooler and pulled on the knee pads. How can you feel foolish when only the sky is watching, or do trees develop eyes, as in children's stories? I walked into a gentle-looking thicket and lowered myself to the ground, suppressing an urge to giggle. I was happy my critics couldn't see me, or my ex-wives, my mother, whomever. I made my way through the thicket, rather laboriously trying to figure out a gait—should I be a trotter, pacer, thoroughbred, or dog? I heard something in the bushes ahead, or thought I did. I stood and walked back to the car with back and butt muscles knotted, as if I were to be attacked and didn't want to know by what. I scraped the pine needles off my palms and went for the wine and my tape machine.

TAPE 5: Edward Curtis owned an etching of a lone coyote, the actual beast, paddling a war canoe upriver with an almost imperceptible trace of a smile. You have to study the smile to see it. What I am saying is, far out in this pine barren Strang might not quite be what I thought he was: an alpha type, a technological genius, at home in any country, the sort that does the core of the world's business, hard-driving, reality-oriented, etc. Writers by experience are over-trained in cynicism, and cynicism along with irony is a device, a set of blinders, to keep the world in its place. Writers pretty much think they are what the total consensus of opinion says they are. It's difficult to avoid this unless they own an additional, secret life, but then their mission is to tell secrets, not conceal them. There is no real consensus about the Strangs of the world because there aren't many of them, they work in inaccessible and unpleasant places far off the usual world capital junket, and those like myself gifted with words (hope-fully) are ignorant of their language. My teeth ache at the thought that I'll actually have to read those technical books he gave me.

I am reminded again that once you get truly out of the circle of your acquaintances, and away from those who bear your professional likeness, you perceive again the mystery of personality. Strang pointed out jokingly at lunch the other day that even the animal world rarely departs from rigidly prescribed habits of feeding and range. Birds migrate to the same place. There are about three hundred Kirtland warblers left on earth, all in three counties in northern Michigan. They join each other for winter on the same tiny island in the Bahamas. So says Mother. Of course, radical changes in climate, food availability, the presence of man, can divert the pattern.

Who is this daughter, or stepdaughter, Eulia? She bears no resemblance to Strang, so she must be a stepdaughter. I'm trying to figure out an acceptable way to visit brother Karl in prison, and maybe at least one of the sisters for a full profile. It would take a boggling courtship dance to get close to Eulia. I don't like to see her underthings on the clothesline, reminding me as they do of my steady march into middle age, and my equally declining, perhaps prematurely, supply of hormones.

It's four o'clock, and Strang has been gone for three hours. I have become morose from lack of food and open another bottle of wine, this one a red. What would it be like to have Eulia fall in love with you? Or someone similar. It doesn't happen to the testy observer; ugly words, senescence and deliquescence, arise. She'd hump your chin when you're tired like little Egypt, Little Cartagena, moist-limbed. . . .

I abruptly put on Beethoven's "Four Quartets," which can be heard in the background should my career arouse enough interest to attract graduate students. The music is the equivalent of a ten-milligram Valium or a mother's lullaby to a three-year-old. I am trying to reduce Strang's notions of the sensuosities of time to a lucid idea. This music is as good as music gets, except up there in the galactic swirl. Life is not segmented artificially by what we call days, months, years, dawns, noons, evenings,

night; rather, life is segmented by our moods,
impressions, traumas, odd transferences of
power from inanimate objects—the aesthetic
principle—dreams, linked by time spans of loves
and hates and indifference, unexpected changes
in the prism of our understanding, areas of passion or lust that disappear in a moment, lapsing
into a kind of sloth, dread and slowness. . . .

It was no use. I got out of the car and looked
down into the gorge. I saw the back of a hawk flying upstream below me. There was the vertigo of a
new mood I didn't understand, caused, no doubt,
by absolute isolation. I wanted to call out
to Strang but couldn't. I opened all the windows
of the vehicle and cranked up a Vivaldi tape as
far as it would go, then walked down the road to
listen. Out there in that vast scrub, a quarter
of a mile was about perfect. I would surely go insane if I couldn't orchestrate what was happen-
ing to me.

Back at the cabin, we had one of the premier dinners of my
life, right up there in the top ten. And this despite my having
eaten in dozens of the best restaurants in the world. Part of the
reason was an irrational hunger occurring in a man who never
allows himself to be mildly hungry. The only title I ever really
admired or envied was Curnonsky, Prince of Gourmands. The
meal explained the odd assortment Marshall had sent. It turns
out that many of the cooks at construction camps come from
Louisiana. Eulia had made Strang's favorite dish: a simple
gumbo made from dark roux, a duck stock where the meat is
reserved for the final dish, garlic, hot peppers, a mirepoix, a
little okra, andouille sausage, then within ten minutes of com-
pletion you add the shrimp, oysters and crabmeat. *Carumba!*

[93]

"You mustn't eat so much," she said, denying me a third bowl.

"What the fuck?" I gulped. I'm only twelve years old when it comes to my compulsions.

"But he crawled all afternoon." Strang came to my defense.

"No, he didn't. His knee pads were barely soiled. I guess seventy-seven feet. The doctors came out just before you came home." She turned to me. "If I give you a third bowl, will you take me on an adventure tomorrow? Robert doesn't like me around when the doctors are here, because he wants to be able to lie to suit his purpose."

"Of course," Strang said, "I'm the director, and I make everything up as I go along. I can tell you what's already happened, but I'd like to control my future." Strang ladled out my third bowl, his glance acknowledging that I'd sacrifice a finger to the hatchet to take Eulia on an "adventure." I merely toyed with my third bowl under the watchful and teasing eye of Eulia; then, in an act of macho defiance, I ate the sucker.

The day with Eulia was radically different from what I expected. First of all, it was raining in the morning when I picked her up. I waited outside because the doctors' rental car was already there. She ran out with a hamper in one of those sportif outfits preferred by foreign girls with dough. We drove in silence all the way to town, and I began to develop a lump in my stomach that quivered to the rhythm of the windshield wipers. I was deep into a Latin problem and recalled that a lady from Rio had ruined my agent's life for an entire year.

"This fucking, dirty rain. I want to go dancing. Maybe the sun will shine later. Where can we dance?" She was cloudy and petulant.

I pulled up in front of the bar. It was midmorning, and a group of retired loggers and commercial fishermen would be having their coffee hour.

"She wants to dance," I said to my friend, the owner. "She also wants a rum and Coke. If she's going to drink, so am I. Will they mind?" I eyed the old geezers, who in turn were staring at Eulia.

"Your money's as good as theirs. They'll have a new story to repeat a hundred times."

She danced for about two hours, pausing only to gulp at a succession of rum and Cokes. It was somewhat of a party: When I became exhausted, a commercial fisherman in his sixties took over, then the bar owner himself. The coffee cups were shoved aside, and I bought a number of inexpensive rounds. The music was severely limited, but Eulia was satisfied with a Beach Boys medley played over and over. I got her out of there at noon when we were both quite drunk, she more than I, on the pretext that the sun was shining. We drove out toward a creek I had selected for a picnic. As usual, I had to get something in my stomach. She decided to talk and laugh entirely in Spanish, and I decided not to protest. The bar owner had made her an enormous drink to go, which she swallowed greedily.

When we got to the creek, the sun was shining warmly and a breeze was blowing. I laid out the picnic on a blanket and decided we scarcely needed a bottle of wine. Without the breeze, the mosquitoes and blackflies would have murdered us; I sensed them lurking back in the swamp at the edge of the small clearing like pilots waiting for a decrease in headwind. There was a fatigued sense that, though I was twice her age, not to speak of twice her size, I was not in control of the situation. I almost yearned for a return to the Latin formalities that had marked the first three weeks of knowing each other.

I looked up to see Eulia leaning naked against an aspen on the edge of the creek, then she made a lurching, wobbly jump, her first ungraceful move in my presence. Her screams were shattering, and I ran over to help her out of the creek.

"Oh madre de mio, oh shit, oh my god, oh I am dying, you bastard, you eveil son of a bitch."

The last patches of snow in the woods had only been melted for a few weeks, and the creek water couldn't be much over forty, the temperature of very cold beer. Her face was contorted and bluish, nearly ugly, and she embraced herself as if to crush her ribs. Naturally, I laughed. If she had had a knife or gun in hand I would have been a goner. Instead she gave me a brutal shove in the gut that took my wind away, a vengeful, nonplayful, double-fisted slug and shove that toppled me backward into the creck. I could have broken my neck or had a heart attack from the icy water. My cavalry twill wool trousers were probably ruined, not to speak of my Cordovan boots. For some reason, I scrambled out on the far side of the creek, which meant I would have to cross it again.

"You shithead, you greaser cunt!" I yelled. I watched her up-end the picnic, wrap herself in the blanket and curl up on the ground. I leaned against a tree until I could catch my breath, then looked for a shallower place to recross the creek. I took off my clothes and stretched them on the warm car hood to dry. She was facing away from me and weeping. Taken to its extreme, alcohol is an utter cliché, especially if the soul is troubled before the first drink. The progression is inevitable: relief, ecstasy, despair, depression, the possibility of violence.

My anger relented, and I knelt beside her and put my hand on her forehead as she shook with sobs. She held out her arms to me and I joined her in the blanket, which wasn't quite large enough. I embraced her and heard a litany of real griefs:

She knew her father would die, and she loved him so much, she would be an orphan "again," a word that puzzled me. Her weeping subsided against my tear-wet breasts.

"You are like a big, warm mamá," she whispered. A hand clutched at my still cool, shrunken member, which began to grow. "Let's not swim here anymore."

My feelings were deeply hurt from being called a mamá but she began snoring against my chest before I could protest. Though the blanket was covering me, my body was pressed against the grass and a number of uncomfortable sticks. Frankly, I didn't want to move and dislodge her hand, which was wrapped firmly and pleasurably around my prick. For want of anything else to do, I stared up into the blue sky and whispered hello to a scudding cloud. I suppressed a voyeur's urge to take a good look at her body for the same reason. A bird in hand, as they say. Dear Eulia, I'm not going to fall in love with you. I just found some work to do, and I don't want to ruin my life. I dozed.

"My head! I must have aspirin." She shook me.

I dragged myself up and got aspirin from the glove compartment and water from the cooler. I knelt down and fed her some, taking two myself. The breeze had subsided, and the bugs were on the attack. She reached out and playfully waggled my hard-on.

"Did you make love to me?"

"Of course not. I'd never fuck a woman who had passed out," I said, with the air of the gentleman from the British Isles speaking to the United Nations Assembly.

"You are a gentleman. Any man in Costa Rica would have raped me, and I wouldn't have known it. You are so romantic."

"What's wrong with now?" I was beginning to feel snippy, betrayed by my virtue.

She pulled herself up on her elbows, the blanket cast aside and her face a tenuous millimeter from my prick. She studied it as if it were an artifact she had just dug up from an archaeological site. She dropped her open mouth on it like a safe falling from a cornice, but just for one stroke. Then she jumped up, drew on her underpants and rummaged through the containers of food on the grass.

"Not now. My head aches terribly, and I'm starved."

I groaned and lay back. It was somehow worse now, the way she squatted with her beautiful ass, and broke open stone-crab claws, dipping them in a mayonnaise mixture and sucking on the shells.

"Oh, you poor, big baby." She dipped her hand in the sauce and grabbed my prick, pumping at it vigorously until I let go with a heartfelt scream. She wiped off her hand with a napkin and continued eating with energy. There was a blissful sting to the mustard in the sauce.

"We're just like your Indians, correct? We are out in the wilderness eating and having sex. We danced and drank. We had a wonderful day!" She did a marvelous little movie version of an Indian dance, similar to what Debra Paget used to do for Jeff Chandler.

CHAPTER X

The new order of the day was swimming, not crawling. Strang was in amazingly good spirits for having spent the previous day being probed by two doctors. I wondered idly what it had cost Marshall to send an orthopedic surgeon and a neurologist this far, but Marshall's life was marked by precise and appropriate gestures. I had heard that Marshall had been offered seven million to syndicate the second racehorse he ever bought. He declined the offer, despite the fact that even the wealthiest horsebreeders syndicated in order to spread the risk. A trainer at Hialeah told me that Marshall was pocketing three million bucks in stud fees per year. Oh, well. To those that have, much is given, someone said long ago, a ghastly conundrum.

"But how are you going to swim? We tried it yesterday, and it was insufferable."

"So did I. I'll have to grease up until they send a wet suit.

The cold kills the pain a little. The orthopede said I'd crawled way too much and built up big bunches of compensatory muscles around the injuries, which is fine if I want to crawl the rest of my life. If I get to walk, it will make me walk like a goddamned land crab."

He thought this was all quite funny.

———

"Is there a new prognosis?"

Oh, none at all. They have no real idea what my chances are. The Swiss chemists haven't had any luck determining the long-range effects of the herb. A company doctor talked to a botanist at Harvard, and the man was encouraging to the extent that he said if you're going to die or become completely paralyzed it happens within a day or so. The intermittent mental effects are totally unpredictable. Right now, they seem limited to my dreams, which aren't conducive to rest. In my sleep I'm a baby nursing at my sister Violet's breast, but she looks too young to have had a baby. To be frank, they are gorgeous breasts, which is a little awkward because she's supposed to be my sister. Then that dream slides into a hiding place I had about a quarter of a mile from the house. It was a small, high place in the middle of a swale, a thicket of aspen and elder. I'd go there and sit on this stump when I was frightened or saddened or just wanted to get away from the family. There's no privacy in a big family. In a hole in the stump, in a metal box designed to hold fish lures, I kept my New Testament and pictures of the actresses Jeanne Crain, Deanna Durbin, and Rita Hayworth I had cut out of *Life* magazine. Also the shinbone of a crow, which Karl insisted had magical properties. You could make a low, scary whistle through it, which supposedly summoned spirits, though I never saw any. One day in October, the October following Karl's departure for the war, I was sitting on this stump, quite disturbed from having caught my sister Lily and her fisherman making love. I don't mean I was offended. I felt I knew everything from Karl's stories, but this was the first time, other than farm animals, I had seen the act taking place. The noises certainly made it sound like they were having the best time possible, say somewheres between a revival and a basketball game. I never went to a game, but one night outside the gym I hid in the bushes and listened to the cheers. Anyway, I was sitting in my hiding place perfectly still one late afternoon in October when a flight of migrating woodcocks landed all around me. First I heard the fluffing of wings and there they were, at least twenty of them. I didn't bat an eyelash, and my only thought was, wait until I tell Karl about this. They spread out to feed with their long beaks, and most of them flushed when I got up to leave at dark. It was indescribably lovely. The trouble is that when this reoccurs in the dream, the birds are all shot up with a wing or head or leg blown off as if at the end of the hunt, but they're no longer dead. Then I wake up.

I'm not superstitious, but it makes one wonder if we ever should have had a part in killing anything, but then I don't dream of dead trout, and trout fishing is where I spent most of my time. If you remember, I was fishing when I was struck by lightning. It was the one thing I could do by myself that made a contribution to the family. After we started picking berries together, I taught Edith how to fish, which pleased her parents. There's not much that is offered as food in the world that surpasses a mess of fresh brook or brown

or rainbow trout caught in the wild. It was the one sermon-
ette my dad allowed us to laugh at when he would repeat
the parable of the loaves and fishes every time we had a fish
dinner. The fact that we had at least thirty fish dinners
between late spring and the end of the fishing season in the
fall did not deter Dad. We had to eat outside unless the
weather was ugly because Jesus had spoken to the multitude
on a hillside. We were limited to homemade bread, the fish
and salt, though Mother in a flight of daring began prebutter-
ing the bread in the kitchen. Dad pretended not to notice
because he loved butter and always helped Mother churn
it. We had two Jersey cows in a shed, and everyone knows
they yield up the best cream for butter.

I should have told you that when Karl disappeared,
Dad began writing our congressman to explain that Karl was
barely fourteen and had, no doubt, enlisted in one of the
services. Mind you, this event was not so extraordinary at
the time. I mean, the age fourteen was rare, but with Karl
that was a chronological mistake. The country, especially
rural areas, which are the best sources for aggressive can-
non fodder, was in a patriotic frenzy. Out in the sticks, there
was the added incentive of seeing the world. If you have to
cut logs or milk cows every morning at daylight, you'll leave
town even if you're going to get shot at. At the time, if you
waved a flag in front of a farm boy, he'd think first of his
nation's honor, then a pliant hula girl.

Ted finally drove Dad all the way down to Lansing,
where they had to wait three days to see our congressman,
who had a pronounced aversion to what he called "hicks."
The memory of being told about this indignity has given me
a permanent aversion to politicians. They tend to waffle
between jokes and lies and can never seem to simply talk.

The test is the quality of the language, and they have simply invented their own. I think Karl somehow had kept Dad healthy, and in Karl's absence, Dad's health began to decline. Well, Karl was located in England and sent home but never arrived. He escaped in New York without difficulty and switched from the navy to the army and ended up with MacArthur in the Philippines, though, of course, MacArthur didn't know it.

God, I can remember a hot summer day before Karl returned and Edith left my life forever. She already knew that they were going to leave, because with the war winding down there wasn't much left to the scrap metal business. It was a hot day in August in the middle of a prolonged drought, which made the flyless woods fine to walk in but the fish hard to locate. It's a rare year that warm water is a problem up here. Trout don't care for water much above sixty, and they'll travel up and downstream to seek the cooler waters of swamps or locales where there are feeder creeks, seeps or springs. Edith recalled an area on Karl's trapping maps, a marked place where he trapped his first otter near a big spring. It was a ten-mile hike, so we left just after dawn. Violet made us a fine breakfast and hugged us good-bye. We packed a loaf of bread, a blanket, a knife, compass, matches, and extra sinkers and hooks in my rucksack. Your best bait in August is grasshoppers and crickets, and Edith could catch them like a martin or swallow. Violet had become a big sister to Edith, who shared our lessons. That summer we were reading the Anne of Green Gables series, Bronte's *Wuthering Heights,* and several novels by Dickens, which we especially loved because so many of Dickens' young people were outcasts like ourselves.

"Don't you two waifs make any babies." Violet waved good-bye.

"Jesus, Violet. Don't say that!" My face turned hot, and Edith covered hers and ran around the side of the house.

"It's not the time to playact, Corvus. If a young girl has a baby, it makes her life impossible. Just be careful, that's all I'm saying."

We were glum on the first part of our long hike to the spring. In fact, we felt like we had been both found out. We were in that advanced stage of impassioned, amoral smooching where only a dainty pair of undies saves a fragile hymen. Sometimes we would open-mouth kiss for over a half hour by my pocket watch. We were going to get married at sixteen and get a job taking care of a rich man's lodge. There would be lots of books and a fireplace, and the world that so totally ignored us would be held at bay. I was already pretty handy, having built three large martin houses for the lawyer's wife, and Ted had promised to put me to work when I hit fourteen.

"Do you suppose Violet ever had a boyfriend?" Edith asked. "She's twenty-seven, so she must have had a boyfriend."

"She seems to know what she's talking about." I put my arm around Edith, who after a full hour of walking was still embarrassed. We paused to take a rest and within minutes were involved in the usual delicate wrestling. There was still dew on the grass, and a marsh hawk made several passes above us, no doubt puzzled by these entwined bodies. We ended up a hairsbreadth from sin and began laughing with delight about our close call. When I think it over, I wonder if everybody's true sexuality isn't private and secret, somewhat in the manner that their actual religion is private and full of peculiarities and secret pacts. It fits their need to survive, for the character of their individuality to survive. This sexuality doesn't yield in any healthy sense to sociological engineering.

I've gone astray. I can see it clearly—how we stopped to fill a small onion sack with hoppers, then began stalking the spring, which had to be just ahead according to Karl's map. It pays to sneak up on trout, then you can catch several before they become even mildly disturbed. We crawled toward the creek along a little ridge and under a blanket of ferns. We were puzzled by a splashing sound and something like puppies yapping. It was a large otter, probably the mother, and a small one. It appeared she was teaching the baby how to fish. They were having a wonderful time. Then a certain shock dawned on us: We had never seen so many fish in one place. The creek in the long drought had dried to not much more than a rivulet, but the spring below us formed a large pool, full of clear water and pale green weeds. The trout were shooting around in clumps to escape the otter, flinging themselves through the water between thick streamers of weed, sometimes out of the water in frantic jumps. There was a small brushpile that saved the trout with enough composure to stay there. Then the otters paused to feed on a dozen fish they had tossed up on a sandbar. I whistled, and the otters scattered, loping up the remains of the creek to a small lake that the map placed just above us to the northeast. It was our turn to catch some fish.

But first we did a little dance. We were simply dry-mouthed and giddy from our luck in seeing such a strange phenomenon. When we calmed down, we decided to take our time. If we caught a lot of trout we'd have to head home right away so they wouldn't spoil. We made our way around to the other side and to the sandbar where the otters had thrown their fish. For the first time Edith took off all of her clothes, and we swam around looking at the fish. The water was so crystalline you could almost see them clearly, and if your movements were slow and easy, the trout calmed down, and the little ones would come close to your face. When we got too cold from the spring, we lay on the sandbar and inspected each other's total nudity somewhat gravely. We started kissing, with Edith on top of me, and then she pushed hard against me, then backed away just in time. We were a little frightened at first, but finally felt betrothed and very serious. We caught a few trout and roasted them, eating them with salt and bread, then dozed on the sandbar, entwined like those on their honeymoon. When we woke we said our prayers, for some reason, including my usual "Oh, Jesus, bring my brother Karl home safely from war." We made a prudent catch, not wanting to be bullies with the trout, which were entrapped there by the drought.

About halfway home, it began to turn cooler, and when we came to the first big clearing we could see a front coming in from the northeast, black with turmoil and lightning. We began trotting along to try to beat the storm, and we almost made it. About a mile from our house, there was a vast field full of stumps that had been used off and on as a pasture. It was late afternoon, and the sky just before the storm had turned yellowish and scary. It was the same kind of day that I had been hit by the lightning. Edith was just ahead of me, and we were nearly at full run, with her long legs kicking up under her cotton skirt, which was whipped sideways by the gale. I caught up with her and asked her to kiss again, but she pulled my ear with a smile and we ran even faster, reaching our gate as the sky let loose with a deluge.

Don't you wonder about these first affinities? I'm sure nearly everyone in the world has had them, with all their frightening intensity, which comes from our vulnerability at that age. We "love" before we know how to protect ourselves, pure and simple. The trout might have collected in the spring like that only once in my lifetime, and the storm on the way home allowed them to leave, I'm sure. The idea that things only happen once used to bother me. One day when the house was empty, Edith put on lipstick and a pair of earrings, and we did what we imagined were the foxtrot and the jitterbug. Dancing was forbidden in our home, though I'm sure the girls learned the minute they left. We promised each other that our lives together would be without rules. Now I can see her knees and bottom and eyes. Life is unbearably vivid, don't you think? I hope I'm not presenting this as a deathbed scene, another thing that only happens once! It's just the nature of being alive. I took my entire savings of seventeen dollars and had Violet buy a selection of ribbons, rings and a necklace from the dime store for Edith. The last time I saw her was in the forest that cold October day. Now I can feel her small, cool, pointed breasts against my cheeks and lips and forehead.

I might be weeping a little, but I'm not unhappy. It's what we all go through, isn't it? It seems that way to me. Well, Karl returned the December of my twelfth year, in 1947, driving a new Chevrolet coupe. He was brutalized and melancholy from war. If you look at a boy between fourteen and nineteen nowadays, it's hard to imagine Karl doing what he did. He gave me a commando knife with dried blood on it, a Japanese sword, a canteen, and a regulation compass. Curiously, it seemed to us, he never spoke much of the war, except to say he had gone back to the navy with the army's permission because he had been trained as a diver in England. In fact, he was still in the navy, and his job was diving down to ships that had been wrecked in harbors or on reefs. He brought out some bodies, but mostly identification tags and documents.

"I like it down there," he said. "You don't see anyone you don't like. And Corve, I've got to get you to the ocean to see the fish. I've seen sharks with heads as big around as my Chevy, and fish in schools of millions. From the ship, I saw a whale you couldn't fit curled up in this house."

Karl took an apartment for a month or so above Brother Fred's hardware store. The town's eyebrows were raised considerably by his affair with the lawyer's wife, which was conducted right out in the open. The lawyer had returned an officer, but a hopeless drunk, having never left the country. Karl had become a hard drinker himself, which added to his later problems. I take a drink now and then myself, but I always noticed that hard drinkers lose their elasticity. If they're in a bad mood, they stay in one; if they're depressed, they stay depressed because they can't quite figure out what to do when they're drinking, due to the sedative nature of alcohol.

Karl did a marvelous thing during the first big dinner after his coming home. It was close to Christmas. Laurel and Ivy came up from Detroit with their husbands, who were also fresh from war but less abused by it. It was Karl's nature to make sure he was in the thick of things. Lily and her husband came up from Naubinway with the first grandchild, named Rexton after the father's hometown. It was strange to be an uncle; it made me feel somehow more significant. I held the baby a lot, somewhat in the same manner that other boys hold puppies. Ted came over from Marquette with a fine-looking girl friend. Dad lifted the household rules to the extent that the men were allowed to take a drink in the pumpshed, and everyone was allowed to play pinochle and Tripoli in the living room. After the utter penury of the Great Depression, the war had brought prosperity to our family. We were much admired in town for the number of new cars parked in the yard. There was a nervous moment when the lawyer's wife dropped off a big roast ham, but Dad treated the situation with elaborate courtliness. Despite the fact we are a melting pot, the social stratification of a small town is rigid, and the lawyer's wife was the only upper-class person to enter our home other than the doctor who had given me pills for my seizures five years before.

Well, Dad could never resist an audience, so one afternoon he insisted on a family prayer service. We all had to kneel on the cold linoleum in the living room. There was much giggling, murmuring and whiskey breath. I was with the men in the back row, with my mother and four sisters and Ted's girl friend in front of us.

"We got to send this geezer a rug."

"I'm supposed to be a Catholic," said another brother-in-law.

"That's quite the row of fannies in front of us," said the drunken fisherman. Lily turned around and stared him into silence. It seemed to me my sisters had their husbands well in hand.

Then Karl came in from outside, red-eyed and mean-looking. I had overheard him talking to Mother about Dad's declining health. The problem was arteriosclerosis, hardening of the arteries, the early stages of what they call Alzheimer's disease nowadays.

"Will you pray with us, Karl?" Dad asked, his voice a little weak, as if waiting for rejection. Those of us who knew Karl felt an unbearable tension.

"Of course I will, Father." Karl knelt beside Dad and stared straight ahead, while we let our breath go.

"Almighty God," Dad began, "to put it straight, we thank Thee for delivering our family more or less in one piece. I thought, O Father, that I saw Armageddon right around the corner, but now it seems things have let up. I saw the slaughter of Thy chosen people, the children of Israel, and I thought, O Lord, how long before you end this carnage?" He paused to catch his breath. Laurel sent us her copies of *Life* magazine, and Dad saw the horror of what is now known as the Holocaust in Biblical terms. "When you allowed your children to die under the fist of the Antichrist, I says this surely must be the Abomination of Desolation spoken of by the prophet Daniel. But now you have returned us home more or less in one piece. You have returned my beloved son, Karl, for whom I prayed without ceasing. We didn't know where he was. He just showed up and made our hearts glad, safe from the yellow plague of the Japanese that sought to destroy us. Can you say something to us, Karl?"

Our eyes were supposed to be closed, but I peeked at Karl, who had taken on that weird, inventive look he had when he took Edith and me out in the swamp to see the giant skull.

"Yes, Father. I can tell you folks a little story about how I came to Jesus. I was down in the South Pacific in a lull in battle on a bright, sunny day. The dread kamikazes had sunk one of our destroyers out in the harbor, and it was my job to go down there and take a look. The water was as clear as the air after a norther down there, and the great ship had found a peaceful grave on the bottom. I opened the main compartment, and there in front of my light, which shone around the room, were a hundred drowned men trapped in the sinking. The captain was in front of them, with the Bible still clutched in his hand. I drew them out, one by one, and sent them upwards, floating slowly to the surface where I could see the bright ring of the sun. One after another, I sent them upwards. It was like what you call the Rapture, when we go straight to Heaven. I left the captain and his Bible for last. I looked him straight in his sightless eyes and said, 'It wasn't all that bad, was it?' then let him go to float up to the sun. Anyhow, that's how I came to Jesus.''

''Amen!'' Dad yelled, hugging Karl and beginning to weep. ''Amen. I knew it would happen. Praise Jesus. Amen!''

''Amen,'' we said, swept away for a moment in Father's joy.

Afterwards Karl and me took a ride in his Chevy. His avowed intention was to get some venison, though the deer season had been over several weeks.

''Did I do okay?'' he asked.

''You did a real good job. Was it true?'' I was shivering and holding Karl's pistol, which was blue and impressive, a service automatic.

''How can anything be true during a war? Bodies bloat so much their clothes burst unless the wreck's real deep where the water is colder. Never saw a body in the Pacific that wouldn't float upwards.''

We shared the unspoken lore of Lake Superior, where the bodies of drowned sailors never float to the surface; the water near the bottom is always too cold for the bodies to deliquesce and gain buoyancy. For some reason, sailors want to be buried on land, say back near the Indiana farm where they started.

"I mean, is it true you came to Jesus down there under-water?"

"No. That was for Dad." He drank from a pint he had in his coat pocket, and the whiskey mixed with the vapor of our cold breath. "Once our ship stopped at the deepest part of any ocean on earth and the captain let us swim. I wish it had been night. I was the only one to free dive as deep as possible. It was like the reverse of floating upwards into the night sky. That's my religious experience."

"You're scaring the shit out of me, Karl. You wouldn't get me to do that."

"Take a drink if you got a hair on your ass."

I took my first drink of whiskey and liked it. We jack-lighted a doe and Karl shot it, throwing it in the trunk. On the way home, we stopped to show the deer to the lawyer's wife, and right there under the streetlight the deer jumped out of the trunk. It started to trot a bit wobbily toward the main part of town. We chased it, and Karl shot the deer in the head again, right on Main Street. I helped him drag it back to the car so he wouldn't get blood on his uniform. The screaming of the lawyer's wife didn't help the situation. Karl and I were laughing, mostly at the embarrassment of not making a clean kill in the first place. Wouldn't you know but the constable showed up?

"You boys are under arrest. The season's been over a month."

"I was out in Fiji getting my ass shot at. I thought when I got home I had some venison coming."

"I should probably arrest you, Karl. You fired a pistol right in town." The constable was confused by the lawyer's wife, who was hugging and kissing my brother.

"There's not a man good enough to arrest me around

here. You know that." There was an unpleasant edge to Karl's voice, and I was scared.

"Just try to behave while you're home. I'm keeping an eye on you." The constable walked off down the snowy street before his dignity could be further wounded.

When we got home, we had a fine feast. Karl gutted the deer outside, then we stripped the loins in the pumpshed while the other men watched with admiration. We all ate the loins and the liver, the preferred pieces, but not before Dad offered a longish prayer on nature's bounty.

The night before Karl left to go back to the Pacific, I heard a conversation when I was supposedly asleep. What kept me awake was the idea that I would be left alone again with Violet, Mom and Dad. Karl and Violet were in the kitchen, and I could tell by Karl's voice that he was drinking.

"You drive me to St. Ignace, and I'm catching the bus. The car is yours."

"I can't take your new car. You're just being kind. . . ."

"God damn you, Violet. I've got no use for a car in the South Pacific. The navy is not in the business of shipping cars. He's almost grown up. He doesn't have to have you here anymore."

"I can't leave him here with Mom and Dad."

"Jesus, I already said I talked to Ted and Ted wants him. It's been over twelve years, and I can't stand the idea of you waiting for the mail to come every day. You got to make a life for yourself. If anyone, whomever he is, was coming back it would have been by now."

"Let me think about it. You're being kind. . . ."

"Stop it, Violet. You're my sister, and I love you. Don't ever say I'm kind again. You said you always wanted to go to college and be a teacher. You're twenty-seven and you better get started."

So Karl left, and it was a decade before any of us saw him again. The drift of the overheard conversation didn't really sink in at the time—I was far too disappointed by Karl's departure to think about anything else. I prayed for friends, but we were too far from town for much chance of that. I studied hard and passed my high school graduate equivalency test at age thirteen with flying colors. Not to be arrogant, but our family didn't realize we were smart until we got out in the world. The high point of that winter and spring were the long rides we took in Karl's Chevy. Ted sent a monthly check, and we lived so simply that there was plenty of money left for gas. Once a week we'd stop at the small county library and see if anything new had come out of interest. We did this during school hours so I wouldn't be running into anyone my own age and incur any embarrassment.

I was thirteen the summer of 1948, the most difficult summer of my life. It was not in my nature to question the way things were, but I was sorely put to the test. First of all, I grew from about five foot five to nearly six feet, and I lost any sense of the perimeters of my body. I had a couple of seizures and quite logically upped my pill-taking to account for my growth. Dad's health was in precipitate decline, so Violet and I switched off looking after him, because Mother had become weaker. Dad had new visions almost daily, many of them including my particular destiny as a great preacher. People don't realize how similar the rural north is to the rural south. It's too cold for writers to live in the rural north, so we get short shrift. Dad put me through several, largely incoherent, hours of Bible study a day. He made me promise to go to the Moody Bible Institute, where he had taken night courses and where he had met Mother. She was an immigrant servant girl from the Alsace and had stopped into the Institute one evening to get out of the ferocious Chicago wind. To show you how bad it was getting, we spent the entire month of June building an Egyptian waterwheel from a picture book on the Bible. The county newspaper had an article about it: "Preacher Invents Egyptian Waterwheel." There was a photo of Dad in a nightshirt, which he wore night and day, and me looking severely embarrassed. I must admit that the contraption did a wonderful job diverting water from a creek to our garden. Dad had to be watched even closer after he showed up in town in his nightshirt trying to pass himself as the prophet Isaiah. Ted, Laurel, Ivy, Lily, everyone came for a visit that summer and tried to reason with Dad, but without luck. Ted, aided by the postwar boom, owned what had become a sizable construction company. When he visited, he told me there was going to be a place in his company for me and dropped off all manner of books on civil engineering so I wouldn't end up as a "laboring stiff."

What forced me back to religion with a terrible energy wasn't Dad's teaching or his visions or the Bible itself, but guilt over Violet. Can you remember when you were thirteen or fourteen and what sex meant to you then? It was a strain that daily tore you to pieces. It had been over a year and a half since Edith had left, and I had no affection whatsoever except for Violet's sisterly caresses. Maybe that potion I took is making me talk about this—you know, like a truth serum—but in the light of later developments, the whole situation must be regarded as comical. You see, Violet was a little daffy and totally without any sense of personal modesty. She thought of herself as an honest drudge, a hardworking young woman, without charm and attractiveness. When anyone would try to flirt, it would pass right over her head for some reason. I can remember brushing her hair after she had a bath when she only had a towel around her waist. I would be looking down over her shoulders at her breasts, which would rise with the pleasure of getting her hair brushed. She would continue reading to me from Romain Rolland's *Jean Christophe*.

One hot day in July, after a long session in the garden, we went swimming at this little lake way back in the woods that only Karl, a few Indians and trappers knew about other than us. After a short dip, Violet lay back on a towel to read a book and drink a bottle of pop. I was swimming around, looking at the bottom of the lake with a pair of goggles Karl had sent me from California. I followed a school of minnows right up to the shallows in front of where Violet lay, reading aloud from a novel by Louis Bromfield. I lifted my head up from the water and saw her legs and thighs and sex through the water-spattered goggles and got a fierce hard-on. This brought tears to my eyes, tears of guilt and shame, so I kept the goggles on, which only put her body at one remove, like a dirty picture. I lay there and ejaculated right under water on the sand. Relieved, I swam around for an hour or so, but when I came back she was laying on her belly and, against my will, I became excited again. Imagine a thirteen-year-old's confused lecture to himself on incest, especially when the Bible came out so directly against it. She turned back over, sat up and brushed the sand from her body.

"R.C., let's go. We've got to pick up the mail and make dinner." She stood and drew on her skirt, then her underpants, with that curious little shuffle women often make. "I guess I got some sunburn on my breasts, or what Karl calls tits."

"I don't want to go. We never get any mail, anyhow." This was the wrong thing to say, as Violet was unnaturally sensitive about the mail. I gave my hard-on a painful squeeze in a vain effort to make it go away. This brought forth an involuntary yelp, and I dropped my face into an inch of sandy water.

"R.C., what in God's name is wrong with you? Are you having a fit? Oh, Jesus, you'll drown."

I looked up as she bent over and grabbed my arms, jerking me to my knees. She tore off my goggles and held my head to her chest, which didn't help matters as she hadn't put her blouse on. Then she knelt down to look into my eyes to see if they were whirling.

"R.C., haven't you been taking your medicine? Are you okay?" Then it dawned on her. She had ahold of my arms, and I couldn't cover myself. I suddenly burst into tears and she into laughter. "That's fine, darling. That's what people are like. All men are like that, sweetheart. You're just growing up to be a man, and I should start wearing a bathing suit. I'm sorry. You need a girl friend. There must be some girl at church you could fool around with, but just be careful."

We finished putting on our clothes somewhat awkwardly. She blushed a little and gave me a hug.

"Robert Corvus, don't let your religion make you mean-minded about sex. The Bible is full of love, but Saint Paul was a little off his rocker. You're a much better boy than your brother Karl. He lassoed me once and took off my pants."

"Jeezo, what did you do?" Karl always went for the immediate solution.

"I kicked him in the pecker, that's what I did. That put a stop to that nonsense."

So I returned to religion with a vengeance, not wanting to be cast into hell for incest and generalized lust. In fundamentalist denominations, to wish to do an act is equated with actually performing the act. Catholics have more sense than to believe that human thought can be significantly controlled for long. When you watched your mother canning tomatoes with a pressure cooker, you hoped the valve on top was working, else the whole works would blow apart. This is a tad corny, but I read in one of those miscellany columns in the newspapers that American legislators as a whole had passed over three and a half million laws trying to enforce the Ten Commandments. It's wonderfully ludicrous, isn't it? This priest down in Venezuela loaned me the autobiography of Saint Augustine, which mirrored my situation. "I came to Carthage where a cauldron of unholy loves rose round about me." It was a horrifying tightrope.

At the time, our church had been through a phase of auditioning new preachers. The elders had just tossed out the kindly old man who had been our preacher for twenty years or so for being too "modernist." This meant that the preacher had been caught red-handed out fishing with the Catholic priest from Epoufette and, what's more, this priest had beer in the rowboat. My father, as daffy as he had become, was depressed in his moments of clarity to see his old friend so flippantly tossed from the pulpit. Violet and I laughed hysterically one day when Dad said of the elders, "Those chintzy bastards ought to be horse-whipped." Deep in the past there was a Chicago street kid who had wanted to move north to go fishing.

Since my father was much respected by the older members of the church as a holy man, albeit a bit of a fool, the new preacher immediately took me under his wing. I didn't understand it at the time, but it was the second occasion where I was being manipulated—the first time was when the doctor tried to wangle out of me our bird-hunting spots. Now this new preacher was from Tennessee and was an accomplished orator. When I was elected the president of the youth group as sort of a cruel joke because nobody wanted the job, he drew me aside and began to lay out the principles of leadership and crowd control. It was a pragmatic amalgam of everything he had learned: look them right in the eye, bring up something to shock them out of the stupor of their last meal, on occasion be spontaneously overcome with tears, pace yourself, use the rhythm of repetition, save a surprise for the end of any talk, let yourself go and Jesus will take over, move around the platform, when you're lost just shout "Come quickly, Lord Jesus!" or "Oh Lord, how long?" and so on. I feel a little odd in admitting now that this training put me in good stead in the world when I became a foreman. You've got to win your men over if you want them to produce. I guess I'm not really embarrassed; I suppose my errors were based on energy and enthusiasm, the discovery that there was something I could do in public after years of suffering a private infirmity, not to speak of those raging hormones plinking around in my system in the manner of the Brownian movement.

Under the tutelage of the new preacher, I perfected a thirty-minute sermon, which I must have delivered, with a few variations, fifty times in two years. If you like, I could probably dig up this artifact. I began with a winter theme and called it "Toboggan Slide to Armageddon" and ran on at the mouth about the atom bomb being the first gong of Armageddon. The mostly pleasant homilies of the New Testament weren't to my taste, other than the Book of Revelations. I preferred the language of the prophets and their keen sense of dire portents. Remind me to dig this sermon out of my papers. We'll look at it like we were these paleontologists I met in the Rift Valley in Africa.

Well, I must say that Violet's advice was right on the money. In no time at all I had all the girls I needed—in fact, far too many to keep my balance. Mother ordered me a pale blue suit from Montgomery Ward. At a tent meeting at the Soo I was a warm-up for a traveling evangelist and was given twenty dollars in an envelope as part of the take. It was at a church group over in Munising that I met my first wife, Emmeline, during what's called "The Invitation." That's when you ask if anyone wants to come forward and take Jesus as their own personal savior. You've seen it on television. The choir sings "Just as I Am," a truly hypnotic hymn, and there was Emmeline, big as life, sobbing at the altar. It was during a church camp revival at a lake near Munising where several hundred people were living in tents, praising the Lord and carrying on, because this was the prime opportunity for young people from far-flung towns to meet each other, to meet someone new. It's deliciously funny when I think it over. We were both fourteen at the time, and Emmeline was what young men call "stacked," still trim in a girlish way but amply endowed. The evening after she came to Jesus we took a long walk around the lake over to where a farmer had cut a hayfield. Our conversation was austere and ethereal, dealing with certain Scriptures that might help us at our troublesome age when, for all we know, the devil might drop the A-bomb square on our heads. Emmeline was in the first glow of redemption, which is, at least partly, a sexual experience. When we reached the still-soft stubble of the freshly cut hayfield we could hear them singing "The Old Rugged Cross" across the lake. The hymn was written by a preacher down in Reed City. We sat down to listen to the music and watch an osprey diving for fish. I remember being attentive to the osprey when Emmeline decided to unburden herself to the "man who saved my soul." I had heard enough of these paltry sins to listen with only half an ear. Emmeline, however, was so original that my hair stood on end and my pecker was at frantic attention.

"Well, Dad died over in Italy in the war. There was just me and my little sister and Mom, who worked at Myron's Wonderbar. Uncle Earl, my dad's brother, had a bum leg and didn't have to go in the service. He looked after us and sometimes would take us girls way over to Marquette to the movies while Mom worked nights. On the way home, when my little sister slept, he started putting his hand on my leg. I sort of knew it was wrong, but I loved going to the movies and, excuse my language, didn't want to piss him off. Everytime we did something, a picnic or a movie or a ride, Uncle Earl was always trying something. Well, this last May on my fourteenth birthday, my little sister got the flu right in the restaurant. We took her home and put her to bed and called Mom and said everything would be okay. So he started sipping at his Guckenheimer whiskey, and I suddenly started crying. You see, I had been invited to the prom by a senior boy, but we couldn't afford a formal—a dress, you know—and Mom didn't have time to make one. I really wanted to go to that dance. So Uncle Earl says, I'll buy you the dress if you do what I say and don't tell your mother.

I sort of knew what was coming and said, you can't make me pregnant—"

"There, there, now. . . . The Lord forgives everything. . . ." Emmeline was crying with more than a touch of the dramatic. I was afraid I wouldn't hear the rest of the story. "It would probably be good to get it off your chest."

"I'm not saying it was all his fault. He limps, but he sort of looks like Tyrone Power. We kissed a lot with our mouths wide open, and we took off all of my clothes, even my underpants. I'd never been that far before with anyone because I didn't want to get pregnant." Emmeline paused again and leaned against me. I was after the story now like a weasel in a henhouse.

"Confession is good for the soul, Emmeline. The Lord died for your sins, and all guilt should be lifted now. Get rid of the old and start anew."

It came out of her somewhere between a shriek and a sob. "He licked my bottom and put his wanger in my mouth!" Then she flopped over like a sack of oats, apparently in a dead faint, with her skirt askew and well up the backs of her thighs. Holy shit, I thought, this is more than I bargained for. I looked to the sky for help, a beseeching prayer for guidance. Being a youth ignorant of the variations of sexual behavior, her announcement was the equivalent of having a hatchet sunk in my forehead. This Uncle Earl would surely burn in Hell, the sooner the better. I helped her up with the slightest peek under her skirt. Lest you think this was a case of child abuse, Emmeline admitted years later she had "more or less" seduced Uncle Earl to get that prom formal. In any event, I was putty in her hands until I left for Africa seven years later. It was on the following evening that we repeated Uncle Earl's moves, under our mutual assurances that the Bible hadn't made any specific statements against it. In this variation to avoid sin, we literally mouthed each other into incoherence every time we met. What grand sex it was, with body and mind sunk equally in the mystery of it all, a true marriage almost impossible to repeat later in life, when dozens of meaningless but inevitable questions arise whenever man and woman meet.

The following October was the coldest on record, without the marvelous fillip or savory of an Indian summer. In addition to preaching, I was studying construction textbooks, learning trigonometry, and digging wellpits by hand for Ted, just as Karl had done. Your basic wellpit has to be underground up here to avoid freezing. You probably don't know it, but down a few feet the earth maintains a basic temperature of about 56 to 58 degrees Fahrenheit. Then I caught pneumonia and had to spend a few weeks in bed. I was just beginning to get around again when Violet showed up in my room one morning at daylight. She was crying, so I followed her in alarm. What happened was that she heard Dad carrying on, which wasn't unusual, but when she went into their bedroom, Mother was dead and Dad was clutching her and wailing. When we got in there, Dad had his face in her neck and was singing softly a popular love song, "You are my sunshine, my only sunshine. . . ." We didn't know what to do, so we got down on our knees beside the bed and I prayed, "Lord, You have taken Mother to Heaven. Bless us who are left behind." Dad finally joined us, and we had to sing some hymns, though at this stage he got the words all mixed up, so we drifted from one hymn to the other until our knees got too sore to bear it any longer. We'd go from "Washed in the Blood of the Lamb" to "Wonderful the Matchless Grace of Jesus" to "Safe Am I in the Hollow of His Hand."

Well, that was the end of my life as I had known it up

to that point. I have thought long and hard about Mother, though it seemed at the time that it was Violet who acted as a mother much of the time. Perhaps it was a matter of exhaustion when you're the last of seven children. It wasn't just that women had no latitude at the time. It was the nature of life then to have to decide rather early the life to be chosen and stick to it, good or bad. The Alsatian servant girl meets the hyperthyroid, religious carpenter. They marry and plunge into their somewhat limited life with touching faithfulness in their capacities and their love for each other. How they loved each other! They were always smooching and taking long walks. Karl said that their noisy bedsprings would keep everyone awake. What I mean is, if you agree with Fate to raise seven children, that has to be your life's work. She was the best cook I've ever known, and I'm sorry I never got to Alsace, as they must surely eat well. Remind me and I'll cook you some of her dishes. I don't know what to say, except I loved her, and sometimes my heart aches at her memory.

Dad had to be put in the county home, but that wasn't as bad as it sounds at the time. He had several friends there, including a goofy old farmer who would wheel Dad around in a wheelbarrow when Violet and I would visit. His brain was nearly gone, but he had a captive audience for his prayers and sermons, and his wild good humor was much appreciated by the staff at the home. In light of a later development, I now recall Violet blushing when Dad introduced me as his "grandson," the "fiery-tongued preacher." Dad died the following May, not six months after Mother, and it was the biggest funeral the county had ever seen. It makes country people nervous when a holy man dies. I was chosen to throw the first shovelful of dirt on his casket.

Violet had been in correspondence with Mother's only sister in Fargo, North Dakota. She left soon after Dad died. I washed Karl's old Chevy and touched up the nicks. At first she was going to go south because she had never been in the main part of Michigan south of the Straits. Instead she went west on Route 2, not wanting to enter the world too abruptly. Ted and his wife, who had come to pick me up, stood on the porch while I walked Violet out to the car. It was a lovely summer morning, and we looked around without a word. Our emotions had carried us well past the point of anything but the simplest speech.

"I love you, little brother."

"I love you, Violet."

Looking back at this with the estranged sensibilities of someone who has spent most of his life in foreign countries, I see that it all doesn't fit together. It's not supposed to. Symmetry is a term better suited to engineering than to people's lives. By the time you wish to become something, you're already something else. In the living nightmare after my accident, I had a dream that we were all black, fertile eggs, each of us encapsuled in our small, liquid universe. I'm aware that everyone sees the world differently, and what I've been telling you might be too peculiar to be of any use. I'm doubtful if I've felt really at home in the world since that summer morning I said good-bye to Violet. I couldn't very well feel homesick when, like so many of us, my home had disappeared. I guess I've moved too fast back and forth across the earth to become preoccupied with the question.

CHAPTER XI

It was a warm June afternoon, and we had been working on the screened porch when we finished the previous segment. I was making notes and watching Eulia and Strang down on the riverbank prepare for his swim. They were speaking in rapid Spanish while she greased his legs and body against the cold water. Thus far the swimming had caused him great suffering; the awkward muscle bunches built up by crawling tended to cramp in the water, but he was sure he could work his way through the problem. The day before a cramp had been so severe that he had broken a tooth while gritting his teeth. I made a note to ask him about this apparent contrast between his intelligence and his optimism. I wanted to say "boyish optimism," but it was both unfair and inaccurate. The forest clearing and cabin had become a bit claustrophobic, and we made plans to visit Emmeline, Robert Jr., and Aurora before Aurora had to return to Italy. I suggested out of maddened curiosity that we visit Karl in prison in Marquette. Strang said it was unlikely that Karl would see anyone, but that I might drop a note proposing an interview. The overwhelming goad behind the long, daily swimming sessions was that Marshall had sent a large folder describing the New Guinea project. There were no photos except a small aerial of the site, the usual twenty-five square miles of green hell with a large river running through the center of it. The rest of the folder was made up of blueprints and specifications, which drew the occasional gasp of pleasure from Strang. Something essentially mean-minded in me wanted to probe deeper for a raw nerve, for the great leveler that is at the heart of all personal journalism, wherein the noblest human might be made pedestrian at least for the length of time it took to read the article: the school of "Faulkner was laughably short," or "Churchill, fat as a toad, coughed up his last bite of flan," or "Eisenhower, despite his questionable talents in World War II, appeared ill at ease and simple-minded during an after-dinner conversation at Stokely Van Camp's winter home at Hobe Sound." That sort of thing, Iago unleashed, the sweltering resentment a pencil pusher feels in a country where politicians keep raising the mythological spectre of the Frontier. Literary biographers have a special talent, too, for making writers more boring than the very least of their work.

There. Eulia was kneeling in her bikini, pointing her bottom at me with telescopic accuracy. If I can't have it, it must be suspicious, I continued my train of thought, then let it trail off into the greenery. It is scarcely the fault of the world that my head weighs a thousand pounds, net. Strang's life seems full because it "is" full, and effortlessly so. Mother used to say "Niggle, niggle, niggle," when I was caught in a fit of spite. My tight heart released a bit, watching Strang kick away at the swift current while he held a rope. He would kick as long as possible, then lie on the bank to warm up and regain his wind. The dog joined in these activities as if they had been designed particularly for her, that is, with a touching air of self-importance. For the first few days of swimming, Eulia was an anxious young mother, but she relaxed when Strang reminded her that he had survived in a far larger river after his accident, and without the use of his legs.

Eulia sensed my current mood and recognized it as a New York relapse, a state of anxiety or disassociation brought on by having to be your own, entire support system, far from your native habitat. Years before I had met two French trout fishermen on vacation in Montana. Their first week had gone splendidly, but then this mood set in, caused by bad food, bad wine and a few days of rain. They were ready to bail out despite the good fishing, so we cooked them a Provençal daube of elk and marrow bones and drank a case of decent California Zinfandel, throwing in a few rancorous, coke-fiend cowgirls who infest the West, and their spirits were restored.

Eulia was full of the emotional subtleties owned by Latin women of intelligence, against which the hardest macho specimens tend to finally shatter, retreat, try to regather their strength by the usual lies, alcohol, sport, violence. I didn't so much shatter as withdraw into a state of melancholy confusion. There was an urge to send this Zen master I had met a half-dozen Latin beauties for a private "sesshin" and see if, how, and why he survived.

Now I felt a harsh lump beneath my breastbone from watching Strang's river struggles: O Jesus, give up, you godforsaken bastard, flatten yourself, subdue your spirit, eat the dirt the rest of us eat from the pot of self-pity. I could hear Eulia's battery-operated tape deck from back in a forest glade where she went every day for her dance workouts. I could make out the strains of Stravinsky's *Le Sacre du Printemps* and left the porch, walking seven-eighths of the way to the glade to be closer to the music, an old favorite.

I could barely see her through the trees, and sometimes my view was blocked entirely. The music had reached a strident, thumping portion, and she was moving to the music by raising her knees to her chin in a pistonlike motion. I moved closer, and it seemed a missed step might break her chin. A third party would have seen the scene as "Susannah Before the Elders," and I felt a little murky: She whirled and flung herself forward, stopped, then repeated this march back across the glade, with her back now toward me, which I used to approach even closer. She was wearing one of those abbreviated leotards, and it was drawn up into the crevice of the buttocks and soaked with sweat. To say I was transfixed would be a euphemism. At first it was curiously nonsexual, similar to the day she stood in the cloudburst, but then the music began to descend from my head into the pit of my stomach.

Abruptly the music stopped, and I found her returning my stare between two clumps of trees. Caught red-handed, I walked over with a faked sense of purpose and a fluttering heart. She, however, was exuberant and laughing with exhaustion. She raised a foot and touched me lightly on each shoulder, resting it a moment on my forehead, where I naturally kissed her ankle, a tripartite blessing from a priestess of an invisible church. Then the dog barked, and we heard Strang's voice. The alarm was immediate, and she ran toward the riverbank, with me in tow at an ever increasing distance.

He had somehow raised himself to his feet by digging his heels into the river bottom and pulling on the rope. He wore a crazed smile and was bellowing a hymn, "Work, for the Night is Coming." There was something ludicrous in the strain required to keep himself upright.

"I would that ye were hot or cold in Laodicea. But because ye are lukewarm, I will utterly cast you out." He had a convincing evangelist's shout, and his head wagged with false but effective rhythm. "So he carried me away in the Spirit into the wilderness: and I saw a woman sit upon a scarlet-colored beast . . . and the woman was arrayed in purple . . . having a golden cup in her hand full of abominations and filthiness of her fornication . . . and upon her forehead was a name written, MYSTERY, BABYLON, THE GREAT, THE MOTHER OF HARLOTS AND ABOMINATIONS OF THE EARTH . . . and I saw the woman drunken with the blood of the saints and with the blood of the martyrs of Jesus. . . ."

Then he lost his grip and shot backwards into the current, going under and bobbing up thirty or so feet downstream. I beat Eulia to the water, making a considerable leap for someone my size, my ears ringing with her screams. I floundered clumsily after Strang, who was floating facedown well ahead of me and approaching a log jam. My heavy, wet clothes and the frigid water made my progress clumsy and exhausting. I was swept into an eddy and found the bottom, standing up just in time to catch sight of Strang as he grabbed an overhanging alder branch. He literally jerked himself out of the water with one continuous movement, the dog scrambling up the bank behind him. Then the dog turned and barked playfully at Eulia and me. Strang disappeared into the greenery. I picked my way as quickly as possible through the swamp with Eulia behind me, crying and shuddering from the cold.

Strang was sprawled near the cabin door, writhing and incoherent, his legs cut up from the crawl back through the swamp. Eulia ran into the cabin while I knelt beside him at an utter loss what to do. I had witnessed a severe overdose on a street in Key West, but this owned the radical difference that Strang was smiling, a fact that frightened me senseless. It took all of my strength and the weight of my entire body to hold his arm still for the hypodermic Eulia brought out of the cabin. The effect of the shot was gracefully immediate: The tremors stopped, and his body went limp, the eyes closing, but the smile firmly in place.

"Jesus H. Christ." I began crying for the first time since my wife asked for a divorce.

Eulia brought out a pillow and blanket and sat beside Strang in silence. I took off my wet shirt and let the sun warm my back, then went into the cabin for the whiskey bottle, which, for a change, seemed appropriate.

"Has this happened before?"

"Twice since the hospital. The last time was the first day we arrived here."

"I'm going to ask him why he was smiling. That sounds insensitive, but I don't mean it to be."

She sat down beside me at the picnic table and put an arm across my bare shoulder. She drank deeply from my glass of whiskey, watching the dog curl up beside Strang as if nothing out of the ordinary had happened.

"The first time happened in a motel room, and I broke the hypodermic. Then I got another one into him and was frightened I might kill him. It was after I made love to him. He was in the hospital three months, so I took him to the hotel and started making love to him as he slept. You should go now. Thank you."

TAPE 5 : It is well after midnight. My watch crystal is full of water, and the alarm clock is in the bedroom. My head was ringing when I left Eulia and Strang. Got back to my place, took a rare Valium and tried to sleep. Is she fucking her own father, for god's sake? Not likely. Or stepfather? Not likely. There is the image of a large, open-air zoo and that I had spent the first half-day on the wrong side of the fence, a vulgarization, but emotionally accurate. I couldn't sleep so walked the two miles down the beach to town, an unexampled act of exercise for me. I wanted somehow to wear myself out—there is nothing quite so fatiguing as real emotion.

There is the problem of keeping Eulia at arm's length when it is your narrator who is in modest pursuit. On my long walk to town I discussed with myself the utter lack of options open to us, or to anyone for that matter. What did you wish to become? Oh, it's far too late for that. The blue, untypically calm, water of the bay reminded me of the Caribbean and what it is like to stare over the side of a skiff during a fast-falling tide along a channel cut. The sun-blasted shallow water yields up nearly everything it holds in a swimming, tumbling stream: nurse sharks, small bonnet sharks, permit fish, barracuda, dollar crabs, minnows, honest-to-god tropical fish, pinfish, baby snapper, needlefish, jelly fish, sponges, unidentifiable flotsam and jetsam, translucent baby shrimp, clumps of sargassum weed, strange wormlike creatures, all stream by for no other reason except that the world rotates and there's a moon in the sky. It is the sweep of this life that gives vertigo, a sense of relentless departure. The rearrival on the incoming

tide is much more gradual and ordered, a proces-
sional, much like the paradigm of our own early
years, which appear so painfully slow when we
live them. No one is ready, it seems, for the loss
of control, the ineluctable character of accel-
eration that gathers around the later years.

The rhythm of walking on the harder sand subdued me to the extent that I felt nearly happy, in
part because the little dog of a few weeks back
appeared for a game of stick-throwing. This dog
evidently spent his life wriggling with pleasure. In my sanest moments, I have not been able to
convince myself that less is more. Once in an awesome palazzo in Venice I had eaten wretchedly
mediocre Italian food. Still, one looks toward
the horizon with a heart willing to lighten,
somewhat like a poor child looks toward Christmas
with a well-suppressed expectancy.

The village was agog with a criminal incident.
Some young campers from Detroit, a full seven
hours to the south, had slashed dozens of tires
the night before. One merchant I had become ac-
quainted with wanted to shoot the culprits. Isn't
that a little radical for the nature of the crime?
I asked. "Don't worry, I won't get caught," he answered, misdirecting my question. Since this
area is virtually crime-free, I wondered at the
strength of the emotions elicited by what anywhere else would be a minor nuisance. Easy question, he says, we're not used to that shit up here.
In other words, these people haven't been desensitized. Reception is so poor most of them don't
even watch television. I'm not at all saying that
they are better or worse than the rest of us, just
not desensitized. It is somehow an appalling notion. My stepdaughter's eyes wandered back to the
television when I explained to her that the old
lady behind the cash register at the deli next
door had to be beaten to death with baseball bats
because a group of young men were victims of un-

happy childhoods. Oh, well. In any event, I discovered how to be exhausted. I drove way out into the outback with a local to "check out" a brook trout spot. From the dead end of a logging trail this involved a three-hour round trip by foot, a real lung-cleanser, an indescribable mudbath trek through swamps, over hills, through swales and marshes. I would have abandoned the hike early, but the prospects of finding the car by myself were dim indeed. Plus, there was the bedraggled remnant of male pride in me. In other words, the experience offered a lifetime of fodder for the whine. But we kept a half-dozen lovely brook trout! Then the blackflies and mosquitoes drove us away. The whole point was the most powerful sense of déjà vu I have ever experienced. We were at the edge of a swamp where the creek opened out into a small meadow covered with sumac. There was a spring and a clay bank with an otter slide—they like to shoot down banks to amuse themselves. We didn't keep one fish out of five that we caught. I was trembling with enthusiasm. Then I knelt down to drink at the source of the spring and saw a trout staring up at me from beneath a clump of water weeds. There was a bird cry, or was it Edith's voice? I could somehow hear the voices of Strang and Edith, especially their laughter. Maybe he was lying in the water while she sat with her legs drawn up on the sandspit. It was uncanny, overwhelming, and I had to breathe deeply to dispel the sensation. Why did I want to dispel it, to draw back? I had had enough and wasn't equipped to handle any more of the purity of this moving picture my mind had devised.

Back to the cabin, finally, with my legs wobbling from fatigue. Though famished, I napped on the couch in my mud-soaked clothes and dreamed of an unapproachable woman I had loved from afar. We are naked and fucking with an energy I have never known in my waking life. I wake up in tears and cook

my trout, make some coleslaw, and warm the bread.
I leave the coleslaw in the kitchen and take my
plate of fish and bread, a cold beer, outside to
watch the evening sun go down. There is no miracle
of loaves and fishes because I am alone. There is
a kingfisher above the lagoon that gets used to my
presence. We are both eating fish. Once again I
see Strang with his brothers and sisters, his
mother, his father trying to summon God down to
the meal. Strang with his tidal insistence that
life allow him to continue to work.

The next morning the cabin, the yard, the river, all looked the same, but there was the sense that a set had been completely restored after a disaster. Strang seemed happy enough, though dark around the eyes, and Eulia was grooming that fat dog as if she were a doll. I was relieved when Strang said it might be a good day to drive down to see Emmeline. All the questions I had prepared were unanswerable, and I wanted to get back to the story he was in no shape to continue.

We stopped in the village on the way through to Manistique so Eulia could call Emmeline. Meanwhile, I picked up their mail, which Strang crammed in my glove compartment without so much as a glance.

"Nice thing about being on a project is that you only get mail once a week. That way it isn't a daily irritation. We used to get mail by company plane on Friday, then you have the weekend to think it over. After work on Monday I'd respond to it all, including a long letter to Emmeline, Bobby and Aurora. Then it was Allegria and Eulia, though I'd still write Emmeline. After that, Evelyn and all the others, plus friends

I had made throughout the world, including children and students I was helping. It was damned hard work, this writing letters, if you got beyond the chatty. I'd hate to make a living at it." He laughed and patted my shoulder.

"It can be terrible when you're not in the mood. Then it's like a root canal at a dentist's. At Harvard in the nineteenth century there was a scientist named Agassiz. In fact, he made an expedition to this very area. He'd make his students do involved descriptions of natural objects to make sure they were truly seeing the objects. He wrote one himself on the common bluegill that is breathtaking."

"I'd like to see it if you can get it for me. I tried to describe an anaconda to Bobby and ended up sending him the dried head and skin."

The anaconda head and skin were on the wall of Emmeline's combination motel–restaurant–service station. It was a much less modest establishment than I had expected and was crowded with cars, patrons and employees. Emmeline was in her office studying for a real estate broker's license.

"If there's money around here to be made, I'm making sure it passes this way."

We made a short tour of the place, mercifully abbreviated in lieu of Strang's walker. It was on Route 2, the main east-west artery through the U.P., a well-traveled road in the summer. The kitchen was huge and gleaming, in direct contrast to the minimalist menu I couldn't help but speed-read.

"You screw up our turkey, Florence, and your big ass is out the door," Emmeline said to the cook with her trademark guffaw.

We drove out to see Bobby and his new skidder. Strang sat up in front while I was wedged between Aurora and Eulia in the back.

"I bet you hate to leave this beautiful place?" Aurora was leaving to go back to Italy that evening.

"Are you kidding? I grew up in these sticks looking at world maps, just like Dad. I might come back here after I see the world. That's why I joined the service."

"Aurora's a real little snot-nose about her hometown. It's not like I didn't go to Hawaii last year." Emmeline was a regular stock car driver on the gravel roads. We fishtailed out of a four-wheel drift.

"Up here in the snowbelt they all want to go see Don Ho, or they go to Las Vegas and see Wayne Newton," Aurora whispered to me.

"I hear you, you little shit. I won't spend money on a dirty place like Italy."

"It's not dirty, Mother. In fact, Italians invented soap."

My attention glided because Eulia's cotton summer skirt was pulled well above her knees as she swiveled to look at the scenery. And Aurora, plump as she was, full-chested and jolly, would accentuate a point by squeezing my leg. Sexually, the U.P. was a sensory deprivation tank. That's why they sedated themselves with booze, my own special poison, and what a friend called "the writer's black lung disease." The moment you left any settlement up here you were smack-dab in the middle of the forest. In the old days there were nymphs and bacchantes in the forest, but they seem to have disappeared to better weather, probably California.

Bobby was delighted to see us at his logging site. There were three other workers who hung back at the edge of the site, bespeaking a certain lowering of the genetic pool in the area. Bobby grabbed Strang's arm and pointed to a huge yellow machine.

"Dad, that's my 130-XL Franklin Skidder. You might say you're looking at twenty grand right there." Strang nodded upwards at the machine, and Bobby grabbed him by the waist and hoisted him up toward a step so Strang could pull himself onto the seat. In his soiled T-shirt, Bobby had the sort of massive build that might give Muhammad Ali pause. He stepped up to join his father, and they went off in a deafening roar. Eulia walked over to greet the workers.

"Isn't it somehow sad to cut down these trees?" I heard her say.

"Guess no one looks at 'em anyhow. Plenty around here, you might say." The worker turned crimson.

When they returned, I politely declined a ride on the skidder. Bobby wondered if it might be possible for Aurora to take a photo of Eulia and the machine for a keepsake.

"All these loggers have closets full of dirty pictures. Don't give him any skin, darling."

"I won't," said Eulia, leaning against a muddy tire. She opened her blouse until a nipple was visible, then raised her skirt just far enough for us to know she wore no panties. She smiled a fake-shy, madonna smile, and the contrast was wonderfully sluttish.

"Corve, what chance does a grown woman have in this world?" Emmeline shrieked.

"Jeezo-peezo," said Bobby.

The lunch was pretty good, if you like hot roast turkey with trimmings and cold beer on a hot afternoon in late June. Bobby said he only killed the turkey on his farm after they had received our phone call. He shot it from a distance in the pen with his .22 because "Fear ruins the meat when you chase them." His two small children were there, and Strang doted on them, his first sight of his first grandchildren. The little boy fell asleep on Eulia's lap. No mention was made of the wife, who had run off with the cosmetics salesman. The stepfather,

Emmeline's second husband, was a mousey, strangely elegant little man, who carved a deft turkey but was given to inanities.

The real shock at the lunch was the presence of Emmeline's Uncle Earl, replete with hair dyed black and a mechanic's jump suit, probably in his mid- to late-sixties, with not more than a vague resemblance to Tyrone Power. He was seated next to me, and his conversation was engaging, given certain allowances to the locale. He told me that he was kept busy by keeping the service station tidy and leading a golden-years polka band. There was the slightest chance, if Emmeline would allow it, that he would play us a tune after lunch. He gestured secretively to an accordion case under an adjoining table. Yet this was Emmeline's seducer! At least thirty-five years ago this old geezer had licked her bottom and put his wanger in her mouth for the price of a prom formal. I was somehow boggled by the idea that these momentous occasions in people's lives usually go unremarked. There is a universe of love and betrayal and death that no one notices. The principals merely yielded to age and, since they weren't particularly attractive or dramatic in the first place, except to themselves, the emotional content of their lives had vaporized. Except to them. Uncle Earl gave me to understand that he was still sexually active. He nodded at a rather doughish waitress who would fuck for twenty Michigan lottery tickets. When this self-same waitress served me a piece of homemade Michigan cherry pie, I looked at her closely for some outward sign of deviance. Uncle Earl added that he and the girl split on any winning tickets. Just last March there had been a fifty-dollar winner, which had somewhat amortized his lust.

After lunch Uncle Earl could not be denied and uncased the dread accordion. He began with "In Heaven There Is No Beer" ("That's why we drink it here"), and Aurora and Emmeline, at her insistence, taught Eulia how to polka. A born dancer, she picked up the steps in moments. I made one pass with her around the restaurant—everyone from Michigan knows how to polka even though they've raised themselves on Monteverdi and James Joyce. I could feel the turkey thigh and its dark freight of gravy swirling in my gut. In my mind, I could see Eulia's beige thighs and a tad of furze against the muddy tires of the 130-XL Franklin Skidder. The question of what we were all doing there only occurred to me much later. I was having a wonderful time, dodging Formica-topped tables with a Costa Rican dancer in a motel restaurant outside of Manistique, Michigan.

There was a blatant, sour note on the way home. I had let Eulia drive because Uncle Earl had come up with a bottle of the Yugoslavian brandy and nostrum, Slivovitz, and the many toasts had left me sleepy. The problem was that Strang had drawn the mail out of the glove compartment and announced that Allegria, his second wife, was coming for a short visit.

"I'll kill her," hissed Eulia, stomping down on the gas.

"You won't kill anyone. She did as much for you as any human being can do for another."

"She let my little brother go to El Salvador to fight—"

"On the wrong side—"

"You know nothing of Central American politics—"

"Yesterday you told me I was a true native. I do know that there's a streak of cruelty down there that would gag the worst Sicilian."

"I'll slap her face."

"Which would get you a quick plane trip to Puntarenas."

Now Eulia slowed the car down and wept a bit. Strang put his arm around her.

"She'll only be here a few days. Typically, she said she had to be in Miami, anyway."

TAPE 6: Midnight. Hope to get Strang back to his story at dawn. This everyday reality pudding is insufficiently soothing. I was a little alarmed to discover when I got back to the cabin that my belt and pants felt loose. My first concern was cancer, then it occurred to me that my drinking and eating habits had been severely tampered with. For nearly a month there had been the long morning talks, the afternoons of organization of notes and possible questions, hikes, walks to the bar. Could it be I was engaged in a project superior to my stomach? Perhaps, but there was also a paucity of raw materials. Romaine lettuce meant a 110-mile round trip. I couldn't loiter at Dean & Deluca's, double-park in front of Zabar's, or stare in the window of Loebel's until I went in and bought something unnecessary. There were no cronies to lunch, dine, and cook with. Yesterday afternoon, while working, I ate my first tunafish sandwich in years. It was a day without garlic. If I lost fifteen pounds a month for a year, I'd only weigh thirty pounds. I could complete this book by November, then spend a month in France playing catch-up football, as it were. There is also the fact that Eulia arouses me far more than is normal for my age, but then what is this passion to avoid feeling foolish? Who cares? Eulia would be the final diet. I'd come crawling back to NYC invisible sideways, scrawny as a POW, a heart like tartare, a literal gruel of longing.

I rowed a boat! Up and down the long lagoon, the first time in thirty years, until some skin started coming off my hands. I did so because of a wave of vertigo over the idea that I had been behaving out of character because there was no

one around that I knew, hence no one who expected
me to act in character. While rowing, I thought
about a floating group of writer friends who
would get together once a month or so for dinner at
one another's apartments. Even the dinners were
competitive. Much of the anxious gossip was who
was being paid what amount for what: articles,
screenplays, nonfiction, novels—the last had
been nearly abandoned as too chancey these days.
I brought up an item I had read in one of those
travel guide books—I once owned a closet full—
wherein it was stated that there was nothing "interesting about Encarnacion," a city of fifty
thousand souls in Uruguay. To my shock, they all
agreed. No one in the group had ever been to South
America except myself and that by virtue of a
fishing trip to Ecuador. South America hadn't
been "hot" for years. There were mumblings about
Mengele, the architecture of Brasilia, the movie
Black Orpheus, mardi gras, Gabriel Marquez's
Nobel Prize, Cortazar lives in Paris, that sort
of thing. Writers can always make more out of
less, so I knifed in with Burgundy energy, ful-
minating about gauchos, pampas, the Amazon
basin, tropical nights full of gorgeous whores
and cheap cocaine (this perked them up), Macchu
Picchu under a full moon, five-pound steaks for
five dollars, cheap rubies, that sort of thing.
But then one of these acerbic wags shut me up by
saying that he was sure that the group could guar-
antee a kitty of fifty thousand dollars, to be re-
paid by advances, articles and so forth, to ship
me to Encarnacion for six months. I bargained
them down to three months, saying six months
would be a financial sacrifice. In the harsh
light of morning, I made reservations for Palm
Beach for medical reasons. Now, while rowing, it
seemed that writers, unlike Strang, were more
than willing to neglect whole continents. Strang
had quipped one day he had never spotted one of our

congressmen in either South or Central America
and had seen no evidence to the contrary that they
were simply a bilious clot of lawyers. There were
water blisters developing on my hands. I imagined
both Congress and the Soviet Presidium being
packed off to a boatless Elba. I saw Reagan and
Andropov mooning each other across the Atlantic,
asses up like huge, pink, metallic scorpions,
while the other continents waited in terror for
the results. I wish Karl would answer my letter.
Think of a man who loved the woods spending his
summers, his Mays and Octobers, in prison.

CHAPTER XII

I don't want to get ahead of myself, but last night I dreamt about ships. Remember when I told you about sitting at the Ojibway Hotel with Karl and Fred and seeing the ships pass? Well, years back Marshall wangled me a ride on this immense oil freighter carrying a full load from Venezuela up to New Jersey. Strange as it seems, I've found few men in the oil business I really cared for. I mean, I'm still open about it, but I've had contact with these people throughout the world, and they're hard to like. I've traced it to the utter greed, the direct venality of the business, plus the idea that there's always been a preconception afoot, an image of what an oil worker is supposed to act like—you know, the hard-working gambler-lover-cowboy with Texas mannerisms, even if they're from Wisconsin. One of our civil engineers formed a small group in a club we used to visit in

Caracas called the Society to Prevent Texas. Anyway, I got a ride on this freighter, and what thrilled me most was the engine, a German-built MAN diesel, actually a K2 93/170, twelve cylinders capable of generating upwards of twenty-five thousand horsepower. The engine itself weighed about twelve hundred tons, you know, equivalent to the weight of twelve hundred Volkswagens, or six hundred regular cars all in one place. I've got the specs and photos somewhere in my papers, and I'll show them to you. I spent a long time looking that diesel over, hoping all the while that it would get me over Allegria, but it didn't. I'll tell you about that later. That engine somehow got into my soul. If you know about such things, you just stand there utterly astounded. The Iracu Falls in Brazil did the same thing, also a blind— they're born that way—freshwater porpoise we saw up a tributary of the Amazon. I'm sure everyone has had these experiences. They pop you right out of your shoes. The same thing happened to me when Ted got me into the real nerve center for the Mackinac Bridge before they really got started building it. You could look out at the empty Straits, five miles wide and hundreds of feet deep, and then look around the room at the architect's renderings, and it was inconceivable that they could put a bridge across it. That day sort of passed as a religious experience. In fact, I was wearing my suit, that light blue preacher suit Mother ordered from the catalog, but I had grown a lot, so it was ill-fitting. I didn't say much that day but hoped I cut a bit of a figure. That must have been about in 1954 when Ted managed to get all sorts of subcontracts for the bridge, from housing to maintenance, to hauling limestone. Ted seemed to know everyone. We ate in a St. Ignace restaurant with a bunch of engineers, and I could hardly swallow food. There was so much excitement in the air and, what with working for Ted, I was to be a small part of it.

But I'm getting ahead of myself. After Violet left for North Dakota, I went to live with Ted and his young wife, Rachel, over in Marquette. We were still late in the postwar housing boom, and I spent three years helping Ted put up houses and buildings. Ted had the only eye for business in our family, and I couldn't begin to estimate the amount of money he socked away. I can't say, though, that he was ever happy except during the building of the bridge. I saw him in Miami last year before he moved to Alaska, and he was a goddamn mess. Of all things, he was envious of my lifelong involvement with irrigation projects and dams. Ted had built literally thousands of tract houses and, later, fancier models. After the bridge he moved to Lansing, then to Detroit. Of course, when I saw him, it was only a few months after his daughter had been raped. There's no underestimating what this can do to a father, let alone the girl herself. Ted wanted to talk about the good old times in Marquette and over in St. Ignace working on the bridge. I have a pretty accurate memory, and talking about the good old days is my weakest point.

I'm not at all proud of those years, say between the ages of fourteen and twenty; most of them seem characterized by selfishness and insensitivity. Work was the excuse, an urge to prove myself at the expense of Emmeline. We got married when we were sixteen, not unusual at the time for people who came from families identified as lower class. By then I was working on the bridge with Ted, who bought us a small house in Epoufette, a lovely little town on Lake Michigan, not far from St. Ignace. It was partly greed over getting a grown man's wages. It was work anyone could have done—road construction, driving dump trucks, build-ing storage sheds. It was only later that I developed some unique abilities that made my labor meaningful. It's said that bridge workers, the bridgemen, are so mean you can never tell if they're sick or drunk or both. I aped these men, including the Mohawks, who are well known for their abili-ties at working at great heights. And the steelworkers who did the marine work off the barges, the caissons, pilings and the cofferdams, seemed wilder yet. It seems it took until Africa before I got over the coarsening effect of those years. I was sick of the cement block tabernacles I had preached in, and the bridge itself represented the slowly building path to the outside world. I would watch the cable-spinners through Ted's binoculars and long to do something high-minded and dangerous so far up there hundreds of feet in the air. At the time, the middle section was the longest suspension bridge ever built in the world, over 3800 feet. All of us on shore were a little tentative, but a lot of the excitement rubbed off. Odd, but I can remember the names of those who died: Frank Pepper, Albert Abbott, James La Sarge, Jack Baker, Robert Koppen. We younger workers wanted to be out there where we might have a chance to die heroically!

Perhaps many of the mutual disappointments between Emmeline and me were inevitable for those who married so young. Most often I was working six days a week, twelve hours a day. My exhaustion was so great that often I'd fall asleep at the dinner table. Bobby and Aurora came along pretty fast, and our main entertainment was playing with the babies. Only the midwinter break, when the bridge work closed down, did we do anything to save us. Emmeline had gotten involved with the young wives of other workers, who

viewed us as laughably old-fashioned. I remember one evening when I came home and Emmeline was crying. It was
in November in 1955 when the south backstay span nearly
toppled in a seventy-five mile per hour gale.

"What's wrong, pumpkin?" I asked. In fact, she had
gained a lot of weight with the births of the children. This
was also my fault, as my complaints about her cooking, so
awful compared to Mother's, had gotten her overly interested in food.

"I drank a glass of beer over at Wanda's today," she
gasped. "I'll go to hell for sure. Save me, Corve."

"A loving God is not going to send you to hell for a
glass of beer."

"Yes, He is," she shrieked.

"A little wine for thy stomach's infirmities," Saint Paul
told us. I was pretty resourceful what with all the Scriptures
at my fingertips. When I didn't feel like going to church, I'd
remind myself that Jesus said, "Work out your own salva-
tion with fear and trembling."

Rachel, Ted's wife, figured we were having problems,
so she took care of the kids and made us go off for a
weekend at the Soo. I hope to tell you we let her rip. We
bought a radio and a phonograph and played records in our
room at the Ojibway. We went to the Antlers twice for
dinner. We did it in the fashion the workers called "dog-
style" for the first time. We bought some beer and pepper-
mint schnapps and sat there in the room drinking and listening to music and waiting to go crazy. We saw my very first
movie, starring Esther Williams, the renowned actress and
swimmer back then. We watched it twice, in fact. I would
get a whomping hard-on watching all of those ladies swimming, and Emmeline would play with me right there in the

[148]

dark theatre. We even danced in the hotel room to a record that was a big hit at the time, called "Sh-Boom," of all things.

That trip helped somewhat, though Emmeline played "Unchained Melody" so much that winter that I finally limited her to once a day. We stopped short of a television, partly because all of our God-fearing acquaintances of the past might see the aerial. We went to the Soo one other time that winter and saw *Rock Around the Clock,* which we thought, despite the wonderful music, was a frightening picture of life in the big cities. We were very moderate in our drinking because my sister Lily had moved to St. Ignace and had developed quite a drinking problem. She showed up at Ted's one night all beaten up by her husband. When I saw her, I just broke down and cried. Ted called the police, but they weren't interested in the problem, so Ted and me went looking for him. We split up and walked the streets of St. Ignace. Until then I had never committed any violence against another man and still think of it as evil unless it is unavoidable, say, if some lunatic jumps you. Well, I found him in a bar and did quite a job, despite my youth, before I was pulled off. Later on they got back together. In fact, they're still married. I asked his forgiveness, but he said I was right to stand up for my sister.

The real problem then was that I had met my first male friend. He was a college kid of Italian descent who had a summer job because his dad was a superintendent for Merritt, Chapman and Scott, the marine contractor. Val, his name was, and we had a great time together. He was from Chicago and treated me at first as if I was a hick, but he was crazy about fishing and hunting, so I was quite a bit of help to him. We'd bring his father a lot of fish on Sundays, and on one occasion we jacklighted a deer. His father was from northern Italy, and I've never seen a man quite so excited about having a deer to eat.

Val's father offered me a job: After Mackinac they were going to do a smaller bridge over the Suwannee in Florida, then on to a larger one in Mexico. I was full of myself for several days until he found out I was married and said a young husband should stay with his wife. Val saw my grief and tried to talk his father out of it, with no success. To tell the truth, I was heartbroken. When Val left, I didn't say good-bye, and when the bridge was done enough to let all the workers make the first trip on foot from St. Ignace to Mackinac City, I played sick and wouldn't go. I lapsed into a long silence and went back to religion. Even Ted couldn't get a thing out of me, and Emmeline took to going out with her friends, leaving me with the babies, whom I catered to in the fashion of a martyr.

This proud murk, or I should say mud, went on for several months until I drove Emmeline, Ted and Rachel witless. Then one day Ted ran into Val's father, who had returned for the bridge-opening ceremonies, and got the whole story. This only served to make my brother angry.

"Corve, there's no real money in being some construction vagabond."

"Not interested in the money. I want to see the world."

"Oh, bullshit. You saved every cent you could since you were fourteen. I'm counting on you for a partner someday."

"Looks to me like I'm going to live and die right up here."

"That's what I'm saying. You got plenty of dough. Why don't you take Emmeline over to Niagara Falls or down to Detroit for a ball game?"

I had something far grander in mind, having called Laurel in Detroit and laid out fifty bucks for a magnificent world atlas. I had outlined a trip that would have required the most manic traveler a number of years. I also bought those books many dreamers buy—*Work Your Way Around the World, Around the World on a Tramp Steamer*—and my secret itinerary included the Gobi Desert, the Transvaal, Tierra del Fuego, Kashmir, the Himalayas, the walled kingdom of Tibet, Macchu Picchu, Kenya, the Sahara, Fiji, and so on. I felt I had two things in my favor. First, I had saved nearly fifteen thousand dollars in six years, an awesome amount for a young man in those days, or so it seemed to me; I would leave thirteen for Emmeline and take the other two to augment what I could earn. And the other point in my favor was that I knew a lot of skills: construction, including plumbing and wiring, heavy equipment repair, regular auto repair, and I could read and follow blueprints, drive shallow wells, drive a bulldozer or a backhoe, finish cement, plus I had modest talents as a machinist. I felt all this should get me around, and I was right for a change, but by accident.

What happened was that Ted had been contracted by an old friend of the family who Dad had helped out. This man had become the director of foreign missions for a large fundamentalist denomination—I won't mention what group because, as you'll see later, these people were truly a bunch of fuck-ups. There's a stubborn irony in the idea that so many of the most compassionate people don't know how to do anything. Anyway, this man sent Ted the plans for a small mission school and suggested if Ted still "loved the Lord" he would be willing to go to Kenya for a few months and supervise construction. The people of the "dark continent" were full of a "longing for Jesus."

"These folks must be real dumb, Corve. We could whip this sucker together in a month."

"With no help at all," I agreed. It was a simple three-room construction—a smallish hall with two rooms in back, one for a clinic and one for storage.

The upshot was that Ted convinced this director of missions that I could do the job, helped a bit by an ample contribution. Ted was a strict tither; that is, ten percent of his income went to the church or to church charities. At the time—it is still true now—fundamentalist groups were insistent that the entire world hear the gospel. The main theological impulse here is that the world couldn't come to an end until everyone had had a chance to know Jesus and, if nothing else, these folks wanted the world to end. You simply can't go anywhere in the Third World without running into these missions. These people go through indescribable discomforts and suffering to spread the gospel. They are scorned by the intelligentsia of every country, but then they could care less about the intelligentsia. Both revolutionaries and right-wingers murder them, but what better thing than a martyr's death? Frankly, these mission schools are traditionally a wonderful breeding ground for revolutionaries because, properly understood, the gospel teaches us to hate injustice and to love one another.

Emmeline cried a lot but had undergone the total indoctrination of the Scriptures. It is said: "Many are called but few are chosen."

"I always knew you were chosen to be something special, Corve. Me, I'm just ordinary. I never give a thought to anything except what I'm doing. Ever since we walked around the lake that day at Bible camp you were my hero."

Late on the eve of my departure I was trembling a lot

and staring at my suitcase and a new brown suit all laid out. At dawn Ted would take me to the bus station in St. Ignace, from which I would travel south to Grand Rapids, where I would be prepped by the mission director. For over a week I had been filled with fear and trembling, mixed with a wild, soaring expectancy. Emmeline and me had simply screwed ourselves silly. She said she would be true to me, which struck me as odd because it never occurred to me otherwise. I kept assuring her that the longest I would be gone would be six months. Later I realized that my departure must have reminded her of her father's fatal trip to war. Late that last night I kissed Bobby and Aurora, and the tears came so strongly I couldn't catch my breath.

So I crossed the bridge going south, and I never really came back until now, over twenty-five years later. A number of things disturb me as I'm saying this, maybe not so much disturb as nag at me. You could almost envision your life as a crèchelike tableau, a series of three-dimensional photographs of the dominant scenes, the bitterest griefs and the accomplishments. I see myself on a rainy summer dawn, embracing Ted and getting on the bus. I can't really breathe or swallow, and my stomach is cramped. Somehow in the diesel hiss and whine of the bus I look east toward the glow of the rising sun. I am murmuring prayers, because I am frightened as if I had somehow allowed myself, a child of God, to be sent back to Egypt. It was as if my yearning had got me out of an imagined bondage for the real one of the unknown. Probably everyone feels this on their first true flight from whatever nest, but it is no less real for being so universally shared! We all have mothers and fathers, and what sweet anguish, sometimes terror, there is in those names. If you give it much thought, the skeleton of life is stupendously ordinary. So much of the emotional content of our lives seems to occur before we are nineteen or twenty, doesn't it? After that, especially by our age, we seem like stone walls, mortared together by scar tissue. The whole point is not to be. From all my reading done in construction camps throughout the world, the main point or challenge is to stay as conscious as possible, absurd as that seems.

Talking to you now I'm getting back some of that vividness. My god, man, look at a map. Maps are comic. Locate Marquette or Trout Lake or Moran or Epoufette in the upper peninsula of Michigan, then look at Kajiado, south of Nairobi, in Kenya. I am barely twenty years old, and the buttons of my new, bargain brown suit are already unraveling. My passport is getting worn from constant rechecking. I am off for a lifetime of work. I say "lifetime" as it is now a question that it might be pretty much over, however abbreviated. South of here, on the Kingston Plains, sometimes on a camping trip if it was raining, Karl and I would burn one of those century-old white pine stumps. I've pretty much burned myself up, and if you looked at a succession of photos of the work I had a part in, it wouldn't mean much to anyone else. Is your true life in those books of yours? It better be. I can flip this photo over in my mind now, the bridges, irrigation projects, dams. We no longer have much faith in that sort of thing in our country, but they do elsewhere. Those triumphs of technology and engineering are easily forgotten when the lights never go out. They are questioned the most by the people who have the most, which is not even a paradox for human beings. It was far simpler for me back in Africa where the drilling of one first-rate well with pure water could save hundreds of lives from fatal cholera, not to speak of any number of slower deaths from other diseases.

Africa was by far the most beautiful nightmare of my life. If it had lasted more than the half-year I was there I might have died, both emotionally and physically. There's simply no preparation for the impact of Kenya, not certainly in the fifty years' worth of *National Geographics* I studied in the Chippewa County library. You said you'd been there yourself, so you know what I'm talking about. But you're a sophisticated traveler, and I was a twenty-year-old stripling who had only been out of the U.P. en route. Manhattan alone seemed a mirage from the airplane, and I swore to spend some time there someday. The church made my travel arrangements with typical Protestant sadomasochism; it was two and a half days of airplanes and airports, with no chance to see any of New York, London, Rome, Addis Ababa. And when I reached Nairobi, my suitcase was at the luggage dock but not my tool chest, which Ted had so carefully selected and purchased. This put a lump in my throat that stayed there until the tool chest mysteriously arrived at the mission three weeks later. Reverend Blank— I must conceal this fool's name—insisted that the power of prayer brought the tool chest to us. The mission wasn't really in Kajiado but well outside a town very similar to it. This is to conceal Sharon's identity—she might have a husband now, or even children.

So there I sat on my suitcase outside the Nairobi airport for more than an hour, waiting for whoever was sent to pick me up. I hadn't had anything but catnaps for more than two days, and my senses were raw and vivid. Twenty-five years later I can still remember many of the faces. There was a group of obviously very rich men from Texas and Colorado being picked up by a white hunter for a safari. One of these men looked at me sitting there in my brown suit with transparent, mean-eyed scorn. Back home you wouldn't look at anyone that way without being in danger of getting your ass kicked. More poignant were two English girls who had been on my flight and were being met by their parents. I had become infatuated with them on the plane, not that they were beautiful, but they were so lively and had extraordinary laughs. They were the sort of upper-crust girls I had never seen before. The true money from mining in the U.P. was limited to a few families on the Keewanaw Peninsula and in Marquette. Most of the mining concerns were Boston-owned, and that's where all the money went. The girls' clothes were strange-looking but lovely. The younger one waved good-bye to me, though we had only looked at each other on the plane. There was a fine flash of leg as she got into the car, the first Jaguar I had ever seen other than in photos. I entered a reverie about taking off her expensive underpants and hoped desperately to see her again. When you come from terribly confined circumstances, the main thing you cannot comprehend is the sheer dimension of human activity on earth.

Then there was a large black man in soiled khakis standing before me and a severe-looking woman in her early thirties in a sun hat and cotton dress.

"Brother Strang? This is Peter, and I'm Sharon, the mission nurse. You look tired. It must have been an awful trip."

"It was a great trip." I bowed to her and shook hands with Peter. There was a thrill here; though I had seen some blacks in Grand Rapids during my indoctrination, I was twenty years old and had never met one. Some fundamentalists think of them as the accursed children of Ham, but Dad had said that was nonsense. After Christ died, all curses were lifted from earth if you wanted them to be.

"I'm glad you're optimistic. You'll need it here." Sharon was giving me that direct once-over that I've come to think of as a mark of an intelligent woman. "I'm sorry we're late. I waited forever at the pharmacy."

Peter went off to check on my missing tool chest, and I had a chance to look Sharon over. She verged on being attractive and would have been so with a minimum of effort. Her surface severity contrasted to full breasts, narrow waist, and fairly full hips. She was a farm girl from outside Stevens Point, Wisconsin, and we loosened up when we began babbling about being from the northern Midwest, not more than a few hundred miles from each other.

Well, the mission was a lot less than I expected. Circled around a huge baobab tree and encircled itself by a kraal-type fence were a small house with a screen porch, a small open-air school, a stucco dispensary, and a miniature motel-like building with three doors. My living quarters were at one end and Sharon's at the other, with an empty nonconnecting room between us. There also was a shed that held a welter of junk and useless equipment. Peter said that no one had been in there for years because it was full of snakes. I immediately shied back, which brought a smile to his face. He was getting the idea I wasn't a total lamebrain, and this was a relief to him.

Reverend Blank was away in Kampala at a mission conference for a few more days, which proved to be a piece of questionable luck for me. There was an old black woman who lived in a hut behind the Reverend's house. She cooked us dinner—rather heated up some tinned stew. Sharon advised me with a twinkle that the Reverend wouldn't trust anything that didn't come out of a tin or a jar. Even the drinking water was bottled, and we were only allowed to run the generator for lights for a single hour after dark. My room had a toilet, but the only shower was in her apartment.

We had coffee outside, and Peter strolled off to his village a half mile down the road. It was twilight in midsummer, and there was a sweet, dry-grass smell in the air. I could stare off across the vast Loita Plains, dotted occasionally by that curious geological formation, the hill of rocks known as a kopje. On our way out from Nairobi during my intermittent dozing I had seen a few giraffes, some deerlike creatures, and now I heard my first coughing, harsh grunt, that is, a lion's voice.

"Holy shit," I said. My hair stood on end.

"It's just a lion. They won't bother us."

Peter had showed me a ten-gauge shotgun and some buckshot shells in my room. He said they had only used it once on a lung-shot cape buffalo that had trotted into their compound blowing blood all over. I knew guns well enough to understand that the weapon would only be useful at perilously close range.

Despite her apparent loneliness, Sharon sent me off to bed at dark—my extreme fatigue was showing itself by my calling her Violet twice. There was a striking similarity physically, but also in attitude: Sharon told me later she had been terribly happy when I turned out not to be a "Bible-thumping nay-sayer." I reminded her immediately of a forbidden high school boyfriend, a football player and beer drinker she could only see in secret. When I slept that night, I had one of those embarrassing dreams that delight analysts. Violet and I were at that lake I told you about—we were naked in shallow, warm water and all greased up with butter, for some reason, and she kept making me enter her in all possible places, over and over, rolling over and over in the shallow water like animals.

It was a real hair-raiser, waking me before dawn with semen all over the place. I lit an oil lamp and studied the rather simpleminded blueprints for the building. I would dig the footings and put in the foundation, gather all my materials, and then, if my tools hadn't arrived, I would see about driving a new well. The current well no longer delivered potable water, according to Sharon, though the natives still drank it. Hence much of the dispensary practice was doling out antispasmodics and other stopgap measures for dysentery and ulcerated colitis. My blueprint study was broken by a lion's roar, the volume of which made the beast seem far closer than it was. I tried to load the shotgun, but the shells were bloated with humidity, and there was only one that fit into the chamber. I began a shopping list that included shells. When you're in my business, sloppiness of any sort can be fatal. Look at me now. Look at my legs. I forgot a prescription for Tagonet in Caracas because I was chasing pussy, pure and simple. We had gone to a Villa Lobos concert, and the music had swept me away. I forgot.

Anyway, I was up at first light with my binoculars to make sure the lion was gone. I took a stick out of the fence and wedged a shovel out of the supposedly snake-infested shed. I didn't have my tape measure, but the intended building was small enough that I could eyeball a line for rough footings while I waited for my transom. After a few hours of hard digging, I was wishing for a cup of coffee. Earlier the landscape had killed my hunger; what an unspeakably immense, dun and bruised-colored landscape Kenya offers in the dry season. How would I have known this world was here all of the time? In this part of Africa all life processes, birth to death, are an open book one is forced to read every day. It fills one with melancholy, but it is a melancholy you owe to life, enshrouded as it is with magnificence. Some people think you can extrapolate all of life from one place. That was Thoreau's mistake, though a very minor one. It's simply not true. The only way to extrapolate the spirit of Africa is to be in Africa.

About midmorning Sharon came out in a robe. She hurried to the Reverend's quarters, saying she would make coffee after she called someone on the radio. It had become so hot that I went into my room and put on a pair of khaki shorts before I went back to my digging. It was Saturday and everyone's day off, but I wanted to work; the rhythm of physical labor can be very peaceful, removing difficult questions such as, What am I doing here? I am building a school and dispensary for the United Nazarene Mission. Sharon's robe had been blue like one of Violet's. There was a certain despair in the beginnings of a hard-on while digging in that sun-baked, rocky soil. Finally she came up behind me with a cup of coffee and a glass of lemonade. She was crying and used the sleeve of her robe to dry her tears.

"Don't mind me. You may as well know I have this boyfriend, this English doctor in Nairobi. On Saturdays he drives out and we have a picnic somewhere in the country because he's married. He's not coming today, so that's why I'm crying. I hope you won't think I'm too much of a sinner, because everybody gets lonely."

"I'm not in the judge business. I'm just over here to work." We squatted down in the dirt near my footings. I could see up her legs, so I looked off in the distance and drank my coffee and lemonade while she continued crying.

"That motherfucker tried to stop me from putting up a

gravestone for my dog in here." She gestured at a large rock in the middle of the school area. "I was in Nairobi for the night, and he was supposed to put the dog in my room for the night. It was a Dalmatian this paleontologist up in the Rift Valley gave me to keep away the snakes. People think Dalmatians are for firehouses, but they're the best snake dog in the world. So I come home the next day, and a hyena or a leopard has eaten my dog, and that miserable little shithead said he was in prayer all evening and forgot my dog. I loved my dog!" She screamed and stomped off to her room.

Naturally, I was a little shocked by her language. I stood there for a while, brushing away flies and wondering what to do. Her rumpled hair and wild eyes had made her attractive, and I have always been an easy mark when it comes to compassion, deserved or not. Her lover hadn't showed up, and the Reverend, through negligence, had allowed her beloved dog to die. I walked over to her screen door and listened to her sobs, which were punctuated by the pumping of the blood in my temples. I called out her name but got no answer, so I went in anyway.

She was on her stomach in bra and panties, which made me an ambivalent victim, somewhere between pity and lust. I put my hand on her shoulder and massaged her neck. She turned over and squeezed my hand against her face, which was a blend of anger and grief.

"I'd like to stake that shithead out on the plains and let the lions eat him. Maybe I'll catch a snake and put it in his bedroom! There's an idea for you." She traced her finger through the sweat on my bare chest. To avoid looking at her body I stared at the full bookcases but somehow couldn't see the titles. "We're breaking the ice in a hurry, aren't we?

[161]

I wish the Reverend could see us now. He can kiss my ass. I bet he'd love to, somewhere back in his weasel mind. I bet he'd like to get right down and bury his face in my ass. My doctor boyfriend thinks I've got a beautiful ass, but his thoughts aren't doing me much good today. I've worked as a nurse at different missions for ten years, and this preacher we got here is the worst little prick I've ever run into. My dad was one of the biggest farmers around Stevens Point, Wisconsin, and he was glad I was going to be a medical missionary. He had plenty of money, and I was going to go to medical school, but my mother decided being a nurse was good enough for a girl. Fuck her, too. I'm never going back. Dad is dead, and I get these fucking, lamebrain, whiny letters from my mother whom I no longer need. Dad fixed her and left me some money she can't touch, so when I get a furlough I go straight to France. I love France, and what's more, I speak perfect French." She emphasized this by quoting a piece. Now I was sitting on the edge of the bed while she was up on her knees sitting on her heels. "I learned that lovely quote by a French poet who wanted Christmas on earth, you know, every single day. This poet lived up in Ethiopia for years, but got gangrene. Your arms and chest remind me a lot of Louis. You called me Violet last night, but I looked at your papers and know your wife's name is Emmeline. I bet your secret lover is Violet! Louis was Catholic, and I was Baptist, so we had to sneak around. I let him fuck me on our high school senior trip down to Chicago. He knew how religious I was so he tried to do it against me with my panties on, but I took them off." Now she put her arm around me and began singing "Mares eat oats and does eat oats and little lambs eat ivy," of all things. I was at a loss what to do, so I turned away from the bookcase and looked at her directly. Come to think of it, no one is ever prepared for this kind of thing. My heart went out to her, but I didn't have any idea what to say. "I don't want you to think I don't love the Lord. I love the Lord by helping to cure the diseases of these people. I just can't stand this small-minded shit anymore. You're looking at me finally. Since you called me Violet, I'm going to call you Louis. We'll organize some drama around this place. I love to read plays. Can I call you Louis?"

"May as well. Of course you can."

"Okay, Louis. Now call me Violet."

"I'm not sure I can call you Violet."

"We're just acting in a play, darling Louis. Call me Violet, and I'll make you happy, Louis my dearest."

"You're very pretty, Violet. I've never seen anyone as pretty as you."

"Louis, you're going to find out in a few days that the Reverend doesn't allow shorts at his mission. He wants you to have skin funguses on your legs. Let's get those shorts off right away."

She prodded me, and I stood up immediately. You might say I was developing a sense of drama. She peeled down my khaki shorts and underpants with a professional air and fondled me.

"Louis, this is a coincidence, but you have an identical cock!" She threw herself back on the bed laughing, then deftly removed her bra and panties. She sat back and put as much of my cock in her mouth as was possible, then took it out. "You've probably never made love to a grown-up woman, have you?"

"Guess you could say I haven't."

"Well, the rule of thumb is to put your heart in it."

[163]

I looked at the slowly floating ceiling fan, then out the screen door at Africa. I was trying to think of a sentence to assure her that I would put my heart in it, but she drew me down on top of her. God, how I loved that woman! I never loved anyone or anything like I loved that woman. I only got to love her a month. Thirty-one days of love before she ran off with her doctor friend to England. Oh, dear Jesus, how I loved her, and she almost killed me, and I didn't care. We had three days before the Reverend returned, and I've never had three days of love like that. Someone asked, "What have we done with the twin that was given us when we were given our soul?" It was a frightening love that I embraced and she ran away from.

CHAPTER XIII

I had to subtly enforce a break here, after catching an appalled glance from Eulia from the kitchen. Strang had jumped abruptly from talking about Sharon to an odd disquisition on the Comsat satellite photos of the Amazon basin and the other river systems he had worked in. He insisted I study this book in order to understand the way in which all of the water on our planet "moves." Being given to picture books, I readily made the promise. There was more than a tinge of the Ancient Mariner to this speech, almost oracular, with some of the rhythms of an evangelist. It came in the middle of my changing both tapes and batteries, but in most respects the speech was of only pathological interest. He started with Violet bathing him in a creek as an infant, then they would walk up the sandy-bottomed creek on hot summer days, sitting in the water where it gathered in a small pool. About ten minutes later, he ended with the nature of the great ocean currents and rivers such as the Humboldt, the Gulf Stream, and others. It was all shape, nature, volume, velocity, behavior around obstacles, temperature, quantity of oxygen, quantity of sediment. I must admit I had never paid more than cursory attention to the subject, but I'll say he made it come alive until I felt a certain vertigo. It seems that water never stops: It is always in movement up into the air, or down into the earth where there are, of all things, underground rivers.

Eulia's alarm increased when Strang lunged upward from the chair and grabbed the edge of the fireplace mantel. He tossed me a small photo album and directed me to a page where, *en face,* I found photos of Violet and Sharon. In the process I couldn't help but notice a photo of Eulia at about age twelve, holding her schoolbooks. There was an eerie resemblance between Violet and Sharon. Both were far more attractive than I had somehow anticipated, though not as full-figured as Strang had described. Was his point of comparison the slender Edith? Sharon was sitting jauntily on the wounded cape buffalo that had wandered into the mission compound and had been dispatched. There was an inscription: "To Corve. Beauty and the beast! With all the love I can summon on earth, your very own Sharon." Violet was in an awkward flower-print dress, sitting in one of those tire swings you see in the yards of farmhouses. There was an air of deep handsomeness and health, not as showy, but somewhere between Gene Tierney and Grace Kelly. Unfortunately for her, there was a specific touch of the otherworldly.

"Where is Violet now?" I couldn't help but ask.

"She's under the ground. Dead a few years back. She had a fine life, teaching at Indian reservations all over the West. She died in Hardin, Montana, while teaching at the Crow Agency. Marshall flew me out, but she was dead when I arrived. Those people really made a fuss over her. She had bothered to learn their language, which is rare, I understand."

"I can't bear this any longer." Eulia snatched the photograph album. "Every day this talk of the past. What are we going to do?"

Strang seemed to think this was very funny. I had watched this ability to parry direct challenges with grace before. "What are we going to do? Have a little lunch, then I'm going to swim a few hours while you do your dancing exercises. I'm real eager for the future. Maybe you should go in town to the beach and take a break if you like. We're going to guts it through, as they used to say."

"You're such a great bullshitter," she said, kissing him.

It was true. There was a smooth, somnambulistic quality to his voice at times that gave the impression, despite his pathetic condition, that he was totally in control. I don't mean there was anything magical or mystical in the man—none of that hokum—but rather a capacity to be all of one piece at any given time. Perhaps he knew that frenetic behavior would increase his suffering, but there was some indication that he had always been that way. As I gathered up my gear to leave, he said he wanted to show me something. He nodded to Eulia, and she brought in two crude walking staffs from the porch. He made his way around the room with these staffs, his face at the same time beaming and contorted with effort. His progress was unimaginably tortured, twisting, shuffling, a drunken, crablike movement.

———

Tape 6: I'm enjoying the satellite photos of earth for the same reason I like to look at the paintings of John Marin, Kandinsky, Poons,

Frankenthaler, Syd Solomon, Motherwell et al. If
NASA takes a writer aloft it should be Mr. Mailer,
who would profit the most from the experience.
Meanwhile I think Strang's books will mean more
to me later in the same fashion that I only really
read Shakespeare after I got out of college.
Right now I crave the topical, the ephemeral. I
often think of the days of the week and month by
what new magazine is available, and there is
nothing of that up here. It's been unnaturally
hot for the area, with south winds blowing steadily over the baked pine barrens. There is some
worry about forest fire, as a fire several years
back burned over fifty thousand acres. An old man
at the bar said his grandmother had survived the
great Peshtigo, Wisconsin, fire that inciner-
ated twelve hundred people.

Putting on my khaki shorts I think of Strang's
trip to Africa, the curious freshness of it that
reminded me of my first stay in NYC, where I had
gone during a summer college vacation to become a
bohemian. I discovered garlic and willing ladies, despite my clumsiness, both in short supply
in the Midwest. But there was also that ineffably
sweet sense of adventure where everything seen,
met, heard, was new. There is also the humor in the
difference in what sex is supposed to be like and
the actual nature of what happens. This is usually presented in a harsh, comic light. Strang
and Sharon are comic, but I scarcely had the
chuckles when I heard the story. The attractive
photo makes me sort through the tale again. . . .

I was interrupted by the arrival of Eulia, suitcase in hand, and
a smile on her face. It seems that Allegria, the ostensible
mother or stepmother or whatever—in any event, Strang's

second wife—had arrived from the Marquette airport via taxi, which must have cost a pretty penny as Marquette is more than a hundred miles away. Eulia somehow made me dither around like a bachelor who is also an only child. We set things up a certain way and aren't very elastic about surprises. There was a smallish spare bedroom, separated by a bathroom from my bedroom. She hoped I wouldn't mind, but she couldn't stand the thought of three nights in the motel. I still hadn't looked her in the eye for some reason. While she unpacked, I fixed us enormous fruit and rum drinks; it hadn't occurred to me yet on the conscious level, but rum might be the secret key to her heart, a ghastly euphemism. I became more conscious when I saw her wiggle into a pair of shorts through a few inches of open door.

"Did you slap her face? You said you were going to."

"Of course not. It was a delight to see a *latina* woman and talk in Spanish. She's my stepmother, and I love her very much." She sat down at the kitchen table, which was covered by the paraphernalia of my work. "I won't bother you. I'll cook and help you write poems."

"I don't write poems anymore." I served her drink.

"Oh, this is too strong. Are you trying to fuck me again? My teacher in Florida said that when a writer stops writing poems, at least in secret, he is dead as a doorknob."

"A door*nail,* is how it goes. Pour the drink out and don't pull any of that prick-tease nonsense, please."

"I'm sorry. I listened to the African story from the kitchen. It was very exciting. I only tease you because you react so strongly. I love to tease, and it is impossible to tease him."

"Is Strang your father?"

"Oh, no. He always supported me since I was seven. Then he adopted me so I could go to college in Florida, but it was a kindness. Allegria is my aunt, and they fell in love a long time ago. He was in Costa Rica to help build a dam, and she was an expensive courtesan, what you refer to as a call girl. She got sick of it finally and wrote and told him in Brazil that she was pregnant, so he sent her money every month. Then he appears again and says, Where is this son Roberto I have heard so much about? Allegria was back in Puntarenas at the time, working in the hospital and having affairs with the doctors. So she weeps and admits her deception. He somehow thought this was funny, to our surprise, because we all knew about it. So they go for a drive and come to our house, which is not much more than a hut, and Allegria paid for that after my father disappeared. There is just me and my brother, my mother, and that dog I told you about that was so nice during thunderstorms. Well, he liked us and where we lived. We went out on a fishing boat with our cousin in the Pacific. We went for long hikes. My mother was quite sick and always depressed about my father running away. About a year later she took her life, which is so rare in my country. Then Strang came back and said to Allegria—I heard them out in the yard from my bedroom—he said, please let me help these children. I love you, and we have no children, so they can be our children. My brother and I had been frightened because we didn't want to live at the Catholic orphanage. Next day, we moved into a nice little house near the sea and near a school. Allegria found an old maid cousin to be with us, but she was there much of the time. We only saw him every year or so. Our relatives used to argue about whether Strang was a fool or not, but one uncle who was religious said, 'The man makes good money and takes no time to spend it! He loves Allegria, and he loves children.' Perhaps that's true, or still true. He married Allegria so she could travel to the States easily and to make our life more dignified. Then when I was fourteen she moved in with a wealthy politician in the capital, but Strang continued to take care of us. He took my brother and me up to Los Angeles for a vacation without Allegria even being there."

She had finished her drink and insisted I take her to the town beach for a swim. There was the disturbing memory of Eulia and Strang in bed in a Miami hotel after he got out of the hospital. Was I being troubled by categories again? A few days back I had asked Strang if he thought of himself as a Christian. This genuinely puzzled him to such an extent that I tried to withdraw the question. "What I think I am doesn't really matter, does it?" he finally answered.

On our way into town Eulia's mood wavered between somberness and gaiety. She had been waiting to see if she were accepted into a ballet and folk dance troupe in San José, the capital of Costa Rica.

"Many of our relatives thought Strang was a ridiculous cuckold, but they were envious of our good luck. Allegria just couldn't stay with him because he wasn't around enough. Some women need what you call proximity, some don't. When he took us to Los Angeles, my brother asked why he spent so much money on us. That upset him a lot. He said he loved us, and he hoped we liked him, and we were part of each other's families. Also he made a joke for us about coming into the world bare-assed, and he wouldn't be needing a wallet when he went out. We thought this was heroic. Are you rich?"

"Not at all. I spend everything, which is a lot, or lose it on investments because I'm a fuck-up, you know, not good at business." I pulled into the post office, and Eulia went off to make a phone call to I don't know whom.

TAPE 6: Continuation: Oh, my god, but my brain is burned. The beach started out well: I finally heard from Karl, who said he hadn't answered mail from me or Corve because he was "somewhat embarrassed" to find himself back in prison. In any event, he was a trustee so we could visit him any day we chose. Hearing from Karl excited me and put me in a fine mood. It was also funny watching the local young men stare at Eulia's half-ounce idea of what a bathing suit was. The same little dog appeared, and I fed him some splendid Usinger's liverwurst from the cooler. He wriggled and rolled with pleasure in the sand. When we got back to the cabin, I planned a nice dinner for Eulia and offered a silent prayer that she would be thirsty enough to become pliant. The bathing suit had also done a very specific job on me. I couldn't remember when I had been so excited. I began to do the preliminary chopping for a Hunanese hot and crispy fish when she announced she wasn't hungry and might she borrow my auto for a "while"? Of course, I said, flustered and feeling the first indications of a wave of disappointment. Off she went, dressed rather too neatly, I thought, for a short errand.

Well, I was so depressed I nearly didn't eat dinner. Then I drank too much and botched the recipe, adding so much hot pepper that I drenched myself in sweat. In the mirror I looked like a marathoner. Then I slept on the couch until twilight, around ten o'clock. She had left at four, and I became alarmed. Had there been an accident and did she lay in some muddy ditch with algae-tinged water creeping up her legs? I had more whiskey with my coffee, lapsing back and forth between worry and anger until I heard the car. In she came as if nothing out of the ordinary had happened.

"Where have you been?" I shouted so loud I nearly frightened myself.

I might have known better than to get in an emotional duke-out with this girl. It was as if she had been waiting in the wings for years for a chance to let go against every wrong that had been committed against her.

"Where have I been? I've been in a motel in Seney fucking Bobby. I called him while you were in the post office. He wasn't there, so I called Emmeline and said, have Bobby meet me in the motel in Seney at five o'clock in the afternoon. She said, oh boy. I knew he wanted me very bad, and we had a wonderful time. He's a big, grief-stricken baby. He's not like you. He has no sophistication. He doesn't have fashionable clothes, bright comments, he didn't make me a strong drink. All you people are alike. You pretend that you don't want anyone, and now you're hysterical because I went to somebody who does want someone. Well, fuck you, big shot. Fuck all you people. I was a poor girl. What do I need with men who think it's smart to pretend they don't need me? Fuck you smart-ass men. Go fuck a mirror. Go make your jokes in a mirror."

That's a fair rendition. It was the mental equivalent of hitting a bridge abutment at seventy. It was time to call in a helicopter, to be frank. I gathered the remnants of myself together and went to the bar. In short, I fled.

CONTINUATION OF TAPE: Awoke at midmorning with a sense there had been a fly in my snoring mouth, tracking out a secret on my tongue. The window was closed and the sun shone hot on my legs. From the living room I heard David Bowie, the androgynous hero, singing "China Girl," a song my stepdaughter played until I was witless. "O Jesu, joy of man's desiring," sang monks in cool, soundproof monasteries. I began to stumble out when she put up her hand, came in with coffee and juice and opened the window. At first there was the air of the self-righteous. Her leotard was damp with her dance routine, and she said she hoped she hadn't awakened me.

"It's an inch better than the 6 A.M. garbage truck on Lexington and Seventy-fourth."

"Should I go after I was so impolite? I drove you from your cabin and made you get drunk."

"Don't go now, my heart might stop.' Actually I was near tears. A truly kind word would have made me break down completely. Her criticism of the night before had stung me deeply, and I would have given anything to be elsewhere. She sat down on the edge of the bed, then stood up and stripped off her leotard. She never said a thing, but she made me eternally grateful, sensing as she did that my soul was wounded and she might do something to help. There's certainly no making a graph or theorem of our passion. I can't think of a single clear statement I've ever read on the subject. One moment you hate someone to the point of tears, and the next moment you're clutched together, writhing in some abbatoir glue, absolutely happy burrowing your face in her hind end and yelping when you come off, as if you've either fractured your leg or made love. I'm sure that Eulia made a practice of saving her soul by giving it up. I studied the fine hairs of her lower spine while she slept. We are all monkeys, I thought, quite happily.

CHAPTER XIV

Sing ho for the life of the bear. The following dawn I dragged
Eulia out of bed and loaded her into the car. It was time to
go back to work, having been put through paces better suited
to someone half my age. Or less. I wondered if I had safely
made it through *latina* undergraduate school, but I doubted it.

Allegria was sitting at a table on the porch looking at
clothing catalogs. She was going to the Merchandise Mart in
Chicago to buy clothes for a boutique in Costa Rica, then
return to see Strang again in August. Her appearance startled
me, not that I had a right to expect anything different. She was
an attractive matron in her early forties, very calm and self-
possessed, the sort of wealthy woman you see in Miami airport
returning home laden with packages. She presented an im-
penetrable veneer of composure and affability. Eulia, at least
that day, softened somewhat around her stepmother, became

girlish and deferential. It has been difficult for me to go through life giving as much credence as I do to people's moods. I handed the ladies my car keys with a reasonable self-assurance that they weren't going off to fuck that lumbering lout Bobby.

––––––––––––––

I hope I can continue telling you stories. I seem to be short-circuiting somewhat, to the point that I waken in the night and think I'm someplace else, not necessarily a place I've already been. The sensation is interesting rather than comforting. Once I had dinner with Marshall and a group of his high-roller friends down in Florida. Most of these men were retired and obviously wealthy. I was just in from Uganda via Brazil, and it was a pleasure to listen to them for a while, but then by midevening I thought, my god, we're not living on the same earth. They were colonialists, of all things, and seemed to love each other for that. It occurred to me they were as simpleminded about life as my father, but a great deal less kind and genuine. One of these guys became a little irritated with me, though still polite, I'm sure, because I was Marshall's houseguest.

"You don't believe a damn thing we're saying, do you? Why?"

"No, sir. You're talking about the world that used to be, or the world you want, but not the world I see in my work." Marshall thought this was wonderfully funny and redirected the conversation to thoroughbred horses. You see, I had been checking out a French hydroelectric project in Uganda to see if some equipment they had devised was applicable in Brazil. The backwater of a cofferdam was full of bloated, decapitated bodies, political enemies of Amin who had come to power. The crocodiles couldn't begin to keep up with the generous, new food supply. God, how it stunk! You couldn't help but retch. Some of the French engineers had quit, and the explanation was that they could no longer eat lunch. Food is the largest morale item at a construction site, just as it is in a prison. What I was thinking was this: I'm sitting here telling you my story, and the story is basically over, though the fact doesn't seem to diminish our interest. I certainly don't want us to become like those men at Marshall's dinner party. After I went to bed, it occurred to me these men held a minimal interest in the world other than that part that immediately touched them. If you think about it long enough, you'll find that the most exhausting part about human behavior is lack of curiosity.

That's what gave Sharon a great deal of her charm. Not a bug or bird escaped her notice. She couldn't bear to play dead, and that's why the Reverend drove her nuts. It was a little like Violet the way we read and discussed books. This was only a year after the Mau-Mau troubles, and our mission wasn't very busy. The poor Reverend lacked dynamism for understandable reasons: He was burned out after thirty years in the field, losing a wife and one of three children to disease in the process. When he returned from his Kampala conference, he was glad to see me, but foremost on his mind was a committee position he had lost. I sat through endless bone-numbing after-dinner conversations with him. His central concern in life was purely theological, the nature of predestination: If God knows what's going to happen, how can we change it? That sort of tautological nightmare. It had something to do with the death of his daughter years ago, though I never got the complete story. She died at the mission at age seven, and I wondered why she hadn't been taken to the good hospital in Nairobi. She was, no doubt, a victim of his theological waffling, and now her spirit was still there, taking its toll.

Sharon had some odd habits that placed her a bit before her time. For one, she smoked "bangi," the local marijuana favored by the natives, in the evenings after the dispensary was closed. She would shower, eat her dinner—she wouldn't eat with the Reverend—then roll this herb up in a cigarette wrapper and puff on it while she read, or we talked or made love. She would become very relaxed and silly and loved to have me just lie there and eat her out by the hour, a chore I relished. God, but what pleasure we took in each other. I've never discovered anything since about love that she hadn't already taught me.

One night she told me a wonderful story about this bush hospital outside Mombasa. Early one morning a boy came to her door screaming. She followed him down the road to where a big group of villagers were gathered near the ditch. There was a man lying there with his left leg swallowed up to the crotch by a huge python. No one could figure out what to do. They all tried pulling on the snake, but they were thrashed around by it and feared further injuring the man. Finally the chief split the snake down the side and freed the man, who hopped around with a leg that had just a few abrasions and looked like it had been soaked in a bubble bath for weeks. This man had been up at a festival at Kaloleni and drank too much "mnazi," which is a fermented coconut drink. Jesus, think of waking up in a culvert with a python an inch from your nuts! Sharon cleansed the guy's leg, then went off with the villagers to a big meal where they cooked the snake. This girl couldn't be stopped, particularly on that night she told me the story. The generator was off, but we had lit an oil lamp. She went crawling around the room and bed on her hands and knees, pretending she was the snake and I was the drunken victim. It was a little scary at first, but I got into it. She swallowed most of my cock, I suppose because my leg was a trifle ambitious. Then she switched around and placed her butt on my face so I could get into the snake business, letting loose with a bloodcurdling scream. Woooeee! This was fine until the Reverend ran in the room with his flashlight. He said something like "My goodness" and ran right back out. Strange, but he never mentioned it to me. I can still see his sunburned, pink face through the crevice of Sharon's buttocks.

During the days I worked as hard as I have before or since. The tropics have long dawns and short sunsets, so I was always up in the cool of daylight. I'd walk around the compound and look for any animal tracks, then go to work. Once I found the pad marks of a leopard in the petunia bed outside the Reverend's house. I didn't say anything, because he was mortally afraid he wouldn't get to retire to Kansas. I wasn't much afraid of dying myself ever since the encyclopedia seemed to doom me to an early death. Come to think of it, I was pretty much following that program Karl outlined for me when I was a youngster.

I was up in Narok one day to pick up some odd supplies and see if I got any mail. It was a Monday, I remember now, because Sharon had gone off on Saturday with her doctor and hadn't gotten back until Sunday evening. I was feeling pretty raw to the extent I had a couple of beers with an English construction worker I ran into. He worked up in the Sudan and was taking a vacation, driving all over Kenya and Tanzania. He was amazed I had worked on the Mackinac Bridge and wanted to hear all about it. Naturally, with the aid of the beer, I made myself a little more important than I was, but that's in the nature of the trade. When I got up to leave, he gave me his card with the number and address of his firm's Nairobi office. If I wanted a job when I finished at the mission, all I had to do was to let him know. The money was good, and there were few places that he, Martin was his name, hadn't been on earth. I was a bit puffed up with this job offer when I left the bar. I had got back in the mission truck when I noticed a well-drilling rig parked down the road at the gas station.

The upshot was that I begged this man, an Irish Catholic from the United States, and his two crew members to come out to the mission and drive us a well. They were en route out to Kissi, but when I offered half the money I brought to Africa, the Irish Catholic changed his mind. In the end he wouldn't accept any money. He told me that driving around in that old truck drilling freshwater wells for the poor was his mission in life. Years later this man became famous for his African well drilling. At the time, the simplicity of his charity dumbfounded me. So much disease and suffering can be wiped out by the availability of fresh water alone.

When I got back to the mission with the well-driving rig in tow, the Reverend wasn't pleased. He had heard about this water missionary and thought it might be the devil's work. I said I didn't care if the guy was a Russian communist, my contract said I had to provide clean water for the dispensary, therefore it was under my authority. Of course, this was a fib, but it sedated the Reverend enough so that he returned to his house without so much as shaking the hand of our Catholic. I apologized, but the man laughed and said he was drilling wells for God, Jesus, the Virgin Mary, and the natives. Sharon had told me that the Reverend had applied for a new well three years before. It would take months or years to go through government or the U.N. field service, but this man showed up and did the job in twenty-four hours. He struck me as a true Christian.

The next day was brutally hot, so I rigged up a hose to spray the tin roof of the temporary school. The Reverend's mood had improved because we had a big Kikuyu audience for the well drilling and he could wander around passing out tracts and Bibles. The half-dozen school children loved this artificial rain on the roof. You could stand inside the school, which was twenty degrees or so cooler, and stare out through the rain at the dusty compound. I laid the pipe and set up a pump at the mission entrance. The Reverend took to hanging out there in his pith helmet so he could talk to the natives about Jesus when they came for fresh water. They didn't seem to mind. The water was great, and we clearly weren't the much hated British.

A man in love at first is ignorant in his passion that the woman involved can choose another option, or even that she might be entertaining another choice. I somehow thought that the doctor was Sharon's weekend toy, or drinking buddy, because she always returned very hung over. She gradually admitted how attached she was to him and that the affair had been going on for three years. He had promised to divorce his "horrible" wife and marry her. I was a little cynical, remembering how many bridge workers shacked up with local girls, then beat town on the last day of the job. Of course, I was utterly frantic and pushed myself way beyond good sense as a lover. I would brush her hair every night after her shower and try to be as bright and witty as I imagined an English doctor might be. It was no use. Letters began arriving every day for her, and I wondered at the duplicity of women, what with the way we spent our nights together. This was a basic misunderstanding on my part. I'd like to know where the vaunted altruism of the male has gotten us? Maybe she hadn't made up her mind, because I also promised to get a divorce and marry her and take her to France, how I don't know. I do know I worked from dawn to dark every day with a lump in my throat.

Of course, to be pompous and wordy runs counter to the particulars of love. It takes years to get the distance to think it over, and what do you have then? You have the distance and your thoughts. The summer before Edith left we used to go into this big shed in town that Ted leased to store heavy equipment. One day it was raining, and Edith and I sat up in an old Dodge Power Wagon, watching the swallows fly around the rafters.

"Dad says we have to move this fall," she said. The idea was so unspeakable that we could only hug each other.

I watched through the screen door when Sharon drove off with her doctor for the last time. It is difficult but necessary to accept the truth of what we are in our loneliest moments. I sat there all day until it got dark, then walked down the road to where the natives lived and got totally drunk for the first time in my life. At dawn Peter and his friends walked me back to the compound. I went to bed in Sharon's empty room to indulge my sorrow in the remnants of her odor and presence.

I finished building the school at top speed with the help of two young Kikuyus in their teens. I still keep in touch with one of them, who owns a construction company in Nairobi. I paid them out of my own pocket, because there was nothing left in my budget and I was terribly homesick, or so I thought, and wanted to get home. I didn't know it then, but I was becoming one of those men who think it's enough to send most of his paycheck home. The day I finished I packed my bags, much to the regret of the Reverend, who wanted me to stay around for the dedication ceremonies. I'm sure he was concerned because for some reason I had become quite popular with the natives, and their hanging around the compound gave him the sense of progress in his work.

The morning Peter drove me to the airport we could see the first rainclouds of the season gathered over toward Mount Eregero and the Lorogoti Plains. I had been so self-sunken I had forgotten the beauty of Africa, and for a change the raw feeling beneath my breastbone was for this beauty rather than Sharon. Those who haven't been there have to try to imagine Montana and the Dakotas in the eighteenth century, or the vast game herds described in the Lewis and Clark expedition. In those days it was pretty grand right up past the Kedong Valley when you were almost to Nairobi. Then, as we drew near the airport, I entered a fateful train of thought. Was I leaving all of this to go back to a late fall and winter in the Upper Peninsula when you mostly drink coffee or beer and wait for spring? The main excitement might be a night in January when the temperature went over forty below. I was lonely for Emmeline and the children, but suddenly I could envision a life building tract houses with Ted, trying to rough them in before cold weather so you could do the interiors in the winter. You build the exact same house forty or fifty times, and you weep with boredom. Was this to be my only adventure in life?

Well, there was a few hours left before plane time that I had intended to use buying souvenirs. I dug in my wallet for Martin's card, the construction man I had met in Narok. We found the building with no difficulty, and I sat in the Rover with Peter, trying to summon up the courage to go in and ask for a job. Peter was all for it, having a great sense of humor about the vagaries of a white man changing his fate on the spur of the moment. In I went, and after I composed myself in this rather elaborately subdued office, I offered Martin's card to the employment manager. Much to my surprise, he said that Martin had told him I might show up and he would "enjoy" having me on his crew up in the Sudan. There was an embarrassing amount of paper-shuffling when I had to admit my life had been without schooling. An engineer was brought into the office so I could prove I knew trigonometry, could read specs and blueprints, and could operate all manner of equipment. I was shown out to a pleasant waiting room with wicker chairs and ceiling fans. A male secretary even brought me a cup of tea. By now I was nearly nauseated by the sheer daring of what I was attempting to do. I pretended to be reading an old issue of the London *Times* when the employment manager and the engineer entered the room with that typically British air that leaves you hanging until you're used to it. Everything was fine. I could rest up and catch a morning flight to Khartoum, where someone would meet me. They would make a hotel reservation for me for the night. Glad to have you aboard, that sort of thing. I chatted with the engineer a little longer about the Mackinac Bridge. There are only so many of these huge projects going on in the world at the same time, and they are the object of intense curiosity with everyone in the trade. I walked back out in the sunlight, having cast a rather large die.

Peter was ebullient and swerved up to the entrance of

the New Stanley Hotel as if he were delivering royalty. We hugged good-bye, and I impulsively gave him my watch. Even the hotel people were polite, probably because this English company did a lot of business with them. Before I went up to my room, I bought a linen sportcoat and a pair of trousers, having sensed in the hotel lobby that my brown suit didn't fit with my new image as a construction vagabond. The man at the shop said that he would have them pressed and sent up to my room, which gave me pause, thinking there might be some swindle afoot. The only hotel I had even stayed at before was the Ojibway in Sault Ste. Marie with Emmeline. My room was rather grand, and I was a little unsure how to behave in it. The towels in the bathroom were huge, and I got a hard-on for no reason. I became a little frightened, so I got down on my knees and prayed, which struck me as a little silly, what with a hard-on like a toothache, but I did it anyway. There was a shocking rap on the door, but it was only my pressed coat and trousers. The man asked me if I wanted anything, and I asked for a Plymouth gin and tonic, Sharon's favorite drink. I can't tell you how giddy I was, just short of twenty-one years, in a fancy hotel, and on my way to Khartoum. I sat here with my gin, wishing that Karl was in the room to share my pleasure. Or Sharon, but the thought of her brought me to tears.

That evening during dinner in the elegant hotel dining room I established a precedent that damn near killed me seven years later. It was drinking, pure and simple. Now you know my system was already less than intact, though that's not central. The waiter asked me if I wanted a cocktail, and I thought, why not? The waiter asked if I wanted a bottle of wine with dinner, and I thought, why not? It had been over three months since I had a decent meal except for one evening that Sharon and I had roasted some zebra steaks over the fire—it was a lot like venison. It was as if I were hypnotized or suffused with pleasure: Indian Ocean shrimp, Tilapia fish from Lake Victoria, which are like bluegills, and a big joint of rare beef. The alcohol blunted, sedated, any normal anxiety, nervousness, the usual self-consciousness. I looked up with some surprise when it was over, and the fear that I was being watched with ridicule was banished by a snifter of brandy. The good feeling returned as the brandy worked its way down through the bellyful. An attractive woman smiled at me on the way to the powder room. I felt I was entering a world where loneliness had been banished, that anything had become possible, that I might meet one of those English girls from three months back—we'd repair to my room, fuck ourselves brainless, and talk about sophisticated things. The bill was a bit of a shock, but I had spent very little of my original grubstake except on my Kikuyu helpers. On my groggy way up to the room, the fact that I had left a big tip made me swagger a bit. The only niggling piece of remorse came from the idea that my dad and mom up in heaven might somehow know the amount I had laid out for the meal.

Every drinker can remember the backside, or the down side, of these first experiences. I awoke at dawn with a parched mouth and an ear-ringing headache. I had slept in my fine new clothes and was soaked with sweat. I puked, wept, took a bath, puked again lying on the cool bathroom floor, inspecting the undersides of the bathtub. I read the Bible, prayed, got a hard-on, whacked off thinking of Sharon, cried again, ordered up oatmeal, juice and coffee. I took a cab to the airport, boarded my flight to Khartoum, and when at midmorning the lovely stewardess asked me if I would like a drink, I thought, why not? By then I was full of piss and vinegar again, staring down out the window at the incredible landscape of the White Nile. A man who pushes himself like I do shouldn't be so hard on himself over a few drinks, I thought.

You quoted someone the second day you were here who said, "The only true aristocracy is that of consciousness." I like that. What else could it be? I'm not going to get preachy about alcohol. It was partly my age, and partly Sharon, whose photo I had already worn until the edges were soft. You take a young man full of muscle, energy, hormones, bitterness, and you either send him off to war, or off to work, the harder the better. I like to think of Caesar's legions going off to Iceland where there was not a single soul to kill. The habit is too predictable; the results gained so carelessly are nearly always the same. You cut off the part of life that irritates you the most, but you have cut off the legs of the horse to get him in the box stall. I am not talking about casual drinking, but the hard-driving, day-after-day variety, where it is the substitute for something, often unknown, that you wished had happened or didn't happen to you. And the British I worked with in the Sudan and India were a special kind of drinker: The purpose was the maximum amount with the minimum visible results. Real drunkenness, except on very special occasions, is bad form. The daily beers and gin, or rum, were a sedation after work. Then came dinner, a little cards and reading, then sleep.

I was less than a year south of Khartoum in the Sudan. We were restructuring a giant irrigation system between the Sennar Dam and the Rosieres Dam on the Gezira Plains between the White Nile and the Blue Nile. At the time this was the second largest cotton-producing area of the world. I still don't like to wear anything but linen and cotton, because it doesn't feel right. Once you move to wool you get the feeling you might be in the wrong place.

I was mostly operating a big shovel or a drag line or installing hydraulic gates on the canal. This part of the Sudan has none of the charm of Kenya: It is mega-agriculture, and only the owners could love the look of it. It is similar to corn in Iowa or some of the wheat areas of the Dakotas, the horizonless monotony of one-crop agriculture, the ruthless banishing of anyone or anything not conducive to the growing of cotton. When we'd get a few days off, we'd go up to Khartoum, where not much fun could be had, or if we had time we would fly over to Addis Ababa or down to Nairobi, the best place for R and R, as they call it. For the much needed prostitutes, I preferred the Galla and Amharic ladies of Addis to the seedy English girls some of the men liked in Nairobi. It's hard to believe, but we lost one of our best workers, a welder from Liverpool, one day over on the White Nile. We were having a picnic and roasting a goat. The locals told us not to swim in the main part of the river, but we were all beered up, and a crocodile took him right in front of us.

"It makes you want to go back home to wherever, doesn't it?" said Martin, who was our foreman. We spent all that afternoon in boats, shooting and gutting crocodiles, trying to find some leftovers to send home to Liverpool for a proper burial. It must have been in the high nineties, and cutting open the stomachs of crocodiles was a sobering experience. Naturally, we never found a thing to send home to his wife and kids. It was horribly primitive but somehow understandable; in the aftershock we felt we had to do something because the fault lay with the whole sodden, incautious bunch of us.

Martin became my mentor. He later died up near Hyderabad of amoebic dysentery, the same disease I caught in India. I must have known him for over half a year before it occurred to me he was a homosexual. There was another homosexual who worked for the firm in the area, a Scandinavian engineer named Sorensen. Curiously, he and Martin didn't like each other. Sorensen got in trouble with the locals for fooling with the wrong young men. Every culture I've been in seems to make a specific accommodation for homosexuals, but it is often brutally limited. I caught on to Martin one week when we were waiting for some equipment to arrive and took a three-day business vacation up in Alexandria, Egypt. After we went down to the docks to check out an arriving freighter, I went for a stroll in the polite side of town while Martin went to a shipping office to do paperwork. While I was drinking some muddy but delicious coffee, I met this lovely girl. We went back to my hotel room, and she pulled the shades, then commenced to give me an overhaul that was breathtaking. She put my dick in her, and I could hardly get it out. Before she left, I made an appointment to meet at the same café later. Well, at dinner I was breathless when I described the girl to Martin, who at first seemed embarrassed, then loosened up with the wine.

"You silly shit, that wasn't a girl," he said.

"I don't get what you mean."

"You jolly well didn't feel her pussy or tits."

"She was shy and didn't want me to." I frantically searched my recent memory for a positive indication of her girlhood.

"They're all over. Don't worry about it. He didn't charge you much because it was a true conquest. I mean, the deception was complete."

To be frank, I was pretty irritated. I insisted we keep the appointment and bet Martin ten pounds, which was a fair amount of money at the time. Well, the girl-boy and Martin figured each other out pronto, and it became quite funny. Martin bought a bottle of champagne, and we drank to my naiveté. On the way back to the hotel in the taxi, I asked Martin not to tell the other guys. He said, of course not. We sat up and drank coffee and brandy, and he confessed his life. I can't say I understood the whole thing at the time, but he was a true friend and I heard him out in the manner that you always hear a friend's most private anguish. Martin was from up near Grassmere in the Lake Country, and his first boyhood lover had died during the Normandy Invasion. It was nearly daylight when he finished his story and we finished the bottle of brandy. In some strange way his first love reminded me of Edith, despite the difference in sex. Naturally, I had heard a lot of stories, but Martin was the first dyed-in-the-wool homosexual who was a friend. When he died in India, me and the crew, who all loved him, put up a stone that said: "This was the noblest Englishman of them all." It was sentimental, but that's what we felt about Martin.

Last night I had a problem talking to Allegria, and that scared the hell out of her. I wasn't saying what I thought I was: a whole stream of disorganized words would come out. It was similar to what often happens to stroke victims. I wouldn't believe it at first, but she recorded my voice on tape and played it back. I thought it was humorous instead of frightening, because I recognized that herb at work again. I guess

I still thank the Lord, or whomever, I didn't take an even bigger dose, which I'm told often leads to almost total paralysis or death. Then this inability passed as suddenly as it arrived.

You should probably stop trying to read that book on dam engineering. It just occurred to me that a dam is more like a movie that you have to see; it can't be successfully described. When you drive back south, take a detour over to Elberton, Georgia, and look at the Russell Project on the Savannah River. It's not a monster, but it's a pretty big operation. A friend of mine is one of the project engineers, and he'll show you around. Or if you're in the area, come see me in New Guinea this winter. A big dam might take more than ten years from start to finish. One of our main problems in India was that we were working too fast. It was in the beginning of Nehru's second five-year plan, and we scarcely drew a breath while we were there.

The real goad to working hard in India for some of us was the hunger you would see all around you. Some of the dams being built under the second five-year plan were basically for irrigation, to increase the amount of tillable land and feed these people. Others were built primarily for hydroelectric power and industrialization, to decrease India's almost total dependency on other countries for any manner of machinery. Starvation in print remains an abstraction, something that can be ignored or dismissed with a quip. You see that in the papers right now: those who are doing well simply refuse to recognize the malnutrition in our own country. It's impossible, they say, because they have never taken the trouble, the unpleasantness, to come into contact with any people but their own kind. Historically speaking, of course, these leaders are swine, utterly contemptible.

You could easily feed the hungry people in this country on the extra dough the defense contractors swindle out of the Pentagon. I read there was a miner over west of here, where the unemployment is forty percent, who was trying to feed his kids on bouillon cubes. A teacher noticed when the kids commenced to faint on the playground. I hope to tell you I sent a check over in care of the newspaper. None of these fat fuckers in Washington or Lansing will ever have to serve his kid a cup of bouillon for dinner a week hard-running. That's for sure, because they're all lawyers, and lawyers think everything is a matter of the right language. The final settlement on the asbestos poisoning case yielded up sixty percent of the total in legal fees. Reporters aren't much better except in city matters; it is an inconvenience to get up in the country where readership is anyhow low. They have largely taken up writing about themselves.

Sorry I got angry, but you got a problem when abysmal insensitivity passes for public wisdom. You know when I talked about Central America where I spent so much time? What if they cut off the balls of our sons or tortured our daughters? I hope to say we'd spend our lives on vengeance. Only they mostly do it to peasants, whom they have long made beasts of burden. In our own Republican and Democrat demographics, the few million hungry can't swing an appreciable vote. The smart political money is after the ladies and the homosexuals. I hope these groups are ready for the mudbath.

Sorry again. Well, up near Amritsar in Punjab we were this foreign legion of workers, paid very well, but not probably commensurate to the damage we did to ourselves. The pleasure in this massive project is to have seen it happen right before your eyes and to know you had a part in it.

Nehru even paid our construction site a visit once. We all stood in long lines in clean khakis to shake this great man's hand. I couldn't wait to tell Violet about the experience, because we were corresponding weekly at the time—me in Punjab, and she in the Dakotas. It's not widely known, nothing of this sort is, but Nehru's big push brought electricity to eleven thousand communities and put ten million new acres under irrigation. Some people are questioning this sort of progress now, and they probably should. I'm in basic sympathy, or why else would I be way back here in the woods in a cabin? But in India it was different. It's one thing to give up the world when you've already had the best it can offer. We always have a return ticket. We are the world's grandest observers and experiencers, though that's a clumsy word.

After we finished the basics on the system up in Amritsar, we moved on down to south of Hyderabad where they were having problems. Our crew was made up of a hundred or so top hands, the men who could handle the intricacies of the heavy machinery and the installation of the German and Swiss-made generators. There was an overall boss, a dozen or so well-educated engineers, then Martin, who delegated the work to the rest of us. It was pretty democratic, though the very top men tended to keep each other's company, due to education and class. This is true anywhere in the world.

In Hyderabad we had to contend with the monsoons and the unusual food of the area. The Punjab climate was less foreign, and the people somehow less exotic than down south. We all tended to drink a great deal more after we arrived, and the summer rains drove us batty. After we were there a year, Martin started being sick. He blamed it on a meal he had at a "western" restaurant in Hyderabad; his usual policy was well-cooked local food, bottled water, and enormous quantities of beer. He became, fatally, his own doctor, which is not surprising as he had spent so much of his life outside good medical help. We were working extra long shifts that spring, trying to repair a faulty twenty-six-foot pentstock before the monsoons could drown out our coffer. I tried to get him to take it easy once I noticed he was sick, because amoebic dysentery can slowly eat you alive. He kept himself going with pep pills, along with opium pills for his guts. He kept saying he'd take a week off when the monsoons came. One hot afternoon he dropped dead from a heart attack brought on by acute dehydration.

I almost quit and went home at that point. Some others who had worked under Martin for a long time shipped out right after the memorial service, including an American from New Jersey, who said, "If it killed the best of us, it's sure as shit gonna get me." A few days later I was handed a note from the boss, an ex-officer in the colonial service named Enright, asking me to have dinner with him and the engineers. The upshot was that I was appointed foreman of the crew. I was dumbfounded and objected that I wouldn't be accepted because I, at twenty-four, was one of the youngest of the whole group. Enright said nonsense, and that I was the unanimous choice of the engineers because I could always see the whole picture, not just my specific job. Way back in Sudan, Martin had entered in my job record that I would make a good leader after seasoning. Oddly, I thought, I received nothing but warm congratulations from the crew. It was a little eerie sitting in Martin's office, plotting work schedules, even though a plaque with my name had been screwed onto the door. The size of my checks to

Emmeline became so much larger that she feared I had become involved in some kind of criminal activity, though I wrote her I had been promoted. Ted told me later that he had checked it out through the firm's New York office. He said it had made him proud that he had helped in my training.

It's pleasant to relive these small triumphs in your life if you don't do it too often. My own was much more ordinary, but I can imagine as a reader what it would be like for you to get your first book printed. Ted had a judge friend over near Marquette who has written some successful books. In a way it puts the place on the map for something other than pulpwood and iron ore.

Three years later the same sickness that killed Martin drove me out of India. They had to drag me off the job. When the first signs appeared, I started keeping an eye on the mess hall. Sure enough, one of the dishwashers was just washing the tops of plates that sat in dirty stacks, plus the rinse water was tepid. People will literally kill themselves from sheer inattention and laziness. The firm gave me a choice of a hospital in London or Jackson Memorial in Miami, where they have some fine people in tropical medicine. I was so weak at the time that they sent an English nurse along to deliver me to Miami.

Years later, when I began seeing Evelyn, I had time to talk, read and reflect on the idea of illness. I didn't come up with anything of any value to anyone but myself. It seemed to me that unbearable longing created my illness a number of times. It was true after Edith left, and after Sharon it was the prolonged but still temporary disease of alcoholism which helped lead to the amoebic dysentery. After Allegria, it was kala-azar and filariasis. After Evelyn it was the accident, because I was untypically reckless. Life kills us. Too much life kills us! What a wonderful idea. Evelyn had me read some novels by the Russian author Dostoevsky because he was an epileptic, though his seizures were far more severe than my own. I loved these books because they possess the most brilliant conversation of any I've ever read. Well, this man contends that to be too acutely conscious is to be diseased. It's a point worth considering, but Evelyn insisted that his own disease deeply colored his perspective. I said, so what, he has given us a great gift. This is probably elementary to a well-read person like yourself. When I was building that mission school, I neglected my medicine for a few days, in hopes I had become well over the years. Peter, my Kikuyu friend, witnessed my seizure and told me about the spirit of "badimo"—I think that's what he called it. The natives think a man who has seizures possesses a certain magic because he can slip through a crack in reality and see the world differently: I doubt if I agree. You don't see a separate world; you only see the same one everyone sees more vividly. The question is whether the vision of a sick man looking at a healthy world becomes, in the rush of convalescence, a healthy man looking at a sick world because he has a memory. Who knows? Evelyn, who could be a perfect WASP nit, claimed that a lot of artists make themselves sick on purpose. I said bullshit, you're missing the point by being a tidy little scientist after the fact. She has the most amazingly brilliant geometrical mind, and she thinks that everything on earth calls for a decision on her part. Her only escape into the irrational was fucking, and I must admit she did a bang-up job at it. To the extent she neglected it on the conscious level it became a repository of energy when she let loose. Come to think of it, I never saw the point of reading those stacks of dirty magazines at construction camps. It was a simpleminded indulgence. You hit Panama after two months in the jungle, and a pair of thighs will pop your skull.

A month ago you said something I brood about, that metaphor was a way to measure things of similar resonance and volume but vastly different shape. Imagine trying to make a blueprint of that statement! We were talking about beauty and the idea if a person, animal, object, whatever, possessed wholeness, harmony, and most of all, radiance, it was likely beautiful. It seems our hunger for this only gets assuaged piecemeal. Maybe we should add "surprise" to the list of requirements. I was thinking that we are pretty blind by habit, and sometimes we are jolted by beauty out of dumb luck or habit. One Sunday an Indian worker from Hyderabad took me up near this small cave in the hills. We were about a hundred feet from the cave when he threw a stone into the entrance. My god, but what a shock! Out of the cave races this king of snakes, a king cobra about twenty-five feet long, rearing up until his enormous hood is at our eye level. He just glared at us, "naga," the Indian called him, letting off blasting hisses and daring us to come closer. You wonder what God had in mind, but you often do. Jesus, that snake was beautiful. Years ago, at Marshall's request, I wrote down all my thoughts on water under the title, which I meant as a small joke, "The Theory and Practice of Rivers." Of all beautiful things, I take to rivers the strongest. They give me that incredible sweet feeling I once got from religion. With the Catholic, the question of whether that little girl actually saw anything at the site of Lourdes ought to be meaningless. You can actually see your foot every day, but that's not what keeps you going. Any metaphor between us and a river is that we can't stop ourselves one bit.

CHAPTER XV

The morning of our departure for Marquette, Strang took me for a walk upstream in order to give me an "inkling," as he called it, of the practical science of hydrology. He had graduated over a period of a few weeks from his set of staffs to double canes, and his gait could best be described as that of a drunken praying mantis, the large insect more commonly known as a walking stick. My three nights with Eulia had soured, frazzled, occasionally delighted me, to the point that my attention span was no broader than an actress's. My pecker chafed from overuse, and my gut rumbled, craving some leftovers from an elaborate southern Indian curry dinner Strang had prepared the evening before. His cooking process had an Oriental concentration and intensity; he was the soul of modesty and, in contrast to so many neophyte chefs, there wasn't a single fandango to impress. It was also the best Indian food I had ever eaten and now, to be frank, I wanted more. I was trying to nod attentively as Strang talked on about the dynamics and morphology of rivers, fluid mechanics, sediment load, the fluvial processes of erosion and deposition, slope and channel morphology.

"What are you thinking about, food or fucking?" He stopped in the path and I bumped into him, nearly falling.

"Pardon . . . actually both at once." There was no point in being flustered. He was amused at my total worthlessness as a student of science. We sat down on a log, and he adjusted his leg braces. The dog buried her nose in my jacket pocket for the biscuits I had taken to carrying for her.

"I bet Eulia got you to promise to take care of her if something happened to me." He didn't wait for an answer, knowing it was true. "She told me her dad used to slap her around as a child. It's unthinkable but it happens all the time. In late May I was here in this clearing with the dog. Over there we watched a raven die. There was a big group of ravens swirling around him up in the tree where he was perched unsteadily, as if to give him encouragement. They made even more noise when he fell down through the branches, but then caught himself, teetering on a pine bough. I held the dog back so she wouldn't torment the situation. Finally the raven fell all the way down through the branches, flopped around on the ground, and then was still. The whole thing took about two hours. I had never seen a bird die like this before. I didn't tell Eulia about it because she is fond of omens and I thought a raven ought to be allowed to die without being compared to me."

The drive to Marquette went wonderfully. Strang drove the first ten miles or so but then gave up when his accelerator foot began wobbling uncontrollably. This didn't in the least diminish his humor, and when I took over the driving, he joined Eulia and Allegria in singing some popular Costa Rican songs. Since I didn't understand a bloody word, I began brooding about whether or not I'd have the opportunity to talk to Karl alone. I had greased the skids somewhat by calling a cousin of my mother's who was prominent in Michigan government. I had always thought the man a dolt but I wanted to ensure that certain courtesies were offered us at the prison.

Allegria insisted we stop several times along the road to pick the wild flowers that abound in the area. She liked to design fabric and was convinced she could incorporate these colors, not found in the tropics, in her cloth. I sat in the car scribbling notes during these plucking expeditions which Strang accompanied. He called my attention to a large black snake which he had caught and soothed by rubbing its tummy as it wrapped around his arm. I declined to do so myself, saying I was busy with my notes. Allegria looked so lovely with her flowers I wanted to trade in Eulia for this more mature, less enervating model. It was impossible to imagine her background as a "courtesan," no matter how far in the past.

When we drove through Munising and could see Lake Superior, Strang was disturbed by a storm front gathering to the north. He said that winds up here have great character and when they start moving up the clock from south to west to northwest, there can be some problems. Allegria's plane would be fine because it was hours before the front would arrive.

————————

TAPE 7 : Returned to the cabin with the sun going down, and a temperature drop from eighty to forty degrees on the first of August. The winds were worse than the night of my arrival, the sea rumpled as if in green torment. A cold sweat from emotional exhaustion, so I changed my clothes, made coffee, poured a whiskey. Eulia's things are here though she went home with Strang. I looked at her open suitcases while I listened to the coffee perk, deciding not to snoop because I wanted no more surprises.

I tended the fire in my small fireplace like a feebleminded boy scout. It cast a circle of warmth that didn't include my back. I felt some of the discomfort but little of the real pleasure that a scientist might feel late in the day after he or she discovered a new species. Some of the items, the wedges of the whole pie, are:

1. Strang's speech became a little garbled after he kissed Allegria good-bye at the airport. I had been in a continuous state of déjà vu since entering Marquette. I hadn't been there in thirty years but memories I had never "remembered" came sweeping over me and I still haven't regained the slightest sense of composure. After the inevitable sadness for Strang and Allegria, even Eulia, at the airport I drove us down to a park by the ore dock. I called the prison from a pay phone to make sure they were aware of our appointment. I turned from the phone booth to Strang and Eulia, who had their backs turned to me and were watching a huge freighter being loaded with the iron taconite ore. For an instant they became my mother and father. We used to picnic at this park in the forties and watch them load the freighters. To the northwest, out on Lake Superior, you could see the blackish gray front approach, with the lead thunderheads rolling and furling over on themselves. Strang turned to me with crazed delight. "I can feel the barometer dropping," he shouted. I watched the other picnickers gather their blankets, baskets, children, and head for their cars. A gust of wind whipped Eulia's summer skirt

around and up her legs. Then the leading cloud covered the afternoon sun, so we headed for the prison.

2. When we passed through the gate, we were directed to the administration building rather than the regular visitors area. This is a maximum security prison, not one of those polite camps where they send the influential dope wholesalers, or the political swine who have betrayed the public trust. I drove by two threadbare and weeping black women, noting that Strang's face tightened perceptibly; Eulia said, "I'm frightened" with a pinched voice. We were shown into a drab lounge by the warden himself, who turned out to be an acquaintance of Ted. He told Strang there was a good chance Karl could be released the following spring if he consented to the custody of Ted up in Alaska, who had pulled any number of strings to make the arrangement. Thus far, Karl had not consented to anything. "He never has," said Strang. We all seemed to share the sodden, pastel, strangulation of institutions as we waited for Karl.

I was fooling with my tape machine when the door opened the same instant the storm hit. The lights flickered out and I could see the silhouettes of Strang and Eulia watching the driving rain and bending trees out the window. I turned back to the opening door and an instant later the lights came back on. I was standing not a foot away from Karl and I involuntarily stepped back with my hand held up in alarm. It was embarrassing so I averted my glance to the guard, who withdrew out the door, though his shadow beyond the steamed glass was visible throughout the visit.

Karl ignored me and moved swiftly to Strang. They embraced warmly and kissed. When they released, Eulia offered her hand which Karl took, making a bow. "Jesus, what a beautiful niece," he said, then turned to me. "Relax, I'm just a big old fucking kitten. You might say I'm rehabilitated." I felt prepped for everything except his actual presence. Strang had told me that Karl had been a diver, an underwater welder, an oil roustabout on offshore rigs, and most lately, a stevedore in Mobile and New Orleans. He certainly looked like all of these, though my frame of reference is limited in the areas involved. He reminded me most of those underground tunnel workers in New York City known as "sandhogs." He gave me a broad toothless smile that crinkled an old scar that followed his jaw line until it flipped up toward his lower lip. There was a seemingly obligatory cobra tattooed on a big lumpish forearm as he offered his hand to me. In his mid-fifties he still presented a sense of threat, though his eyes twinkled. He was Strang's height, about six feet, but thickish, nearly massive, and the hand he offered had the heft of a shot put. Again, in contrast to his visitors he was warm, almost radiant.

Strang launched into a soothing, but never pleading, number of reasons why Karl should accept Ted's custody. Karl smoked one of my cigarettes and blew childish smoke rings toward Eulia, who couldn't help but stick a finger in one of them.

"Well, Corve," Karl said, "Just sitting here looking at you I see you've got the living shit kicked out of you. Remember when we met in New Orleans and you weren't too impressed by my bimbos? That was three years ago. Right now I could cry seeing what's happened to you. I agree. I'll go up to Ted's. Maybe I'll start trapping again after forty years. Neither of us like the cold weather but it beats the shit out of this place. I just hope you get well enough to come for a visit. Bring Eulia here," he pronounced it "yew-lee" like Bobby, "and maybe we'll find her a skull as big as a car."

They lapsed into a longish brotherly reverie

ending with a discussion of Strang's physical condition and prognosis. They caught me glancing nervously at my watch. We only had an hour allotment and forty-five minutes were used up.

"What did you want to know?" There was a slight edge to Karl's question so I decided I better go for the liver, reducing a dozen questions to two.

"Why are you in prison?"

"Dozens of reasons. I had a very happy childhood as Corve will tell you. My parents and brothers and sisters were marvelous. I had a long and wonderful war which I joined at fourteen, and stayed in until 1948. They wanted to send me to Korea and I said nothing doing, so I did six months in the brig. An officer friend interfered and I got an honorable discharge."

"Why did you refuse to go to Korea?"

"The situation didn't appeal to me. Korea wasn't trying to take over the world like the Japs and Germans. The Pentagon, you know, all the officers, just wanted another war. It's their job."

"I'm not sure I understand. Could you clarify?"

"Sure thing. You're Corve's age. When since World War II have they not been trying to get us in a fight somewhere on the planet? At the time I didn't feel obligated to take part. I don't feel obligated about a lot of things, you might say. I've been in jail and prisons here and there, to be sure, but you pay for the way you live. To be specific, two years ago I came up to see a girl friend in Detroit. Outside a club I was attacked by four plainclothes policemen. Me, an older man. I got in some good licks, too good in fact, so they had to set me up to look like a bad-ass to avoid embarrassment. So I got a three to five in Jackson Prison. While I was there, I heard about what that street gang did to my special niece, Ted's daughter, my darling, Esther. Sure enough those three guys got sent up to Jackson so I evened the score and was sent up here."

"I don't understand. What did you do? Were they black?"

"No they weren't black," Karl laughed. "What an asshole question. What does it matter when they raped your niece, give her a few cigarette burns, and stick a pop bottle in her ass? One by one I gave them a squeeze with this good right hand here. Burst their nuts is what I did. One of them damn near died, and the other gang members who were in prison got on my case. So the state sent me on up here for my own protection."

"Jesus, Karl, that was a terrible thing to do." Strang was standing and shaking his head. "I'm ashamed."

"Of course you're ashamed. You're a fine Christian person. I'm not. I didn't think eighteen months of free meals and sleep were an adequate punishment for those fuckers. The counselor asked me if I didn't think the world would be a horrible place if every one acted like me. I agreed, but said everyone is not me. I teased him by saying I had read too many Zane Grey novels. Besides, they all know worse things than that happens in prisons. I had seriously considered killing them. 'If thine eye offend thee, pluck it out,' Dad used to say. I just helped the process along."

"Would you mind leaving the room for just a minute?" I asked Strang.

"That's okay. I know what you're going to ask. Was Violet my mother?"

I nodded assent. For the first time Karl looked very grave. He took another cigarette and stared long and hard at Strang, then at me. I was more than ready to withdraw the question when he began to speak.

"I promised Violet never to tell even after she died. Remember when you asked me in New Orleans

when we were drunk? At least I was. I didn't say a
thing because she was still alive." Now he gave a
weird smile that reminded me of Corve's stories
about their youth. Karl stood, closed his eyes,
swaying his head back and forth, "O dearest Violet, O beautiful Violet, wherever you are in the
spirit world, but probably right here, I feel
your soul right in this room. Forgive me now for
breaking my vow to you. Yes, Violet was your
mother." Now he opened his eyes with a full smile.
"When she was fourteen she worked over at this
camp on the other side of Kingston Lake where university students come in the summer to study the
flora and fauna of the area. She worked in the
kitchen and was real proud to have a job. I was only
five or six at the time. She fell in love with this
college guy. I found out much later that it went on
all summer. So he left and she was pregnant.
Mother and dad up and moved us all away down to
Moran so mother could pretend it was her baby so as
not to spoil Violet's life just because she fell
in love with someone. I'm the only one now who
knows the guy's name because I found Violet's
diary in her bed springs before I went off to war.
Her secret interest in the mail used to drive me
crazy with anger because she never got an answer
to the few letters she sent. In the early fifties
I tracked the guy down to East Lansing where he was
a professor of botany or horticulture, something
like that. I was drinking a lot at the time. I sat
across the street from the guy's house. In fact, I
held a tire-iron in my hand as he walked his kid
down the sidewalk. Something held me back, probably the kid. Years later, when I visited Violet
out west I confessed this and she made me promise
on the Bible that I would never harm this man. Not
ten years ago, I passed again through East Lansing intent on killing him because number one, I
don't believe in the Bible, and number two, Violet was in Montana and would never hear of the mur-

der. But he was dead already, so I sold the rifle and scope and got drunk. She certainly was a good mother to you Corve, a fine mother. I wish you had got to be her son, but people did such things back in those days."

"You have to let me ask this. My dad taught botany. Who was the man? He had to be a friend of our family."

"Nothing doing. I broke one promise and I couldn't break another. Besides he's dead." Karl was impassive.

Out in the parking lot, after the farewells, there was the unendurable sensation that I had just swallowed a chunk of ice. Of course there were no sidewalks where we lived in Bircham Woods in East Lansing. I knew my father had been to that camp as a student because he tried to get me to go, but I was interested in James Joyce not plants and trees. I quickly computed that the timing was right, then dismissed it all as rather breathtaking nonsense. Who knows the actual lives of our parents? I sorted through the memories of my father's colleagues wondering who could have been Violet's lover and Strang's father. In the somewhat hysterical aftermath of the funeral, my mother had assured me that she was the only woman my father ever "knew" in the Biblical sense.

Strang's arm was around my shoulder when I returned to Earth. I was evidently mumbling and staring at all the storm-ripped maple leaves pasted against the cement at my feet. "Is something wrong?" he asked. We drove home in almost total silence and now I'm sitting here before the fire, wondering how close this story has come to me. I see Karl standing there, impassive as a pre-Columbian, or Oriental figurine, neither of which are known for the answers they offer.

CHAPTER XVI

I awoke at noon to a cold, blustery day, wrapped in fetal delight with every blanket in the cabin piled on me. I had just had one of those undeservedly pleasant dreams our brains give us to keep us from ending it all. I decided not to go out to Strang's since I was already five hours late. There was an ugly knock at the door and I trotted through the frigid cabin, wondering why pioneers had stuck it out in a place where good tomatoes couldn't be grown. It was only the landlord asking if my propane heater was working. Frankly, in two months in the cabin I hadn't noticed the contraption. He lit it, departed, and soon the cabin was toasty. I had eaten less the day before than any day since a severe bout of flu years back. I set about making a "putanesca" sauce for pasta, a kind of Italian version of soul food that lifts the spirits of weary streetwalkers, not an inaccurate metaphor for journalism: the sauce includes sausage, wine, capers, anchovies, tomato paste, a liberal sprinkling of hot pepper flakes. When it was done and the pasta was nearly cooked, I opened my last bottle of Barbaresco. How can I convince anyone of the splendor of this breakfast when I ate it alone and shot back to bed?

My second sleep was interrupted at midafternoon by Eulia, who was giddy and full of frippish excitement. She brought a bottle of cheapish champagne, the only available in the area, stuck in a sack of ice. She pushed me back to the bed and joined me with two glasses. The joggled bottle fired a Freudian squirt against the far wall. There's nothing quite like twelve hours of sleep to get you ready for love. It lacked the blurred, fumbling of the post-multi-cocktail-dinner-drinks-nightcaps-half-mast screwing stupidity. The occasion was the new that she had been accepted into the dance troupe in Costa Rica. Later on I would question a certain artificiality in her whole performance that afternoon, a quality of design. For the time being, I was a carb-loaded marathoner, at least for my age. The first one was accomplished with me in my robe, and Eulia bent over a chair with her jeans around her knees in front of the door mirror. This was her idea, and after our eyes met in the mirror I was sent reeling backwards like a squid in the general direction of the bed. There's no question that dancers are different. An hour later, when she left me steaming there like freshly butchered beef, I was able to sleep again.

Quite naturally I was trying to avoid the loss of coherence brought on by the day before. Now, I've never been tempted to write a detective or mystery story but I've read hundreds of them. I don't care for the English style where, in a state of bedtime drowsiness, I never get to figure things out. I prefer the riper colors of evil, sex, utter mayhem; I want the characters to remind me of those I've known or seen. No one can have read John D. MacDonald and not cast a colder eye on the citizens of Florida. But the genre was limited and, finally, tended to attach itself to an excitement with a rather low metaphysical lid. Strang's story was immersed in love, work, and death; its lack of decor was made up for by the tired, aforementioned saws of wholeness, harmony, and even, at least for me, a modicum of radiance. In short, the mystery of personality, of life itself.

My wariness began with Eulia's behavior, that of a not quite well-trained actress, the kind that can talk about her problems with intensity but can't deliver a convincing, "Hello. How are you?" Throughout the late afternoon and evening I tried to lucidly identify all of the elements of the situation. Eulia was leaving in two days to be replaced, according to her, by Evelyn, Marshall's daughter and Strang's third wife, who had taken a month's leave. Allegria was coming back, and Emmeline was in Manistique. There was me, at least temporarily. It's a cliché that truly sick people don't appreciate visitors to the extent that visitors think they do, that a sick dog seeks the solitude of his hiding place under the porch, or in the clump of burdocks behind the barn. Strang in his right mind couldn't really think he'd be ready to join a new crew in New Guinea this winter. How, if, and when, was he in what one might think of as his "right" mind? Where was the still and stable point, or could there be one for any of us? He was in an obvious cul-de-sac with friendly attendants massing at the entrance, but also blocking the way. I was there taking it all down, which was of questionable help in the situation, though it passed for the idea of work he so much admired. There was, however, nothing in his life that bespoke the sedentary victim. What was to become of him when the story, unlike a river, ended with the present? What is he thinking about tonight in the cabin now that he knows his beloved, dead sister is his mother?

All of these considerations, understandably, brought up the question of whether I had reached any conclusions. That's my job, I thought; it's premature to try to foreshorten all of the perimeters of what could happen. I then lapsed into the vertigo of Karl outside a house in East Lansing years ago. It wasn't the thousand-to-one shot that my own father had been involved— I had tried to comfortably dismiss this possibility. It was the utter proximity, the onset of the chill when life loses its flippant anonymity and all faces become recognizable; that life, which passes us by so casually, could try to draw us into its current.

CHAPTER XVII

It was the coldest morning yet; my fingernails made a bad implement so I used a spatula from my cabin to scrape the frost from the windshield. As a friend in college once said, "everything was new, like a warm rain after a movie." It wasn't surprising to me when Strang was evasive about continuing his story; or not so much evasive, as lacking any current specific interest in his past. Years back I had interviewed a prominent French politician who spoke with delight and animation of his youth in Castelnaudry, but treated his central five-year role in Indochina as a slice of torpor, and dismissed his heroism during the Algerian crisis with a series of filthy quips.

Sitting before the fire with Strang, I waited patiently for the strong coffee to take effect. Perhaps the knowledge that Violet was truly his mother had released the tension essential to his telling the story. Meanwhile, he told me about M.

Freyssinet, a Frenchman who was, of all things, the "father of prestressed concrete," who consequently made possible such items as bridges, air terminals, parking ramps; the sort of things I think of, being literary, as urban eyepoppers and neo-blight. But if nothing else, this story had taught me that such attitudinizing was of no particular value other than as fodder for witticisms. Then he took a peculiar turn into a Tolstoy version of Christian behavior: what Karl had done to the three young men was horribly wrong, and his own feelings about vengeance in Central America and for blacks and Indians was wrong headed, keeping as it did, the wheel of Kharma spinning out its usual freight of human guts. Without knowing it, he presented a fresh but classic defense of nonviolence.

"There, now I feel better."

"Why? Vengeance is usually thought of as satisfying while forgiveness is an intellectual effort."

I feel better because I changed my mind. It always works that way. It removes a clot in your head and shoots in a little oxygen. When you didn't show up yesterday, not that I blame you, I was overcome by the idea of how much illness and injury limits freedom. This was propelled by a curious insomnia the night before, where all my thoughts illustrated themselves by vividly colored pictures. I'm sure this happened because the truth of Violet, long vaguely suspected, was finally revealed. Freedom was that day fishing at the spring with Edith. I could see her tummy as if it were just an inch away. And the opposite of freedom was digging a well-pit with pneumonia after Edith left. I would lay my forehead against the cool striations of earth down in the hole and wonder why all my strength had left me. I could barely pull myself out by the rope I used.

It was the same in the hospital in Miami, you know, when they were curing me of that severe case of amoebic dysentery, and a half dozen other parasites and elements the flesh is heir to in the tropics. The trouble was, I couldn't accommodate my emotions to hospital life because my body was too weak to organize a feeling of hope. Then one day Marshall, who was in mid-career in making his company one of the best, showed up, saying he was a friend of one of the owners of the British firm. This friend had asked as a courtesy that Marshall look in on me. Two of his aides stood in the doorway waiting, but Marshall and I hit it off for some reason. He gave me his card and told me to call the moment I was ready for work. "It's time for you to change continents," he said. So I had a glimmer of hope despite the deenergizing character of my treatments. A day or so later several cartons of brand new books arrived with his compliments. I began to get better faster. Then a series of specs were sent over of different projects up for bidding in Mexico, Central America, and South America. I could see what he wanted was the opinion of a working foreman, rather than the readily available ideas of engineers. The upshot was that Marshall put me on the payroll for a full month before I got out of the hospital, then moved me over to an apartment in Coconut Grove for my convalescence. I drove the yachtsmen down at the marina there a bit crazy trying to figure out the specifics of why one sailboat was better and faster than another. Several of them took me out on rides, and I became much in demand for my ability to repair diesel engines, especially for free.

You got me started again, though I'm not sure my heart

is in it. I walked better than ever yesterday and this morning, and I'm not sure why. The goose that laid the golden egg shouldn't be checking out his ass too often. I know you've been thinking "he's never going to make it to New Guinea." Well, I think I will. Maybe not right away. I've got a little farm up near Nicoya, north of Puntarenas, that's run by one of Allegria's relatives. If I have to, I'll go down there and reinvent the Egyptian waterwheel. You might say, I'm not dead yet, and even that might be preferable to stopping my whole life in lieu of illness. But I don't really want to leave you in the lurch, what with two wives and five dams to go.

So Marshall got me started again. First I went over to La Paz in Baja California to check out this reservoir for a few months. Then I was called off that job and sent to Costa Rica for the preliminary work on a hydroelectric project.

It's curious to me that I never really got started drinking again like before. Perhaps I had exorcised the demon of Sharon by becoming too worn out for longing. I'd like to meet her now and start out all over again. I've never been partial to younger women because they're usually too full of themselves to talk about anything. It's amusing to me that everyone in town, not excluding Emmeline down in Manistique, thinks I sleep with Eulia! Even Allegria asked me. Eulia and I keep each other alive, that's what we do. She showed up at the hospital after I was flown up to Miami from Venezuela and said, "If you let yourself die, I'm going to die and I don't want to." Perhaps this is something the peasants do to each other down there in the mountain country. I've never inquired, but it would be unthinkable for me to give up. It's commonly known that a friendly dog can keep a person alive. It reminds me of a profoundly sad woman I saw in my hotel lobby down in La Paz. The first day I noticed this woman, who was in her late thirties, she was arguing with two lady friends, but then I didn't see them anymore. One evening at dinner I couldn't stand her despair and I approached her table.

"You shouldn't feel so bad. This is a beautiful place," I said.

"You could try minding your own business."

"It is my business. I'm a psychological counselor from Miami."

"No you're not. I'm a psychiatrist from Chicago and you're a construction worker. I asked a waiter. Please sit down."

"You caught me in a bald-faced lie. I'm not past fibbing once in a while to keep the spirit going."

She had come down to La Paz with two other recent Chicago divorcées and they hadn't thought the place sufficiently interesting. I took a day off and we had that, plus three fine evenings. At first she wouldn't let me make love to her because she was a tad plump and said I was just being nice. This was a subtlety I hadn't encountered before so I put her hand on my hard dick and told her to try to be nice to it. We were driving back from the beach at the time in a Volkswagen but we managed to make love right there in the car. Neither of us had made love for several months so we had a fine time. That was fifteen years ago, but we still keep in touch though we haven't met again.

The years in Costa Rica were the best of my working life. I'm shocked you've never been there, because I'd say it's my favorite place on earth. I worked three years on that dam up in the mountains practically nonstop, but it was lovely and owned none of the usual tropical nightmare, the insects, heat and vermin. Few people know there's some pretty good trout fishing in those mountains. There's great beef and seafood, and dozens of kinds of fruit. It was the only job I've been on, before or after, that we didn't lose a man. If you got a day or two off you could go down to Puntarenas, then travel north or south on this overwhelming Pacific coast. Or you could go over to Limón on the Caribbean, an old banana town, where Marshall would stop to fish tarpon when he'd fly down for a visit. For some reason the rich of this world haven't discovered this country, but then they usually defer to their travel agents, rather than do any off the cuff wandering. Why does anyone want to know where they're going to sleep a month in advance? If you're civil, you can always find a bed and something to eat.

I remember very well the day I met Allegria. It was summer, we were winding down the job, and I was down in Limón making sure our freight helicopters got packed on a ship for Brazil, my next destination. I was shaky, giddy with exhaustion and not a little with regret, but somehow in the prime of my senses, so that everything was fascinating without judgement. It was the feeling I used to get just before a seizure, that is, before I took medication. Even when I was frightened by those men and the approaching bird dogs in that thicket, there was a beauty and clarity to the dead wild flowers, and the leaves, and the dogs running with their tails outstretched. That day in Limón it was so hot the ocean herself had a scorched odor. Off the pier the horizon fell right into the ocean so that there was no differentiation between the sky and water. It was cooking up for the coming hurricane season. In a half-trapped eddy of the falling tide there was a deliquesced jelly fish or perhaps a fetus. I decided on jelly fish as I had just eaten lunch. It occurred to me that it must be ninety eight and six-tenths degrees because when I waved my hand around it was the same as the air. My lunch partner, a local civil engineer, said that it was believed thereabouts that the ghosts of mad dogs roam the streets in such weather looking for their bodies. I asked him why and how people could believe such a thing, and he replied that it was a little less improbable than the Virgin Birth, a fact dear to the hearts of Christians. I was in my early thirties and it had never occurred to me to think about or question the Virgin Birth. Come to think of it, it's a strange idea. The real mystery among many mysteries, it seems to me, is that life exists in the first place, don't you think?

Anyway, a chopper pilot took me back up to San José. Marshall had gotten me a fancy room at the Grand Hotel of Costa Rica, and invited me to an elaborate dinner he was giving for politicians and the top men on his own staff. My male secretary had even measured me for a tuxedo, which would be a first. To be frank, I didn't care about the dinner when I got up to my room at the hotel, which was actually two rooms. I had instructed the pilot to fly low through the mountains from Limón to San José, following the railroad bed all the way. It is characteristic of one age to forget the engineering marvels of another age and this railroad was a spectacular job. I had a rum and fruit concoction and fell asleep. At first it had the quality of a dream when I answered the door and there was this astonishing woman standing there in a ball gown. I was so drowsy I didn't realize I was buck naked. Well, she just came in, called for drinks, and told me to get ready for the dinner. She would be accompanying me and her name was Allegria. I was a little startled when she stood at the bathroom door while I shaved, and then helped me get into the tuxedo. I had assumed she was some sophisticated friend of Marshall's and didn't for a moment think she was a call girl or whatever. She was pleased that I spoke fluent Spanish and then tried her English out on me. It was a little rough so I told her I had a few days off before flying to Belém and would help her out. Her voice had a marvelous hush to it, like seeing a dull amber light across water. I thought we cut quite a figure in the hotel lobby.

Well, Allegria seemed to know everyone at the dinner. It was a case where I was proud to have the most beautiful woman on my arm. She was very attentive to me and we left early at her insistence. I told the company driver we were taking her home but she said no, we wanted to go to the hotel. Then she gave me a kiss that blew my ears off. I asked her out to a concert at the Opera House for the following evening and she said she doubted she had the time, which was puzzling. It was quite funny and embarrassing back at the room when she explained the whole thing. Marshall had given her a large amount of money to take care of me and she meant to do so. We had a grand time. Once when we were up and down on each other I asked her opinion of the Virgin Birth for some reason, probably proximity. She was pissed off for a while because she's quite religious, then figured out that I actually meant the question. Allegria never had a heart of gold and I had to rent her time for years—until, by persistence, I got her to love me at least a fraction of what I loved her. You know the rest of the story. She'll be back early next week, at least I hope so. I'm also hoping she'll get along with Evelyn, who insists on coming tomorrow, no doubt with elaborate plans for me.

Brazil was a grim contrast to Costa Rica, except for the few times I got down to Rio. When a key worker would start to go nuts in the Amazon Basin, or suffer from what's now known as clinical depression, we'd send him on down to Rio for a few weeks. I've never figured out the specifics on the curative power of this city; I don't much care for cities but Rio certainly took ahold of me. Off and on for years I've been studying a Portuguese grammar and dictionary in case I want to go back. I've got some friends among the engineers at Eletronorte so I could always get work.

Marshall's firm had a large consulting, troubleshooting contract in Brazil. Now Brazil has no oil reserves of its own so they properly decided to develop the hydroelectric capacity of the Amazon Basin to reduce the debt incurred by a dependence on foreign oil. There's a fine article by a woman named Caulfield in *Natural History* about the problems involved. Of course billions of dollars would have been saved had we known about the problems fifteen years ago, but this mammoth hydroelectric system in a tropical rain forest was without precedent. I can't imagine dams being built under more adverse conditions. It didn't seem necessary to clear the site of the vast forest, but when the water began to gather there was a sulpherous stench around the Tucuruí and the Curuá Una for fifty miles. The water was rich with decaying matter which promoted the growth of the dread water hyacinth, which is choking Florida waterways right now, and also ceratopteris, a water fern. There was a reasonable protest against the use of defoliants because that would have poisoned the river system, as we've seen in the aftermath of Viet Nam. It's a matter of some conjecture whether that country will ever get over the chemical onslaught of Agent Orange. Anyway the decay of the trees was slowed by the overlay of vegetation. The water, deprived of oxygen, became acidic and began to corrode the generators, which broke down. The huge reservoirs supported mosquitos, and spread malaria so that one of every five workers at Tucuruí had the disease. At certain dam sites the still water promoted the growth of the snail that spreads the disease schistosomiasis, otherwise known as bilharzia.

I was in Brazil for over seven years before I got the disease. In a way, it was a repeat of India. Strangely enough, after Costa Rica, Marshall had given me a choice of Brazil or that huge project up in Quebec. Maybe I chose Brazil because of nearly killing Violet and mother in that snowstorm. Evelyn gave me that poem of Frost's about "Fire and Ice" when she treated me for bilharzia. Anyway, there I was, back at Jackson Memorial over ten years later. As usual the pain of the treatment is as bad as the disease, whether it's injection by sodium antimony tartrate, or you take lucanthone or niridazole orally. The side effects indicate the severest abdominal pain and nausea and temporary madness. The madness wasn't so bad because, just like now, I can endure what's going wrong in my brain, because the brain has a capacity to accommodate madness better then the body can illness. In a note of wonderful absurdity, Marshall told me that they recently have had good luck in Tucuruí with manatees, the big water mammal, that loves to feed on water hyacinths. Marshall, typically, is now involved in a manatee breeding experiment.

I think I told you that it was during my bilharzia episode that I met Evelyn. She was interning at Jackson in tropical medicine. Anyone a mere foot to the left or right of us could have seen it was a bad match. The attraction of opposites you hear bandied about is suitable for short and intense love affairs rather than marriage. This is no less true for being so commonplace. Evelyn can't help herself any more than I can help myself when it comes to the inevitability of character. There's probably no creature on earth who is less susceptible to change than an only child who is also rich and brilliant. We had our talks, our books, and our lovemaking. Marshall was not so much against it as he was amused that two otherwise intelligent people would even try it. From the beginning neither of us had any intention of following the other around the earth so we immediately went our separate ways, as if that were the natural thing to do. In the entire brief marriage we only spent any real time together in Holland where she was doing postgraduate work, and I had been assigned to help on a subcontract for the Delta Project.

The Delta Project is the only unique engineering marvel I've ever been privileged to work on. The idea was simple enough: dam the estuaries of the Eastern Scheldt south of Rotterdam and prevent a repeat of the 1953 storm that killed eighteen hundred people. Halfway through the project, the Dutch, unlike we ever do, changed their minds when they discovered the first two dams destroyed the rich marine life of the estuary, the mussels, cockles, and oysters. They spent nearly a billion more dollars to protect the eleven million dollar annual gross of the Scheldt seafood industry. This sounds a bit insane if you have the soul of the accountant. The engineers erected about sixty 25,000-ton piers with gates that slide up and down as a storm surge barrier. This was a visionary act, so much so that all the major equipment had to be invented. Where are you going to find a floating crane that can move that pier into place, actually half that weight as the pier is partly submerged. We've become friends, haven't we? You said you're going to Europe in November to eat? Well, promise me one thing; promise me you'll go up and see this project. The other thing, If something happens to me, promise you'll take care of the dog.

CHAPTER XVIII

Naturally I agreed to both and, to my minimal credit, fulfilled both vows. The idea that the story was nearly over filled me with what is coyly known to all but the victims as free-floating anxiety. It can't end! What do we do when we arrive at the present? Strang spoke of alternatives but didn't mention particulars, other than an Egyptian waterwheel on a farm in Costa Rica. My god. We were interrupted so I could take Eulia down to Engadine to catch the bus. Strang would be left alone for a short while but Eulia didn't want to chance a meeting with Evelyn, whom she despised as a soulless manipulator. I took a short walk with the dog to allow them a proper farewell. Within fifteen minutes I became quite lost; I had been sunken in my thoughts and inattentive to landmarks. I sat down with the dog and drew out some possibilities in the dirt with a sharp stick. It was hopeless. Then it suddenly occurred to me that the dog knew I kept biscuits in my vehicle. I said "bisquit" somewhat tentatively and she lunged, slobbering all over me. I said, "Where are the bisquits?" and she trotted off with me in tow, reaching the cabin in less than five minutes. I hugged the dog vigorously and dumped out a half a carton of the biscuits for her, congratulating both the dog and myself for our ingenuity.

TAPE 8: Eulia is gone, probably forever. It's extraordinary that at my age, forty-six, it can be literally too much bother to love someone. No, it's not extraordinary, it's ordinary. I'll stick to the facts despite this full bottle of whiskey. On my way back from Engadine, I saw Evelyn's cab entering town but she was looking the other way. She appears as out of place as everyone else that travels to that cabin except Emmeline. One afternoon they were upset at the tavern because a cab came and left without anyone knowing what passenger was dropped off. I suggested a hired killer, which was met with general interest, adding that I had interviewed a number of them years back and they all looked as solid as your average lawyer.

In the hour's drive to Engadine Eulia was largely noncommittal, nearly forlorn. I had made a writer's classic mistake and entered fully into the lives of my subjects to the extent my skin was going to come off when I tried to get out. It would be any day now I sensed, and it likely wouldn't be as clean and melancholy as Strang felt when finishing a dam. There was the vertiginous sense that when we part, we let each other drift off rather aimlessly into the future. At least most of us do.

Eulia's insistence on taking a bus still seems odd to me. She claimed she wanted to see the country and also stop and visit an old exchange student friend in Madison, Wisconsin. From there she would fly from Chicago to New Orleans, then on to San José. She certainly wasn't a bus-type person. She was wearing the summer skirt, now clean, she had muddied against the tire of Bobby's skidder. There was the urge to drive off on a side road, tell her I needed her, and make love. For some reason I chickened out. Back to business I thought.

"Are you Strang's lover? I've never figured that out." I croaked.

"You are disgusting. You are a pig," she shrieked.

"But you said that in the hotel in Miami . . ."

"God is blind to what you only do once out of passion. I'm leaving. Don't try to make me unhappy." She leaned over and kissed my ear. I put my hand on her knee and slid it up her thigh, but she shook her head no, and looked out the window. When she turned back, there were tears in her eyes. She didn't, however, pull her skirt back down. There was the odor of lavender, her scent, and I felt congested as if I were about to cry. I waited until after I flagged down the west bound bus on Route 2, and kissed her good-bye.

I just fried my first hamburger in memory. It looked boring so I fried an egg and put it on top of the meat along with a slice of onion. I've finally run out of wine. I hankered for sweetbreads but this would have to do with a glass of whiskey. There was the unmistakable sound of Strang's truck in the drive though it was after midnight. Sweetbreads had made me think of Eulia's promise to visit me in New York, where I would certainly keep her away from my friends. I properly guessed the truck to be Evelyn. She barged through the door with scarcely a tap, and a smile that was resolutely false.

"Still eating I see." What a charmer!

"Fucking right. Didn't Strang tell you? I've become a part time lumberjack."

"You're not fooling me in the least. You're killing him."

"Now why would I try to fool a nuisance? You haven't been around. I haven't had the occasion to remember you existed more than once or twice." If she wanted a bitch-out I'm not exactly harmless.

"I'm taking him away as soon as possible. You won't be seeing him again. That's final."

"Can the shit, Evelyn, I'm not the butler or the upstairs maid. You don't mean a fuck to me, if you mean that much to anyone. You know he won't leave without seeing me again."

Not surprisingly, tears were the next tack though she wasn't very good at them because, for obvious reasons, she only used them rarely; I poured her a big drink while the tears weren't working. I looked out through the screen door at the night where the northern lights were gathering in a fluttery green haze. I would miss them. I permitted myself a smile as my ballbreaker guest continued to snivel. The voice came hard and clear, though there was an effort at charm.

"You can have one more day. I'm taking him to Switzerland. I stopped there for a week on the way back from Africa, and we've decided on a course of treatment."

"What would that be?"

"Well, simply put . . ." She was gathering strength again. "In layman's terms it would require at least a year of absolute rest, of semisedation. His attempts at walking are horrible. We need to weaken the muscle groups and restructure them if he's ever to walk normally."

"Have you told him this?" I interrupted.

"Of course not. He's not in his right mind, and he's not a doctor. He's certainly not able to determine his own best treatment, as you can see."

"That's quite a pile of negatives. It might be

worth it if there was a positive chance of getting rid of the effects of that herb."

"That's, of course, the ultimate point." It was as if we both exhaled and decided, at least for the time being, not to be contentious. "His medical history is a horror show and that's an understatement. The particular combination of tropical disease plus epilepsy makes the situation problematical. You doubtless know that epilepsy can't be cured, only the symptoms can be alleviated to the point that they don't exist. Sometimes it just disappears. The Swiss firm has done all the preliminary work on *Aristolochia medicinalis,* I mean the exhaustive process by which it's reduced to its pure form, also the whole battery of biological screens. We have nothing to really go on so we don't know if an important alkaloid might have been lost in the purification phase. They've just begun to run tests on animals, but these have been inconclusive. The herb has never been considered valuable by the field people who explore herbal passibilities, particularly in tribal cultures wherever, so none of the work had been done."

"What does it do to animals?"

"In layman's terms again, they either die in a state of paralysis or go crazy. We're trying to define specific effects and determine dosages. The consensus of everyone involved is that a long period of rest under sedation, and reducing all stimuli to a minimum, would best prepare him for the eventuality of experimenting with antidotes."

"And he's not aware of what's coming?"

"I wish you'd stop that for god's sake. I've told him the basic facts and he seems agreeable. Stop acting like I've come to take a prisoner. Simply put, I love him and want him to be well."

"Frankly, he seems well enough to me. There have been some occasional bad times but he seems

quite happy, more so, in fact, than anyone I've
ever met, including you and me."

"You have a charming circle of acquaintances
I'm sure. I'm also aware of what people like you
think is well. Just don't try to interfere." And
on she went.

CHAPTER XIX

The good doctor Evelyn was no doubt doing the Third World countries a lot of good, I thought in the morning. One of the curious effects of a bad hangover it that you think you're wrong whether you are or not. Not wrong in particulars, but wrong in general, wrong about everything. If you had saved a baby from a rabid dog or a bull rattler the night before, it would still be wrong. The hangover had started early enough so I thought I was wrong before Evelyn left. There can be a desperate inelasticity in alcohol. Everyone has heard a drunk friend repeat a story until you want to jam him with a cattle prod with the voltage to the max. By the time she walked out the door, I was "feebed out," as they say in Los Angeles. I had even consented to help her out if Strang proved recalcitrant. Marshall was sending up a plane in two days and would I take them to Manistique? Later I could drop the dog off with Emmeline or take it to the pound. She had a few drinks herself and there was a moment when I thought we were going to end up in bed, or on the floor, or on the Formica table, but now I guessed this flirtation was part of her art of persuasion. Such is our deference to the arrogance of doctors that the average mother might sit in an examining room and watch her child's limbs get hacked off without protesting. This overstatement is another symptom of a hangover. I was going to say that a mad doctor had finally been arrested in New Mexico for prescribing the ingestion of dog turds for cancer. He had been closely watched for seven years, had hundreds of patients with abdominal complaints, and a Lear jet.

As you can see, my drive to Strang's hadn't been going well. I stopped and opened all the windows to increase the oxygen. Nothing would work. It wasn't just the hangover. I found myself wishing that Strang were my brother so the story wouldn't have to end, so that I would have a brother's definite and legal prerogatives in the matter.

At the cabin I was shocked to see that Evelyn already had a number of cartons packed in back of the truck for shipping. She was extremely cheery and treated me as a coconspirator. It was a fine morning so we sat by the river for our final session. The dog brought me a stick to throw in the river. She made one of those grand, absurdly energetic leaps into the current that made me feel better. Strang gave no visible evidence that he was being bullied into a long trip to Switzerland, and I deduced she had prepared him for the inevitable in correspondence.

———————

This is a melancholy occasion isn't it? Dire portents, as Dad used to say. My memories of the accident aren't very precise; the event that might have ended my career is more a series of fractional images. I had a small crew up on the Rio Kuduyarí putting the final touches, some cosmetic and some necessary, on a dam in preparation for a government inspection and ceremony. I remember talking to an electrician from Wyoming who was busy rigging a cable and switch for the usual general to pull from the usual platform. It was near the end of the rainy season and I had a number of worries. The project engineer was vexed beyond belief because the volume of runoff in the watershed had somewhat exceeded all predictions. You had to shout to communicate anywhere in the vicinity of the dam because the overflow and the river were far beyond the thunderous. Dams don't stop rivers, they just control them on a temporary basis and the control in this case didn't seem much beyond the tentative. My main worry, I think I mentioned this before, is that I had been without my seizure prescription for three days, having forgotten it in Caracas. I had tried to radio it in by chopper, but the weather had been so foul with wind, rain, and fog, that the safety factor prevented the use of helicopters. What I did sounds incredibly stupid but it seemed better than staying in bed when there was work to be done. I had done the same thing in India when I had run out of pills with no adverse effects. Now the presumption of the act boggles me, but I suppose it was in character.

Here's what happened to me. I had dinner every evening with this Venezuelan engineer who was also an amateur anthropologist. He was an outsider, partly because no one shared his interest in the local Kubeo Indians. The day before I had asked him to check out what the medicine men gave their people for epileptic seizures. He showed up with this small packet of ground root, and after I talked to the electrician that day, I went to my office and took a minuscule portion. The engineer had no real notion of dosage and had advised against the whole thing as foolhardy. At one time he had eaten a mushroom the medicine man had given him for depression and it had radically altered his mind for some months. The cure had been almost unendurably strange, he said, and for a while he yearned for the simplicity of depression.

So I swallowed the tiniest mound of bitter powder and drove my jeep over to the dam. For some reason people think that dams are concrete all the way through, but there are tunnels, passageways, for a variety of maintenance reasons. I entered the main tunnel where security is quite stringent for obvious reasons: a guerilla group could only truly damage a massive dam from inside. I walked through the narrow tunnel at the dam's base for about three hundred yards. It was dimly lit and fogged by condensation. My stomach was quavering a bit, but I attributed it to a local hot pepper sauce I was fond of. You could feel the vibration of the river and overflow despite the immensity of the structure. I took the elevator up about twelve stories, or two hundred feet to the top of the dam.

Now the top was only a hundred or so feet across, enough for a roadway but not much more. My crew was winching up the guardrails that had arrived by barge across the reservoir. It was not a place for anyone with a fear of heights, what with no guardrail. It was a smooth concrete surface with the reservoir on the upstream side a hundred feet below, and the river at least two hundred feet down on the other side. Not far under us the overflow passed in huge flumes, increased vastly by the rains. The overflow dropped until it hit what we call the flip-bucket, which is an upturned lip, an energy dissipator, because straight falling water at this location would undermine the foundation of the dam.

I stood on the unprotected edge staring down at the ponderous overflow. There was a Spanish worker next to me who was always singing love songs. Sometimes I would tease him by singing Emmeline's favorite, "Sh-Boom," the only popular song I could remember, or some hymn. He didn't speak English but I told him the Doxology was a famous love song and we'd often bray out together, "Praise God from whom all blessings flow. . . ." We were laughing and doing that while watching the overflow, though we weren't audible above the noise. Then I cursed, because there was a thunderstorm moving up river toward us from the west. I motioned to the Spanish worker, Luis was his name, to get the crew off the top of the dam since it was the highest point and lightning would be a factor. It was twilight anyway and they weren't far from dinner break. I was alone then, and though I don't remember feeling immobile, I just stayed there watching the marvelous bolts of lightning against the black clouds. Even the thunder was drowned out by the power of the water.

Then it was that the drug must have struck hard into my system because I felt violently sucked outward into the storm as if I were seven years old again, flying outward and down into the lip with the water moving so quickly I didn't penetrate it, then shooting up and out as if I were taking a catapulting, tumbling ride on a flume of water. The velocity from the rainy season was such that I was shot far out into the turbulence of the river. Any other time of year the life would have immediately been crushed out of me. I remember in the river that my legs wouldn't work but my arms would, so I swam a long time with the rushing current until it eased and I nudged against something solid and fell unconscious. I guess it was lucky for me that I was a night-swimmer because I swam toward the ease of pressure in the current until I reached an eddy and the bank of the river. A Kubeo Indian found me seven miles downstream at dawn.

That's all there is to say. And now I'm here. Five months in a hospital and four months here. Do you realize how unspeakably grand it was to come up to this cabin, the area of my youth, after that long in a hospital, which is so often—and I thought it would be for me—the house of death. That's why I refused all those drugs after a while. I had to be conscious. That's all. How could I bear not being conscious? Last night I was swimming in the dark in my dreams and it was wonderful.

———

Doctor Evelyn interrupted us for lunch but we all knew the story was over, especially the smiling Evelyn who saw no reason for me to tarry though she was being civil. Her cooking was Waspish—a cold cucumber soup, a sprig of broccoli, a minuscule, unadorned veal chop. She reminded me that I had agreed to pick them up at ten the next morning to meet a charter at the Manistique airport. I had been so subdued that she allowed me a few minutes alone with Strang when he walked me out to my vehicle.

"We might not have much of a chance to talk tomorrow. I'll keep in touch. Meanwhile, have a good year at that Swiss hospital." I blurted the latter out with an ache in my temples. Strang embraced me, then held me at arm's length and smiled. That's all. Not even an enigmatic smile, just a smile.

CHAPTER XX

I went home and began my minimal packing. I was giving up the cabin the next day, after nearly three months, for an elderly couple who had spent their anniversary week there for the past forty years. Being a resolute sentimentalist about such matters, how could I interfere with this precedent? My mother's comment about how unfavorably I compared to a dancing woodcock came back to me. If nothing else, the summer had made me fifteen pounds closer to flight. The heat had returned so I reread Joseph Campbell's *The Hero with a Thousand Faces* for the umpteenth time. Mythology is a soothing hobby. There aren't any old myths, just new people.

In the evening I fished for a while without success, then went to the tavern for my last all-you-can-eat whitefish special. I took the precaution of carrying a bottle of Pickapepper sauce and waded through five pieces, which would serve as a sleeping pill. Home to the cabin and a single nightcap while reading an interview with a porn star named Rhonda in one of the magazines I bought the first evening in town. And hence to sleep with a vision of a buttocks as big as the Ritz.

There was Evelyn, beside the bed at first light, her hiss rising to a shout. "He's gone. Where is he, goddamn you! He's gone."

I followed her to Strang's cabin, half wishing that the old pickup she pushed to sixty would go into one of those endless cinematic tumbles. Sure enough, there at the riverbank were Strang's clothes and leg braces.

"He's gone," I said with purposeful vengeance.

"Oh god, he's dead. It's your fault. He fixed me the rum drink we used to have and made love to me. He put something in my drink. I finally woke up before dawn and he wasn't there."

She began weeping and I couldn't help but put my arm around her. She got control of herself, then ran to my car, swerving out of the yard. I stooped beside Strang's clothes and petted the dog, who was lying there looking disgruntled that she hadn't been taken along down river. I looked in the door of the pumphouse and saw that the wet suit was still hanging on the wall. This depressed me for a moment, but then I noticed the can of grease Strang used before the wet suit arrived looked recently opened. For some reason I closed the can and stuck it behind some paint cans on the shelf. Then I made my way with the dog through the swamp down to the log jam. The dog scrambled out on the pile of half-submerged logs wagging her tail excitedly at the scent. She looked at me to see if I understood. I walked back up to the cabin, poured a drink, and looked at a topographical Strang had showed me of the area. It was an extremely unfriendly stretch of water, but not impossible for a man of his capabilities.

———————

TAPE 9: I am in the motel now with a soundless television on for comfort, my first viewing in nearly three months. I had pretty much forgotten television existed and now it has all of the charm, but none of the color, of a city dump. Evelyn returned with two squad cars in tow, one was a county sheriff, and the other was from the Michigan state police, a stunning title if you think about it, but an efficient group of professionals. I was questioned for an hour, then sent on my way.

The town was abuzz with excitement the next few days. Drownings are not uncommon in the area but no one had ever seen, including me, this kind of search. By late afternoon a private jet made several passes down the river and over the town. I properly guessed it to be Marshall, who had flown in from a horse sale in Saratoga, New York. By dark Marshall had managed to summon in three helicopters, which swept up and down the river and bay with spotlights before landing on the beach for the night. There were state police divers and a diving club from Marquette. Marshall's efforts reminded me of the news stories of Nelson Rockefeller combing New Guinea's beaches in a chartered 707 looking for his lost son.

Not surprisingly I was cast as the villain. I waited to be summoned or questioned again, and when nothing happened, I drove out to the cabin in the middle of the next afternoon. I was met by what is called unbridled hostility from Evelyn, Emmeline, and Bobby, though I noted that Bobby was a little less than convincing. There was the slightest tinge of the soap opera to his anger.

I walked over to the picnic table where Marshall was having a pow-wow with the police and a detective brought up from Lansing. Marshall somehow had managed to wear one of those Orvis outfits, viyella shirt and pressed khaki trousers, not to be cynical. His aide was in the usual MBA, not quite tailored, suit. The detective was saying that there were tire tracks on the two-track going to the river about a half a dozen miles downstream, the next access below the cabin. This was inconclusive as it could easily been a trout fisherman. Again, I was surprised that no one bothered asking me any more questions though I suspected Evelyn had poisoned that well. The police accorded me the respect given to a cub reporter with a bad complexion, though Marshall gave me a seemingly friendly nod.

I drove to the bar but left immediately when it was full of diver, pilots, and onlookers, one of whom said to me, "This beats the shit out of the Fourth of July."

Back at the motel I had my own, private victorious wake. Of course I couldn't be absolutely sure that Strang hadn't been swept by the current out into Lake Superior, where he rested cold and intact in two hundred feet of water. I doubted it. I constructed a scenario where Eulia got on the bus in Engadine and got off in Manistique, where she was met by Bobby. I could see Bobby standing there in the glare of headlights at the end of the two-track waiting for his father to come down the river. I didn't in the least feel bad about being made the villain. I felt quite calm, in fact. It had happened frequently: You write about something that happens and, for various reasons, people are so forgetful they confuse you with the cause.

Marshall stopped by the next morning after I had bribed the lovely desk clerk into going out for coffee. He had brought the dog for me and wanted to say good-bye. The dog seemed content in her new surroundings, jumping on the bed for a quick nap.

"You don't think he's dead, do you?"

"No, not really."

"Would you share your reasons?"

"No. You're too powerful and that would tip you off. It's obvious that he wanted to get away from all of us and this is the only way he could manage it." I was looking out the window at a police car that held the driver, Doctor Evelyn, and the spiffy aide.

"That's true. You must know him as well as anyone by now. If you hear from him, we can send his checks through you. I looked at his account books last night and he's given everything away to wives, children, students, organizations. He wasn't very worldly."

"I think he probably was."

Marshall laughed then, and began to leave. "I'm the only one who doesn't think it's your fault. Give me a ring in Florida."

"I will."

Driving south out of town that evening I tried to imagine what it would be like to swim down a large river at night, but couldn't quite make it. You had to see the dam or work on it yourself to really understand it: There was less than a half-moon and dew on the grass. You would shiver involuntarily when you took off your clothes. The water would be cold, but not the bitter cold of June, and the grease would insulate you for the first few miles. Then the scramble over the log-jam, and back into the current. Since you couldn't see what you were doing, you would seek the strongest part of the current for speed of travel, guiding yourself with strokes of your arms, your legs, twin rudders. You would aim by sight into versions of black. On corners you would run the inside banks in the chutes, then strike across where the power of the river made its swirling turn. You might hear the wolves a trapper said lived in the delta. You would see trout rise, perhaps disturb a family of otters, hear an owl's call above the rush of water. The fatigue would be sweet when you saw the light diffused upward in a bright haze downstream. Your son and Eulia would help you from the water.

ABOUT THE AUTHOR

JIM (JAMES THOMAS) HARRISON was born on December 11, 1937, in Grayling, Michigan. He received his B.A. in 1960 from Michigan State University and married Linda King in the same year. They have two children, Jamie Louise and Anna Severin. He obtained his M.A. in 1964. In 1965 he met poet Denise Levertov, who helped him find a publisher for his first book of poems, *Plain Song*. He published two more books of poetry in the next three years, *Locations* (1968) and *Walking* (1969). By 1969, aided by NEA and Guggenheim grants, Harrison left his teaching job at the State University of New York at Stony Brook. He wrote and published steadily after that, two more books of poetry and three novels: *Wolf* (1971), *A Good Day to Die* (1973), and *Farmer* (1975). But when *Farmer* was remaindered almost as soon as it was published, Harrison found himself facing financial ruin and unable to pay for his daughter Jamie to go to college. In order to make more income, he began writing Hollywood screenplays. Through his friend, writer Thomas McGuane, he met actor Jack Nicholson who "found it offensive that an artist he liked couldn't make a living at his art." He advanced Harrison enough money to finish the three novellas included in *Legends of the Fall* (1979), Harrison's breakthrough book. The title piece appeared in *Esquire* magazine and the three pieces were all sold to the movies. *Warlock* appeared in 1981 and *Selected Poems* in 1982. Harrison lives on his Lake Leelanau, Michigan, farm and keeps an isolated cabin on the Upper Peninsula.